I0831917

Manstress Diaries

A novel:

Darrell C. Scott

DSEPublishing@gmail.com
https://www.dsemancipatedpublishing.com

ISBN 978-0578684451
2023 Edition

Disclaimer

This is a work of fiction. Names, characters, businesses, places, events, locales, and incidents are either the products of the author's imagination or used in a fictitious manner. Any resemblance to actual persons, living or dead, or actual events is purely coincidental.

DEDICATIONS

Superwoman: Thank you for being my rock. Without you, none of this would be possible. Thank you for the unconditional love you nourished me with for 25 years and counting. And though at times I take it for granted, thank you for knocking down barriers, so that I do not have to. My heart beats for you unconditionally. I love you, mom.

Pops, Big Bro, and my Aunt Chilli: Thank you for your continued love and support over the years. This project would not be possible without you guys serving as the foundation of my support system.

@its_jerry97: My cousin and my best friend. Thank you for your effervescent spirit! You have brought me so much laughter and real conversation over the years. You have been one of my biggest supporters and sources of inspiration. Keep that hustle.

@Dra_boogie: I owe you a car wash!

"Fly abandonedly into the sun.
If you should return to me,
We truly were meant to be.
So spread your wings and fly,
Butterfly…"

-Mariah Carey

The Entries

The Closet

Hoe -Tale

Blurred Lines

Crossing Lines

Bad Decisions

The Warning

The Agreement

Triggered

Instagram Flexxx

Man's Best Friend

Ghostin

The Widow

Stay The Night

Walk of Shame

Baggage

All I Want For Christmas

The Ultimatum

Don't Forget About Us

West Dallas Street

Broken

Break ur Heart Right Back

When Love Calls

Looking In

Bitter

Manstress Diaries

The Closet

I've always liked older men.

Normally, when you make a statement like that, people assume you have daddy issues or that you're on the prowl for a sugar daddy. I don't have the balls for that, although shopping at the Galleria or strutting down the palm tree-lined streets of Highland Village (which is kind of like the Rodeo Drive of Houston), would be a lot more fun on someone else's dime.

My affinity toward older men started in middle school. Well, I wouldn't say it started (I've come to understand that the attraction was always there, lying dormant, waiting until I was old enough to know what the word gay means. Remember High School Musical? Troy Bolton, AKA Zac Effron? Yeah. He was cute, but I was more interested in seeing what his dad (Coach

Jack, AKA, Bart Johnson looked like without a shirt. Blue eyes, dirty blonde, and shaped like a dad that played basketball in college.

Remember "Baby Boy?" Most people lust after Jody, better known as Tyrese. Nah, I was into the man playing his stepdad, Melvin (Ving Rhames). The one who was in the kitchen cooking breakfast butt-ass-naked and drinking all the Kool-Aid. Prison muscles, tattoos, built like a football player, (not the big burly linebackers, but the quarterback), full goatee, and a 5'o clock shadow. Mmmm, aged and a little rough around the edges. That's how I liked them.

I would later find myself wondering what it would be like if I was the love interest in these love stories. I remember thinking how I'd rather have the attention of those guys than any girl I knew at school. That's when I fully realized my unusual attraction toward other men. Something about the thought of being held by an older man felt safe. Soon after that, I learned that Google Images has pictures of all sorts of fine, naked older men. And by older, I mean at least 20 years older than me. I googled so much, I discovered gay porn. "It was a whole neeeew woooooorld!" (in my Aladdin voice).

At times, after the deed was done, I was disgusted with myself. But I would grow out of that phase. After that, I discovered the gay chatrooms that dominated the early 2000s. A few scrolls past daddies with big chests and full beards, and they soon finagled their way onto my playground. Some of you may remember the G.Y.C or Adam 4 Adam. I was always browsing, but never acting on any of my homoerotic impulses. Hell, I didn't know how. I always felt like I was doing something wrong. Something shameful. Yet, it felt as natural as any straight man lusting after breasts. All the while, I stayed with a girlfriend on my arms all through junior high and high school, but I digress.

During my Sophomore year in high school, the iPhone was only three-years-old and had taken the mobile phone industry by the balls. The App Store changed not just the tech game, but the gay hookup scene was flipped upside down. In came the infamous... Jackd and Grindr, the virtual playground of choice for *men seeking men.* I'd mention Craigslist, but that's where weirdos, serial killers, and pedophiles like to play... allegedly. For some odd reason, the black gays flocked to Jackd and the white gays played on Grindr. It was almost an unspoken rule at the time.

I got my first iPhone when I was 15. A sleek and glossy iPhone 4. And so, long story short, I downloaded Jackd. Jackd is where I met my first, a Spanish-American guy named Rick. Rick was a mere leaf on a tree. When the wind blew hard enough, he would surely go with it. Rick was 19 at the time and hanging on to his college ball player label by 1/10 of a point on a 4.0 grading scale. Something like that. I was never good at math.

Because of the age gap, I didn't give him any more of a reason not to take me seriously. I didn't want him to see me as some cliché high schooler, who was still getting grounded for high school drama like missing curfew and getting bad grades in math. Lame. I had to be "mature". More mature than I was capable of being at that age. And so, I did what I did best back then. Lied. We've all told a lie at least twice in our lives. Some lies are potentially more dangerous than others. The ugliest lies tend to steer us into complicated situations and inevitably, internal suffering.

I told Rick that my parents pretty much let me do whatever I wanted and that I was 17 because I had convinced myself that saying I was 18 would have been pushing it a bit. He never questioned me, though. I thought it was because I was really convincing but now, not so much. Reflecting on it, I should have run from a grown man willing to "date" a 17-year-old. But hey, if Mariah Carey doesn't know numbers, then why should I? Did that make me complicit in my molestation? It's still molestation in the eye of the law, right? I don't know. I'm no lawyer.

My birthday rolled around and that's when things got interesting. I can still say it is the bleakest birthday of my 25 years of strolling around without a clue. I had been carrying the closeted homosexual burden for about a year at the time. I managed to snag my first boyfriend thanks to Jackd, and still maintain a heterosexual charade for my friends and family. With my knack for lying, I thought I had control over everything. Nobody suspected a thing as far as I knew. During school hours, I was dating a girl named Melanie, a biracial girl with long hair and sassy. I had a whole routine.

After my track coaches blew the final whistle for the team to hit the showers around 5 p.m., I'd kiss Melanie goodbye, then dart across campus to freshen up in a restroom that was almost always empty around that time. After, I'd hop in the car with Rick, whom Melanie believed to be my cousin. It worked for a while until Progress reports rolled out. When my parents saw all the A's printed on that thick green piece of paper, were stained by the letter D, my life was over. They confiscated my glorious iPhone 4 I begged them to buy me for Christmas and imprisoned it inside the junk drawer in their bedroom.

My weekends in front of the 65-inch TV screen in the upstairs theater room with surround sound, catching up on Pretty Little Liars, Sex and the City, and The Real Housewives of Atlanta, was over "dot com" (as Tamar Braxton would say). My relationship with Rick would suffer from neglect and I worried he would likely move on in my absence. On top of that, I wasn't allowed to participate in track, which meant my chances at qualifying for the Regional track meet were, as my mom put it, *"ain't gonna happen"* if I didn't get that damn math grade up before they mailed out the final Report cards for the grading period.

None of that mattered. My birthday was the exception to the rule (in my naïve opinion), and so I figured I should have my phone and all the freedom in the world on my birthday. Sure, I would have to sneak down the stairs in the morning while my parents were sleeping and steal my phone out of their drawer without them noticing, but it hardly seemed like a challenge. My dad's snoring was sure to mask any noise I could possibly make in the effort of being stealthy. He only ever snored like that when my mom slipped a little something extra in his drink to help him sleep.

All the stars were aligning in my favor. Getting caught would have its consequences, but I had convinced myself of a lie: *Mom and dad want me to have a good birthday. Having my phone would ensure that. Therefore, they wouldn't mind. Hell, they're probably planning to give it back to me for my birthday anyway.*

After saying repeating it in my head a few times I believed it was the truth, knowing damn well that it could all blow up in my face. Still, salvaging what I had left with Rick was more important. For some reason, I've always been utterly submissive in relationships. I was very much all about doing what it takes to please my man. In most of my dating experiences, it was obedience. I didn't mind the headache. Rick talked a lot about a future where we both would move to California and start a life together. He would become a big-time filmmaker and I would be free to train for the Olympics. The way he used to describe it, made it sound like a fairytale. My very own love story. I was and still am very much a believer in a Cinderella Story and Prince Charming.

That said, getting my phone taken was literally the worst thing that could happen. Stealing the phone was a success, though. When I got home after school that day, I wore an unbuttoned red Polo shirt, pinned with dollar bills from friends and a smile. My mom, however, sat at the bottom of the stairwell, wearing her power suit and a scowl. *Remain cool, calm, and collected.* I remember thinking. "Heyyyy, ma!" I said, trying to pretend as if I had done nothing that warranted the soul-crushing glare she was laying on me.

"Where is your phone, Khai?" My mom was never one to beat around the bush when she was pissed. I lied, of course, and told her I didn't know. She hollered for my dad. He got all up in my face and asked the same question while he placed his thick hands on my small shoulders and gripped them like a stress ball.

"Y'all had it. The last place I saw it, was in the drawer."

At that point, my mom decided to negotiate with me. She said she would look around for the phone one more time, and she had better find it, or, "Ima have ya ass on the bed in silky underwear!"

My dad stood behind her, holding a thick orange extension cord that belonged in the garage and not on my ass. My mom made no empty threats. I had to do something. I was not about to be like my brother when my dad stuffed a sock in his mouth and my mom whooped his ass with a fat switch for trying to hide his Report card. No, ma'am. I wasn't there for it.

She had me stand still next to the dresser while she and my dad looked around the room for it. They were all under the bed and peeping behind the headboard, searching high and low for my stolen phone. My heart was palpitating, but I managed to keep a poker face and shrugged every time she took a second to glance at me and raised her brow. My dad lectured me background about lying. All I did was nod and said, yes sir, when I felt it appropriate. Finally! My opportunity arrived to salvage the crisis. They both went into their bathroom and checked the drawers and the closet. So, I took the phone out of my duffle bag and tossed it across the mahogany wood flooring and it slid underneath the dresser.

I cringed at the thought of the scratches that would be on it later, but it was desperate times... They emerged from the bathroom and my mom told my dad to check the junk drawer one more time. This time he looked behind it. It was a solid wood piece with brass accents and handles and a white marble top they bought while in Korea during their military years. The legs were shaped like the flexed paw of a lion with brass claws that gave the illusion that they were digging into the floor.

The sharp tips taunted me and the more I stared at them, the harder it became to stand. As my dad was moving the dresser, the light exposed the shadow that was hiding my phone and my mom spotted it. All hell broke loose after that. I had a grin on my face and was eager to gloat.

"Told you so!" I said, with my chin in the air. My dad shook his head. "So, you mean to tell me if I turn it on and go through the messages, there won't be any from today?" Time slowed for a split second and my head was spinning like something out of "The Starry Night" before my heart fell to my feet and my body was thrust headfirst back into real-time. Damn near fainted. With eyes big as Krispy Cream donut holes, I said, "Nope. Not a one."

I was bluffing. It failed. Miserably. My dad turned the phone on and demanded I unlock it. For half a second, I ransacked my brain for ways I could wipe the phone clean with what little time I had to unlock it with him hovering over me. "WHO. THE HELL. IS RICK!" I was determined to deny it until all four wheels fell off the wagon, going uphill with a load of river rocks.

"Just my friend."

"You sure he's just a friend?"

"Yes, sir," I said through the lump forming in my throat. My mom snatched the phone and read my dirty text messages to Rick aloud. It was embarrassing as hell. They sounded so much better in a text than read-aloud. That's for sure. My dad asked me repeatedly, "Go on and say it, you're a faggot!" To which I just kept saying no. I wouldn't say it out loud. Not to him.

"Fuckin' flower child! Own up to your shit!" The next thing I knew, he launched himself at and me, slapped me so hard, speckles of light danced behind my pupils. He was in my face and I was cornered. My head banged against the wall when he head-butted me like a stranger in the street who had just hit on my mom. My flank grazed the corner of the dresser where the junk drawer lived, causing a stabbing pain in my side that lingered for several minutes. An aged photo hanging on the wall of my parents holding hands and kissing on a yacht in Miami dug into my scalp.

My face twisted up and I closed my eyes. I couldn't make eye contact with my dad. I thought if I clenched them together hard enough, the tears, and the shame that tugged at the apex of my heart would cease. It didn't. It only intensified and birthed one of those silent cries that leave you gasping for air as the ache in your throat chokes the life out of you.

"Eric! Please!" My mom cried. His eyes were beaming through mine like lasers. I broke out in tears and kept saying, "No! No! No!" As if I were trying to convince myself. My mom finally pleaded for him to put me down long enough to irritate him. When he did, he stormed out of the room. My shirt was all twisted up, a few of my dollar bills were torn and I just sat there on my knees in total disbelief. Nothing could have prepared me for that moment, but it would have been nice to have at least seen it coming.

My mom embraced me and kissed me on the forehead, falsely reassuring me that everything was all right. There was no evidence to prove that. She swore that my dad was only angry because of the lying. "We always knew you were…that way." Something about the way I carried myself and my obsession with Carrie Bradshaw and Mariah Carey had everything to do with it. She said that they just hoped that they were wrong. I couldn't respond because I thought it ridiculous. Can't a guy watch Sex and the City and idolize one of pop's most notoriously glamorous divas and not be gay? My mom walked me upstairs where I would find that my dad had taken all the doors off their hinges in my room, including the bathroom! He insisted that they had given me too much privacy… Still makes no damn sense today.

What hurt the most, was seeing my mom cry. It made my stomach hurt. I couldn't bear the sight of my mother's pain. Especially when I was the cause of it. After that, my dad made me call Rick and tell him that I was not allowed to see him again. I was relieved that he didn't answer, even after 3 attempts. "Leave a voicemail!" My dad ordered. I would see Rick for a few weeks after that, but I had hoped that I could fix it later when things cooled down.

My driver's test was 2-days away and my mom had convinced my dad to give me one last lesson. I had to ask her to do it for me because I was afraid to ask myself. After my coming out, he just isolated himself from us. He'd sleep all day in the guest bedroom and would leave to go to work around 6 p.m. 3-days out of the week. My mom spent most of her time in her office and I hid upstairs in my room as long as I could. I'd only come out to eat and do my chores. My brother had moved in with his fiancé, a year before my life went to shit and I grew to resent him for it. I had no one to talk to, so it was just my mom and I sitting at the dinner table most days, talking about everything but what mattered.

Usually, we used my mom's Escalade for my lessons, but this time, he decided to pull out his 99 Corvette. It mostly stayed in the garage. I would say it collected dust, but he cared for it like it was his child. He had just installed brand-new Goodyear high-performance tires. The black paint was so shiny it looked wet and the bold yellow letters on the tires, made my heart race. I couldn't believe he was about to let me drive it. "Are you sure about this?" I asked. He nodded and started typing a message to my mother on his phone. He frowned at it momentarily, as if he was unsure if he should send it or not.

"Don't be all timid and take forever to turn like you always do. I don't have time for it today. I'm tired." He said, just before I heard swooshing from the message being sent. That was the friendliest he had been in a while, so I let it roll off my back and laughed. He didn't. He just stared blankly out the window. It was a nice spring evening, with low humidity, so he told me to drop the top. We were pulling out of the neighborhood when he said" Let's do something different today. Turn left."

Normally we turned right and drove down the back road to Walmart and back. The rumble from the exhaust was exhilarating. I had never been behind the wheel of something with so much power. It was getting dark as we drove down the eerie backroad about 5-miles from the house. My dad had the radio tuned to Majic 102.1. Maxwell's "This Woman's Work" was playing quietly in the background. It made me think about how odd my parents had been acting toward each other. So, I figured I'd ask because if they were talking divorce, I wanted to know sooner rather than later.

"Everything all right with you and mom?"

"You need to stay out of grown folks' business, boy. I perched my lips and refocused on the road. The clouds were threatening to dump a shower on us, and I had never driven in the rain in a car like that.

"I think I'm good," I said.

"Good?"

"Yeah. Looks like it's about to rain, and I don't feel comfortable driving your baby in it, to be honest."

"Can't be a sissy all your life!" He said. "All right, pull over here." He pointed at the side of the road. I did as he instructed, and we swapped seats. As soon as he pulled off, the sky was purple, and heavy rain fell. The way it hit the windshield, you would have thought someone was dumping a garbage bag full of skittles on the car. The revving engine resonated on my back as it vibrated the seats and my dad turned the music up louder, so loud, it was deafening. I remember reaching for the volume knob only to be thrust back into my seat. I was begging for him to slow down and before I knew it, I woke up 3-days later in Memorial Herman Hospital with a shiny laminated band on my wrist and my mom at my bedside in tears and a firm grip on my hand that told me she would never let go.

My mom hardly cries. I knew it had to be something terrible for her to be balling the way she was. I couldn't believe it when she told me my dad died. It was surreal, like a lucid dream. Just a few moments ago, we were just together and he was breathing. Now, he was gone. I scanned the room to avoid eye contact with my mother. There was no sign of relief in her grieving eyes and face. Only devastation.

I didn't know where I was going to go, but I had to get the hell out of there. I couldn't breathe. I pressed that damn call bell at least 50-times until the nurse showed up and sedated me. My mom and I stayed home for about two weeks after that. No more, no less. I'll never forget the day she snatched the blankets off my shivering body, flicked on the lights, and told me I was going back to school. She was fully dressed in her power suit with her hair all done up in a tight bun.

"The show must go on, baby. The world doesn't stop just because you need time to cope with your hurt feelings."

Her eyes were unreadable. It was the toughest love she had given me, but it was the reality of the situation. She had a family practice to run and I had an education to get. We still had to survive. All I could do was nod and say, yes ma'am.

On my first day back, I skipped track practice to catch an Uber to see Rick. I was still trying to maintain some order. That turned out to be a mistake. Uninvited and unannounced, I stood outside Rick's door. Knock, knock, knocking. Hope burned like fire in my chest, that he, would not be as deceitful as I hoped him not to be. I didn't want him to be responsible for damage that I feared would never fully be repaired. He did not answer the door. I called. No answer. Instead, I got a text.

RICK: I'M IN CHURCH!

ME: Prove it! Send me a photo!

RICK: No. I'm done, bro. You doin too much. Acting childish!

He claimed to be at church, so the driveway should have been empty. Yet, there was an unfamiliar gray Camaro parked in front of the garage. Still, there was no sign of the Nissan Altima he and best shared. It gave me a small glimmer of hope.

But it kicked. Kicked, kicked, like an unborn child. My gut ached and my eyes watered. I knew something was not right. If he wasn't home, then why was the A/C unit screeching and rattling inside his bedroom window? He was always saying they wanted to cut down on the electric bill. Running the A/C in an empty home hardly seemed like the way to go about it. I called repeatedly. As expected, he didn't answer. I pressed my ear against the dusty hardy-planked wall and held my unsteady breath, listening for the truth. I listened and prayed that I wouldn't hear what I thought I was going to hear. The pounding in my chest was deafening, but I was able to mute its, thump, thump, thumping, for a brief moment. And a brief was all I needed.

Voices… I heard Rick's. It was deep and wrapped me in familiar warmth. Then, the voice of a stranger. I couldn't breathe. An ongoing Final Destination-style 20-car pileup was taking place in my mind. Millions of irrational and destructive thoughts, bred from a place of hurt and betrayal, crashed into each other without mercy. I couldn't move. Moans of pleasure enraged me. And so, I found the biggest stick I could find in the yard underneath a massive pine tree that stretched over the driveway and jammed it repeatedly into the A/C unit until it started hitting high notes like Mariah Carey. Briefly, I fantasized about them both dying from heat exhaustion or something. I was dizzy and short of breath running back to my car and there, in the middle of the pinecone-covered driveway, I collapsed. With the neighbors as my audience, I wept so hard my throat throbbed.

The strained relationship with my dad, eating at a vacant dinner table, witnessing my mom's heartbreak, and feeling every bit of its crumble. After that, I spent 2-years changing in a separate bathroom before track practice, so that the other guys wouldn't get the chance to second-guess changing in front of me… All of it, for nothing! I wanted to hide.

Rick made a fool of me, and I made a fool of myself. I wanted to believe Prince Charming was real. But in a world riddled with drugs, sex, murder, Jackd, and Grinder, holding on to optimism like that, is easier said than done. After Rick's little stunt, I decided that maybe some men aren't made for relationships. They're made to be played. For years after that, I was hooking up every chance I got. 7 or 10 guys in a week. I was having hot-boy summers before Meg the Stallion could coin the term. I thought my heartbreak story ended with Rick. Nobody was allowed to get close.

It was all fun and games until I played with the wrong one and fell stupidly in love with an adonis named Terrence. Two years have flown by since my days with Terrence without stopping for me to take a beat. Meanwhile, I remain stuck here in my loveless suburban condo battling self-pity from my memories of love unrequited.

Hoe -Tale

I met Terrence in the summer of 2016. We should have followed the rules of hookup culture. No. Strings. Attached. Night fell and it was time for me to treat my reoccurring nightmares with sex, as the prescribed medication it was pretending to be for me.

Mesmerized, the first time I looked into his green eyes…We stood before each other in a filthy Palace Inn Motel in a questionable part of north Houston: Somewhere off 1960 and 45–Greenspoint, or "Guns-point," as some like to call it, about to sin. I had strayed too far from the suburban safety of The Woodlands. Courtesy of the infamous, Jackd. Jackd is an app that I and many others like me, visit frequently in search of a quick fix. It's a virtual black hole full of half-naked bodies and damaged goods Admittedly, it is not the most effective way to find love…if that's your thing. It used to be mine back in my Rick days. When I was with Rick, I was but another hopeless romantic looking for love that conveniently led with sex on the first date. On our first date, he took me to see the remake of Alice in Wonderland and told me that he wanted to make movies like that one day.

He was so passionate about it, it made him excited. I believed in his dream and we were in the bathroom stalls after that, making very bad decisions with our phone cameras. Spoiler, we were not making anything remotely respectable as Alice and Wonderland. And that was pretty much our relationship. Sex, lies, and videotapes. When it got old, I guess he looked for a new co-star. I've come to expect that sort of inconsistency after that. In a world riddled with hookup culture and *no-fucks-given* attitudes, romance is pretty much a thing of the past.

Terrence and I never had a first date. We did not get to spend the night before, anxiety-burdened and pondering over how good or tragic things could go. We did not get to romanticize about a happy ending in which a beautiful relationship blossomed, and about how we would spend our days traveling and sipping fine wine while someone serenaded us in an Italian accent on a gondola ride through the romantic waters of Florence Italy. We were as far away from Italy as you could get.

An open gravesite of dead roaches and ants resided in damn near every corner of the room. It reeked of cigarettes and stale cheeseburgers and the AC blew hot air. As much as I love to deny my stuck-up tendencies, at that moment, I was well aware that random sex in a cheap motel was beneath me. None of it mattered because Terrence stood before me with his black square-cut tank looking like it was painted on. I loved the way it hugged his chest and complemented his golden skin as it radiated under the dim lights. With one of those strong jawlines you only see in magazines, he formed a sly smile.

This was the sort of distraction I needed to keep my dark cloud at bay. It was dense with unexplained night terrors, obsessive thoughts, and the occasional shakes when driving in the rain. It made me want to lock myself in my closet and never come out of the house. Sex was my outlet for when my cloud was becoming too dense. I had to have him. Granted, I would have him. Soon. He sported a diamond-encrusted watch, which nearly blinded me when the light hit it just right. His golden Cartier Love bracelet could have been a sign of wealth or a front. I had no way of knowing. Although he seemed so together, something about him whispered scum bag in my ear. It was likely because he was the one to blame for having brought me to that grungy ass hotel. His place? Not on the table. My place? Not on the table.

He reached out to pull my slim figure towards him. His gold rings and a tasteful gold chain pressed up against my bare chest. A brief chill amongst my waist made me jolt, but only a little. I licked my lips as I admired how the outline of his pecs seem to thrust forward through all of the fibers in his shirt, daring me to touch. What drew me to him was the way his masculine gaze was peppered with a taste of unapologetic sexuality and maybe a hint of narcissism. I wasn't sure, but he seemed like the kind of guy who would fuck you good, and leave you hanging high and dry with a wet ass and fucked up credit. I took one look at him and wanted to taste him.

"So, wassup witcha, playa?" He said, his voice deep and naturally sensual. "I don't have a lot of time." He slid his shirt up the muscled ridges in his stomach, to reveal a large sculpted chest, with a tattoo of a maleficent viper. The way it slithered up and down his torso, had my eyes scanning down just how far the snake would lure me… Maybe it was the size of his arms and the sensuality in his voice, but something about his aura suggested he was a man's man. Maybe even… Charming? Dangerously so. To this day, I cannot take that away from him.

"I dunno, you tell me," I said, trying to be nonchalant like I wasn't itching to be with him in every way possible. I nearly choked on my own words from trying so hard. He was the fairest of feats I had ever laid in bed with, and that by no means, was an easy crown to dawn (if you're catching what I'm throwing). I was prepared for this to be the experience of a lifetime. As he laid on top of me and encircled his tongue behind my ear, below the lobe, and down the side of my neck, he paused to look into my eyes.

Quivering, I tried to follow the rules of hookup culture: little to no eye contact, don't ask questions, wear a condom, and most importantly, no kissing. It was all for nothing because he broke all the rules when he placed two slow kisses on my unsuspecting lips, igniting a lust so ravenous, I was compelled to kiss him back, returning the illusion of passionate love.

"Ima make you mine." He whispered in my ear. His warm, modest, Jack Daniels-scented breath, sent welcome chills down my neck.

I knew better than to believe that bullshit. But it still turned me on. And so, he went on to ravish me like we had known each other for years. He was selling a fantasy because that's how he preferred to get off. It was fine with me. It would have been selfish of me to have denied him the pleasure he was seeking. You can imagine my dismay when his phone started ringing. The first two times, he let it go to voicemail. But the third time, he jumped up so fast from in-between my cheeks, he had to have been light-headed for a moment.

"Everything alright?" I asked. He looked at me and shook his head as if burdened with the stress I had not the age or experience to understand. Meanwhile, I eyed in between his legs. It was starting to look more like a gummy worm the longer he stood there swiping on his phone. Whoever had been trying to reach him must have been fed up, because when he called back, I heard it go straight to voicemail. Then, there was a hollow and rapid knock at the door. "Jasmine!" He said in a harsh whisper as if we weren't the only two people in the room. It all went by so fast, because the next thing I knew, I heard a nagging voice piercing through the walls.

"Terrence, Mothafucka! I know you're in there! Open this damn door!" I rummaged around on that nasty ass motel floor and grabbed my belongings. I was about to high-tail it out the front door, when he grabbed me by the collar of my crisp Polo dress shirt and snatched me back so fast, my eyes danced around like a camera out of focus.

"The fuck iz you doin'!" It had been knocking on three days since I achieved more than 3 hours of sleep. I was irritable enough as it was, his pronunciation choices were disrespectful to me at that point, and none of the mess that was unfolding was helping my headache at all. I had come in an effort to force my body to sleep. Sex usually exhausted me so much that even my nightmares couldn't wake me. I can't say it was, R.E.M. because I always woke up the next morning, groggy and worn out as if I hadn't slept at all. But it was sleep, nonetheless.

"Leaving! Where the hell else would I be going?" I yelled back. "Not my woman. Not my problem. I did not sign on for this shit."

"You ain't going out THAT door!" He insisted. I looked around the room confused as hell. Was there a back door or something I didn't know about? "There's only one way out. And that's exactly where I'm going. You've already been caught, so I meannnnn...What's the point of all this extra?"

"Just hold on a sec, playa." he pleaded. He looked so terrified and beautiful at the same time. I almost felt bad for him. If the eyes are indeed the windows into the soul, there was the most curious view of a desperate and troubled little boy in his that made me willing to toss what little morals I had to the wind out of pity. He released his grip on my collar, walked over to a duffle bag he had stashed under the bed as if he had nowhere to be, and pulled out a bottle of Jack that had maybe one good shot left in it. I guess he figured he needed it, before opening that door and dealing with what was clearly, a scorned black woman. And she had every reason to be as angry as the blood vessels popping out of her neck suggested. The moment I opened the door, all hell broke loose.

"Jasmine! Whatcha doin' here!" He yelled from the other side of that dreadful spring mattress. He was acting like a fuckin' coward.

"I came to say goodbye! I'm going back to Chicago and I'm bringing Dwight with me!" She yelled back. Even with her mangled auburn-colored weave draping over her petite shoulders and the straps of her tattered red mini-dress, Jasmine was still radiant. Stressed out and scorned as hell but still beautiful. Her lightly bronzed skin and her hazel eyes were captivating me from the distance. Who cheats on a woman like that? I looked beyond her to see a drizzle wet the ground and a red Impala parked under the one street light in the parking lot that worked.

"Daddy! Daddy! Daddy!" I heard a little boy call from the back seat of the Impala. "Daddy! Daddy!

Daddy!" A little mixed-looking boy emerged from the car. He had to be around seven or eight-years-old.

"Get back in the car, Dwight!" Jasmine yelled. Terrence put his hand on his forehead as if he had a killer headache. "That is MY boy! You can't take him!"

"You lost that right when you blew off the custody hearing for a piece of ass and party favors!"

She pointed at me with her squinted evil eyes and rolled her neck as I was coming through the door. Then she pulled a bottle of pills from her purse and launched it at him. He ducked and the bottle hit the wall with a hollow clack and rattled like maracas. I tucked my head and zipped my lips. I was just about to take off sprinting to my car when "Wham!" A loud thud ricocheted off the walls and carried out the doorway. Imagine my shock when I turned to see Terrence out cold on that dirty ass carpet. Jasmine did all but run my little ass down in the doorway with a bulldozer to get to him. The little boy came running to his dad's aid in a stream of tears.

It was heart-wrenching. The poor little guy probably thought his dad was about to die before his innocent little matching blueish-green eyes. Apparently, they had a protocol that usually worked for this sort of thing because the son instinctively darted toward the mini-fridge for some ice water and dumped it all over his dad's face. Meanwhile, Jasmine continued to slap him in the face and demanded he wake up.

"Not again, you son-of-a-bitch! Don't do this to us again!" She screamed out in rageful tears. I could see her face was blood red from the parking lot as I made my way to my car. Trying to escape. I'm no good in emergencies. I get all jittery and short of breath, to the point I would need medical attention myself. It's the whole reason nursing school never worked out for me.

There was a whole lot of screaming for help going on between the two of them. I figured there wasn't too much I could do but call for some professional help on my way out, and maybe the Maury Show.

I'm sure had I gone over there with a pathetic attempt to perform CPR, his wife would have mauled me and left me for dead in a ditch somewhere. Or, I'd get all choked up and faint my damn self. I panicked and did the absolute worst thing one could have done during these "Stay Woke" times. Called 911. I was thinking that at the very least, they could get the medical attention he needed, but I was dead wrong!

I stuck around to watch from the safety of my car. After about 15-minutes, a police car and an ambulance pulled up to the scene. One of the officers rushed to the scene while one searched Jasmine's car for no apparent reason.

Another one of the officers pulled the little boy away from Terrence's side, kicking and screaming. That's when I realized I had made matters worse. Paramedics jumped from the sides of the truck and darted toward him.

"Please! Please! Don't take him! Don't take my son!" The woman cried. The officer put the boy in his cruiser and after necessary but degrading groveling on her hands and knees, he allowed her to get in the backseat. The cruiser pulled off and it started pouring down rain! Terrence had finally come to and at the right time. The paramedics stepped away to give him some space. Several of them ask the stupid question:

"Are you alright, sir?" He stumbled around, trying to find his balance before finally falling to his knees, with hands of prayer raised to the heavens begging God for mercy, as he witnessed his son be driven away in the backseat of a police car.

"Is that your Impala?" one of the officers asked. He glanced over at the car and nodded his head. As his hands were held high, the men in blue cuffed his wrists. I could hear the revving engine of an old Crown Victoria, which grew fainter as it sped off into the distance, and the sounds of raindrops falling from the rooftops pounding the pavement. Suddenly, it all seemed to be happening in slow motion. What an ugly sight it was to see a 40-something-year-old man in hysterical tears. Droplets of dirty rainwater poured relentlessly from the leaking roof and onto his face. Guilt compelled me to leave the safety of my car. I could not stand by while they took him to jail and it all has been my fault.

I sprinted from my car to the entrance of the hotel room. "Get. The Hell—Out!" He snapped at me as I was approaching the scene. I must have startled the officers because they were quick to draw their hands back to the guns tucked in their holsters upon my abrupt arrival. I stopped dead in my tracks and put both my hands in the air. The rain drenched my clothes. My heart was pounding and for the first time, I realized just how much danger I had put myself in. I shouted that I was unarmed and that I was the one who made the call.

"I'm his therapist!" I blurted out. "He needs medical attention!" I would have reached for my work badge, but I had been watching too much shit on Youtube about cops murdering people and I'm one of those people who are quick to jump to the worst-case scenario. Whether my fear was rational or not, I wanted to avoid giving them any reason to think I was a threat. I was and never will be in the mood to become another face of the Black Lives Matter movement. "Step away, sir," one of them said. His hand was gripping his holster with force and his arched eyebrows dared me to make one wrong move.

"Check my pockets, please!" Their white faces eyed me in disbelief. I couldn't imagine how they could look at me and think I was a threat, but I can only imagine the amount of fear they might battle with daily, with having to enforce the law in a world where we are being taught to not trust men in blue no more than politicians.

I knew fear can make people act irrationally at times. But had I been shot, not even I, with my privileged and sheltered suburban kid lens, could justify or even begin to understand why. I was dressed in labels, as Carrie Bradshaw liked to call them. My nails were freshly manicured, and my naturally soft-spoken voice couldn't have been any less intimidating, even while yelling. I was no threat, but they had no way of knowing. My thumbs trembled and I broke out in a cold sweat as I invited them to search me. Who knew what that would bring? A face full of concrete? Bludgeoned to death with a club? Or shot in cold blood? The news had me thinking the worst.

"Please!" I begged.

"Hey! I think I got something!" One of the officers called from behind the bed. He was holding a bottle of pills in the air. "Looks like prescription Xanax! No name on the label." All I could do was shake my head and drop my shoulders. We were surely going to jail.

Blurred Lines

Weak knees and all, I kneeled to offer Terrence a helping hand. Years of elite track and field will do that to you. Part of me was expecting a thank you for having called in a favor from my mother to have him admitted to the psych hospital she often referred her patients to. I had to convince the officers that this was a suicide attempt and that he needed help. Not jail. Even with the smudges and dirt on his face, and the pungent stench of alcohol and deadbeat dad on his breath, I could still appreciate his beauty. All of it–wasted.

When I reached out for his grimy hands which were covered in dried-up traces of alcohol and tear stains, he shoved me away so hard, I nearly fell back on that rank-ass carpet.

"What part of get the hell out did you not understand!"

Raising one brow and folding my arms, "Make me." I said. He fumbled around on the floor some more, before rising to his feet. "Don't trrrrry me, bruh." He said, his speech slurred heavily and his head swaying to the right and then to the left.

"I just saved your ass! Apparently, there's a warrant out for your arrest. The leeeeeast you could do is let me help you and maybe say thank you. The whole paramedic crew stopped dead in their tracks as if they were about to place bets. I did not know him from a can of paint, but after seeing a man lose his son, I figured he would need somebody to just be present. The paramedics convinced him to get in the truck and I hopped right in along for the ride. He ignored me the whole ride to the hospital. I wanted to ask him about where the hell he got Xanax from, but it wasn't the time. Patients come to my office all the time, totally dependent on that stuff. God knows what reason he had to be on it.

When we arrived, Terrence was sitting up on the stretcher at the back of the truck refusing to go inside. He insisted that he was fine and that he would call someone to pick him up. "It's either the hospital or jail," I said. Wrinkles formed on his forehead, "I'd rather take my fuckin' chances" The fact that he'd risk going to jail was enough to convince me that he was a lost cause. Eventually, he conceded and the men escorted him to the ER waiting room. While he checked in and waited for one of the doctors to do an assessment, I made a stop by the food court and grabbed some square-cut pineapples and a pack of Nutty Buddy Bars from the cafeteria. I hadn't eaten much of anything all that day.

When I got back, Terrence was missing from the waiting room. I hurried out the sliding doors and found him outside sitting on the curb. A tall skinny man was standing near him carrying a briefcase in one hand and holding an iPhone to his ear with the other. He stunted in a dazzling Dior suit. I knew it was Christian Dior because I spotted the gold cuff links, with the iconic

CD initials engraved in them as I approached the scene. He had creamy skin and looked to be mixed with Indian and something else, maybe black or Cuban.

"You look a mess," Terrence called out to him. He was sitting just outside the entrance to the emergency room, holding a bag of ice to his forehead.

"You get all cleaned up for me?" The man said. He stepped onto the back of the truck and I got a glimpse of his shiny pair of Louboutin loafers. They were black with the signature Lou- Spikes spiraling over the toecap. Tasteful. They were classic. I had a pair just like them. Red with gold spikes. Worn once when I hooked up with a lawyer who invited me to a country club, only to show me some vacant area behind all the machines in the laundry room and drop his load in me. I formed a fake smile as the man narrowed his gaze at me.

"And you are?" he asked. Sassy bitch he was. His attitude suggested that he was judging me and so I did what I always did. Pretend to be unbothered. I sat down on the curb next to Terrence and crossed my legs. This time, however, I wanted him to see my red Giuseppe sneakers. The two gold metal plates that wrapped around the top of the shoe, bounced the moonlight off their glossy surface and made me proud. "I'm a friend," I said, knowing damn well all of a few hours ago, I didn't know his first name.

"And you are?" I sassed back.

"Jarvis. His—sponsor."

I couldn't believe it. A man like him, a sponsor? He seemed so—together. Then again, I briefly thought Terrence was charming in a weird I don't give a fuck kind of way. What did I know? Not a damn thing. I guess it's true. You can never know what demons people are hiding from a single glance at their red bottoms. We're all fighting something. Chasing, something.

Longing, for something. And that unsatisfied hunger influences our actions every day.

God knows what Terrence had going on and how long it took to drive a man to drink his life away, or whatever substance abuse problem I assumed he had going on.

"You can just leave, Jarvis. The both of you." He snapped, "I'll call an Uber."

"Then why would you have me come up here and waste my time, Terrence?"

"Wait, you told him to come here?" I interjected.

"Yeah. I got the messages right here. Not that I need to show you. He rolled his eyes at me and shook his head. It was clear that Jarvis had built up some sort of immunity to Terrence's episodes, because his deep brown eyes only looked at him with what seemed like endearment and empathy, instead of shock and disappointment. He stroked his trimmed goatee and took a deep breath. "Substituting one for another? You know you can't recover that way." Terrence kept silent and avoided making eye contact with both of us. Out of shame or annoyance. I wasn't sure.

"I'll take it from here, Mr. uh…"

"Khai," I said. "Right." He said. "Looks like you've got your hands full." The judgment behind his eyes recognized me for the mess I was. I realized I looked ridiculous holding my plate of pineapples and Nutty Buddies. Labels be damned. That was my cue. I had done enough. I had no business there. Terrence may have broken all the rules back at the hotel, but me calling the police which resulted in his son being taken away, inviting myself to his trip to the emergency room, and talking to his sponsor, I had re-written the rules.

It was dark and I had no way to get home. My car was still back at the hotel. I called an Uber back and sat in my car for over 30-minutes trying to muster up the strength to pull out of the parking lot. The rain was still coming down heavily and it was pitch black outside. Only one of the three streetlights in the parking lot worked and it flickered, spending more time off than it did on. I was damp, cold, humiliated, and sexually frustrated.

The rain eventually died down to a drizzle and I was able to get on the road with fewer nerves. I spent the drive home in silence with not even the steady blow from the air-conditioning as my soundtrack. I always liked to take the back roads home. There's something nostalgic and calming about the tree-lined roads and bluebonnets in the pastures when spring was in full effect. It was always quieter than the main freeways and less crowded in terms of traffic, better suited for my little problem with anxiety.

I was the only car for as far as my eyes could see. 30-minutes in and my eyes were heavy. I got a glimpse of them in the rearview mirror and wasn't surprised to see they were suffocating in barbed wire veins of red. They were begging to close for just a moment. The lines began to run together until it was all one big illuminated, yellow blur. Thump-Thump. Thump-Thump. Thumping, my tiers went as they veered on and off the rumble strips lining the side of the road. Before long, my head became a block of led and planted itself onto the horn. My eyes shut and all I could feel was the sway of my car shifting back and forth. My tires let out warning screeches as the Lane Assist tried pulling me back on the straight and narrow. Money well spent.

If you have experienced sleep paralysis, then you know exactly how I was feeling. Fully aware of what was happening, but incapable of moving a muscle. This induced a state of panic. The most silent and helpless form of panic one can ever experience. It's like I was listening and visualizing my death as it was happening, and I was unable to do anything to stop it. Something straight out of the Dexter Morgan plastic-wrap playbook.

Images of a winding back road and pouring rain flashed in and out of my mind with each crack of thunder. My mind imagined the endless yellow lines ahead of me, but my hands were not steering and my foot was not in control of the gas. I did not recognize this road and it was evening instead of night. Things were not making sense. I had seen these images before in a reoccurring dream but none of it had any meaning to me.

A puff of warm fermented breath passed behind my ears and across my nose, and a young boy's voice, crying: "Wake up, daddy! I'm scared!" The thunder cracked once more, and it all faded to blackness again. Only the sounds of the crying boy remained. Tears fell from my sealed eyes. I was preparing for the worst. Those expensive ass computer systems could only do so much and were reaching their limitations. I heard a long honking from what sounded like an 18-wheeler getting closer and closer. I squirmed and squirmed in my mind helplessly as if tied to a railroad with a runaway train headed in my direction. My mind willed my body to move something. Anything! But nothing worked!

Just as my car was veering off into the oncoming lane and the wailing horn was at its peak, I came to and was able to grip the wheel and swerve into the grassy pasture. My heart was thrashing behind my chest, trying to escape its boney prison and my arms were shaking as I held a death grip on the wheel. I couldn't move. This time, by choice. I needed to catch my breath. After several nervous minutes, I exited the car and assess the damage. There was nothing but clunks of mud and grass wedged between my tires and fenders, but I still had to call a tow truck to pull me out of the mud.

It took 2-hours before anyone showed up and I didn't make it home until a little after midnight. After a hot shower and picking over my fruit salad and baked chicken mom brought to the office for me because she knew I still used my oven for decoration, I crawled into bed. Maybe I should have popped the Xanax my mom prescribed for me, but I feared the side effects, so I kept them locked away in my medicine cabinet. A glorious California King hugged my body with silk sheets, 8 fluffy pillows, and a warm weighted mink blanket that my mom bought in Korea. It had been in the family for over 15 years. Sleep? I would never know it. Every night, a nightmare. I usually like to scribble little details about my dreams in my journal to interpret them later but there is one that I always try to forget. It's this reoccurring one that I was terrified of what it might lead to if it dared to explore its origin. Too much blood, too much rain.

I would stare at the ceiling and fantasize about what it was like to sleep peacefully. An hour went by and my eyes finally shut. Just as I felt myself drifting. I saw a blinding light shine behind the blackness of my eyelids. I thought about Terrence. A replay of his desperate hands reaching towards the sky in between the pouring raindrops towards the flashing red and blue lights as they pulled away with his son. Something about it was familiar. The lights flashed and flashed behind my eyelids with complete disregard for my need to sleep. Terrence's deep, but weakened voice pleading, only to fall upon deaf ears, made me identify with his feelings of failure. I would lie awake that night, tossing, turning, tossing and turning, and glaring at the clock as what remained of the night seemed to fly by. I remained with my eyes peeled open, forced to look into the mirror of yesterday and try to piece together the origins of my madness. Then, trying not to remember when things became too vivid.

I wanted to log on to Jackd, get my fix and call it a night, but the thunder outside my widow punked me. I settled for porn, a bottle of Stella Rosa, and two shots of Vodka. Most nights, I still lie awake thinking of that day. If things had worked out with Terrence, I would have probably had a very different night. The fact that I was still thinking about him was weird to me, but I tried to ignore it. Still, my little hoe-tale and lost battle with blurred lines will forever be marked as the beginning of a tumultuous series of bad decisions that would ultimately result in my self-ruin.

Crossing Lines

I should have followed my mom's rules. They were simple. See 8 patients a day. Report to her. Don't make any clinical decisions regarding a patient's care plan without consulting her. Show up to Sunday dinner and most importantly, don't get too close to the patients.

My mom, a seasoned psychiatrist, owns a thriving family practice. I was working in my mom's clinic so that I could complete the remaining clinical hours I needed so that I might receive a piece of paper qualifying me to treat the mentally ill. My mom's hard work made finding a clinical site so easy it was almost unfair. She's all the educated black woman and business savvy everyone likes to imagine when they think of Black Girl Magic.

In exchange for the hassle-free and paid clinical hours she provided, I agreed to work in her office as the onsite Counselor for a year after graduating. In the meantime, she paid me to manage the clinic. It was her dream fully realized. Every time I walked into the office; her honeydew eyes lit up like a star on a Christmas Tree. Lord only knows how many nights she stayed up dreaming about the day her baby boy would join the family business.

Although I wasn't completely on board emotionally with the career path ahead of me, I thought maybe I could be the Elle Woods of therapists. If I was going to spend the rest of my days behind a desk, why not be fabulous doing it? Would you believe it? All the sparkling pens, velvet lounge chairs, Giuseppes, and optimism in the world turned out to be no help at all! I was struggling to finish my hours because the closer I became to a very special patient, named Jane Mallard, who other than myself, was probably the loneliest person I had ever met, the less motivated I started to feel.

In my first year of working, I quickly learned that you can never truly know what demons people are battling. And in that time, I would find myself burdened with this haunting sadness that had no origin. Exploring the sea of my suppressed emotions sounded better when I encouraged my patients to do it.

Some days, I'd feel so low that I wouldn't even bother to come into the office. My mom was mostly sympathetic when I asked for mental health days (a perk you get when your mom owns the practice). She always called to check up on me every hour as if I had the flu or something. When I insisted I was fine and that she didn't need to worry, she'd say "I just worry about you sometimes, Khai. You don't handle stress well." Then she'd bring up nursing school.

I guess the little problem I developed with anxiety which resulted in an embarrassing panic attack that ended my nursing career before it got started, did a number on her. I was in mostly better spirits than in the nursing school era, that's for sure. Patients would come from all over Houston, carrying trauma ranging from rape and molestation to bankruptcy, murder, suicide, and kidnapping. More times than not, I felt like a fraud. I didn't feel comfortable telling people how to cope with all the ugly realities happening before their eyes. 25 years of coddled life. What did I know about real pain? If anything, I wanted to learn from my patients.

I was firmly planted on a career path that had been laid out for me before I knew what a college credit was so I missed out on the normal high school experience for the most part after "The Closet" days. The social aspects of it, that is. Because of it, I was able to graduate well before I would have planned for myself. I resented my parents for a while back then. I blamed them for making me grow up too fast. Maybe it's because of the fast-forward on everything, that I always felt I was just going through the motions. Not really experiencing things. Same as now—still going through the motions. Patient in. Patient cries. I give a sympathetic ear. Offer advice they surely will not take, nor should they. Go to school. Contemplate my poor life decisions while doing so. Leave the office. Jog down at Buffalo Bayou Park. Go home. Shower. Eat. Hook up with some random guy on Jackd. If the first fix wasn't enough, I'd hook up with two more. Watch Housewives. Wallow in self-pity, close my eyes, and hope not to have the same nightmare. Wake up screaming and sweating. Stare at the clock until my eyes burned. Get up. Do it all over again.

I had many patients that came in and out of my office. But of the 20-plus patients that I was responsible for, only one would stand out above the crowd and that was Jane Mallard. The absence of Steve, her husband of 20 years, broke her. Jane and I formed a friendship during our sessions together, one that I would go on to cherish very much.

It was early September of 2016. Jane and I were scheduled for our usual meeting at a local animal shelter. Every Friday, we always sat outside on a bench across from the entrance and watched as stray dogs and cats were brought in. I'd always bring a caramel macchiato for her and a raspberry passion tea, with 8-pumps of classic and added lemonade for me. This time, before joining her on the bench, I observed her for a moment from my car. It was getting cooler outside and the air was dry. Occasionally, she'd have to stop and dab her nose with her pink handkerchief. After lightly beeping my horn to let her know I was there, I stepped out of my Benz and walked up to her with a smile. My scarf blew in the wind, but I didn't mind. "I'm here for the drama, dahling." She said.

"It's all for you, my queen." She took a sip of her coffee and exhaled deeply.

"Mmm. You know just how to order it, hun. Thank you." I followed her lead, sat down, and sipped my tea.

"Anytime."

"I sure hope when December rolls around, you will stop ordering that fruity ass tea like it's the middle of spring." Her voice was a horse. I could tell she had been crying. Her cheeks and eyes were still a little puffy.

"Why do you drink hot coffee outside in the summer? If I remember correctly, I think you owe me a pair of shoes. Or, did you forget?" I said, recalling last summer when a bird flew too damn close to our heads and I wigged out. I knocked her boiling cup of coffee out of her hands and onto my white Giuseppe sneakers with gold zippers on the side. "$1,500 soiled with caffeine!" She batted her eyes and sipped her coffee once more.

"You're far too intelligent to have such an irrational fear of birds, hun." I smiled and nudged her with my shoulder.

"Look!" She exclaimed. Her thin eyebrows raised as she pointed with one and while she held down her orange French beret. The wind blew the floating strands off her curly grey wig in my face. It smelled like strawberries. I had to swipe the flyaway strands off the bridge of my nose and the tips of my eyelashes to get a glimpse. The dog catcher had just pulled up and was fighting with a spunky black and white Jack Russell. It escaped its cage somehow and darted out the back of the van the moment the man swung open its doors. No matter how much he yelled, griped, and pulled on his hog holder contraption, the little guy would fight back. The man cursed like he stole something before finally yanking the rod hard enough that his four legs took flight and dangled like tassels in the wind. The little guy yelped, but he was unharmed. We both laughed and took a sip of our drinks. "Aww! Poor fella!" I said.

"That one's a fighter. I like it!" She said back. I knew I was not supposed to be there and was under strict orders to only see patients in the office, but Jane had stopped taking her meds. And from my mom's final progress note in her chart, it sounded like she had no intention of ever taking meds again. Her recent diagnosis of Lupus did nothing for her Depression, she had sworn off all psych meds after her battle with dependency. I never understood her attachment to the shelter, but it seemed to bring her joy.

"How are you?" I asked. "I'm worried that with Steve gone, you'll…ya know. Are you having those thoughts again? You know to call me, right?"

"Calm down, hun. I'm lonely. But I'm coping." She said. "Besides, I have you and Scandal. I don't need medication, hun. Stop worryin'. Matter of fact…" She paused for dramatic effect. "Consider it…"

"Handled!" I finished for her. We both laughed and talked about how Kerry Washington was born to play that role. But that word, lonely, loitered around in my mind. "Well, Jane, I think it's time you found a hobby."

"A hobby?" Her southern bell accent slipped a bit. "I have hobbies, hun! I like to bake and play Bingo down the road there off I-45 and 1960 every Friday night." Her eyes were big and full of awe. I smiled and shook my head.

"First of all, you didn't start going to Bingo until I mentioned it."

"Okay, annnd?" She said tilting her neck. "Moral of the story, I got hobbies."

"I'm thinking something more long-term. You know, to keep you busy, make you feel loved. Oh! I know! Maybe a new puppy?"

"You mean, distract me."

"Maybe a little."

"I'm tired of hobbies and I don't need distractions, hun. That's the problem. Steve and I used to travel the world together. From the Eiffel Tower to the white-sand beaches of Greece and Costa Rica, I've seen water so blue it'll make even the most macho of men gushy.

It sounded like a dream. "What happened? Why did you choose to stay behind this time?" She looked down at her coffee, cupped between her hands and resting on her lap, and shook her head.

"I can't get on a plane. I'm just tired, hun. Tired." I found it hard to believe Steve would leave her for a vacation in her time of need, but I went along with it.

"Does Steve know?"

"Steve is still full of life. I try not to worry him these days." she said as she clenched onto the black silk tie with a gold airplane clip that was engraved with the initials, S.M. "I don't want to drag him down with my —" She hesitated. "I can't keep up. My body aches all over, I can never seem to get enough rest, my memory is fading, I'm losin' my hair and with these spells of nausea and dizziness, hun, I am in no condition to travel."

"I don't understand how he could just leave you knowing you clearly haven't been feeling well." Her eyes watered and she wiped the tears before they could fall. She missed him. The twinkle in her eyes as she recalled the glory days told me everything I needed to know.

"Damn wind, dryin' my eyes out." She was holding back something. Something painful because I saw her grip her gut at the thought of it. I chose not to pry. She would eventually come around to telling me the truth about why Steve has not been home when she was ready. I didn't know what to do, so I just hugged her and promised I would be there for her if she would have me.

"I see you, hun." She said. I tilted my head and scowled.

"What do you mean?"

"Maybe you should consider the dog. Or, maybe a boyfriend. A real one." She said.

"Ha-ha! I'd be a terrible dog owner. In fact, how do you know that's not my dog giving that man a hard time?"

"Well, please promise me you'll think about it." She said.

"Hmm... Only if you promise me you will think about it as well." I said.

"The hobby or the medication, hun?"

"Both."

She nodded and we both finished our drinks and rambled on about what kind of dogs we've always wanted. She told me she wanted something small so that she could carry it around like the baby she and Steve could never have. And I told her I wanted something with stamina so that I could take it on my evening runs down at the park.

The clock struck 1 p.m. and after an exchange of hugs, Jane was gathering her things when she received a phone call that made her gasp and clench her invisible pearls.

"Is everything alright I asked?"

"I'm not sure." She said. "H–Hello?"

A man cleared his throat on the other end of the phone.

"Hello. Is this Jane?" The man said.

"Yes. This is she. May I ask who's calling?"

"It's Jim. Afraid I got some troublin' news for ya." Jane sat down and took a deep breath. A few seconds later she hung up the phone without a word.

"Everything alright?" I asked, placing my hand on her shoulder.

"It's Steve! He's not coming back!"

"When is the last time you heard from him?"

"Got a postcard a week ago. Said he was in Nevada for a hiking trip. But he's been gone for a while now. I hired a PI." I had known Jane for about a year and had never met Steve. He was always away on a trip.

"Maybe there's an explanation. Besides, it's not the first time." I tried to reassure her.

"Maybe he just went on another bender and will turn up soon," I said, remembering when she mentioned how many times they used to miss flights back in the day because of his hangovers.

"Maybe so." She said. I could tell she wasn't convinced. "It's my fault he's even out there. I didn't know what that meant. Without any more formalities, she got up, wiped her tears, and headed toward her car. I worried as I watched her pull away in her old white convertible 1970 VW Beetle. She must have been able to tell I was concerned because she waved behind the glass of her cracked windshield and smiled at me as if it were supposed to give me some sort of reassurance or something. I was supposed to be the one comforting her. But I had no idea how. Regardless, it would have to wait.

It was time for my meeting with Dr. LeRoy. He was my assigned clinical supervisor and family friend. I met him through my mom. He used to work at the clinic but he left to work in a substance abuse Residential Living Facility in Midtown. I was only required to report to him once a month, but because he was the only other gay professional I knew at the time, I'd visit with him often. He had an office out in Montrose, the gayborhood of Houston, where he also saw patients for therapy.

It was an old brick building that looked like one of those former single-family homes that had been repurposed. It smelled like old oak with a hint of vanilla. Unlike most head doctors you go to, he did not have all his degrees on the wall. Instead, he had one massive mural on the accent wall as soon as you walk in.

The oil painting appeared to capture the silhouette of a nude man sitting in Indian style with a green glow, meditating in a serene garden. It was eye-catching but unusual in my opinion, given that it was the only thing on the walls. A warm brown coddled the other walls like a childhood blanket. On his desk, stood a few framed photos of him with his two older children and wife riding horses on what I assumed had to be Galveston beach, given the water in the background looked like chocolate milk. It all came together to create a sense that this is a safe place. An open space. He invited me to take a seat and I submitted to his command. He stood up from behind his desk and joined me in the center of the room. I sat in the gray loveseat facing the window, and he planted himself in a matching gray chair with a high tufted back across from me.

Dr. LeRoy is the kind of man that appears intimidating at first glance. Tall, slim, yellow, handsome, but more importantly black and educated. He's the kind of guy my mom would want for me: *You need to bring home somebody who brings more than dick and balls to the table.* She would always say. I was so used to being the one behind the desk, it started to feel like a scene straight out of Freaky Friday.

He sat quietly for a minute. Perhaps, observing my body language. That would have been my first instinct as well. The best time to observe someone's body language is when they are not aware of it. That is the closest one can come to decoding the true nature of a person without having exchanged any words. *Words can tell lies, but body language tells the truth.* That's what LeRoy always remembered to tell me at the end of our meetings. Suddenly, every time I sat down with him, I felt like my every movement was analyzed. It made me feel the need to be more put together than I was capable of being. It all went away the moment he asked me, "How are you breathin', my brotha?" I wasn't even sure what he meant, but he always seemed sincere when he said things. He leaned in towards me and searched my eyes.

I needed to avoid eye contact, so I scanned the walls. "I'm alright," I said, still observing the room for anything other than his eyes.

"That's a nice bag. What is it?"

"It's Coach."

"I shoulda known. You and your Labels."

"Don't do that?" I said, with my face all twisted up.

"Do what?"

"Belittle me because I like to shop. We all have to find something we enjoy on this earth while we wait to die."

"I wasn't judging. I think it's cute. You always come in here fly. You just have this confidence about you. It's infectious." That caught me off guard. If only he knew I wore labels because they gave me the boost I needed to make it look like I had confidence."

"Thank you. Sorry, you know I can overreact sometimes."

"I'm right here." He said. I was avoiding eye contact more than ever at that point. I was staring at the clouds behind him and following the birds that flew by until they were out of my line of sight.

"I know." I finally said.

"Then what's the problem?" He was distractingly handsome. That's what.

"Just looking around."

"You say that every time you come here. Surely you've made yourself aquatinted with my office by now. Do I make you nervous?"

"Meh, I see something new every time I come in."

"Oh yeah? What did you notice this time?" He raised one brow and smiled at me. Well, in that photo of you with your family at Galveston Beach, you're not wearing a ring."

"Interesting. What else?"

"You and your wife are apart."

"So what?" He quizzed.

"So, there's trouble in paradise. But that's just a guess based on what little information I have to work with." I thought he'd be offended or a little defensive but oddly, he smiled.

"You and I both know you'd be right to guess that."

"Jokes aside, I'm sorry to hear that."

"I'm not." He interjected. "We were both miserable. We didn't want that energy to infect our kids."

"Oh, okay. I thought I—" The notebook he was fiddling with fell from his lap. He interrupted me to lean over and pick it up.

"You still seeing that one patient, with the missing husband?" He opened the notebook to a blank page and started jotting some things down.

"Yeah," I said. "My mom says if she continues to be non-compliant with meds, she will discharge her."

"Do you not agree?"

"I just don't feel comfortable giving up on her like that. I dunno. Something about it felt like abandonment."

"Khai, your heart is in the right place. But the toughest reality in this line of work is that you cannot save everybody and that you cannot force someone to accept your help. You also have a duty to protect yourself, your license, and the integrity of whatever practice you're working with." He sounded like my mother's minion. But what could I expect from someone that she mentored?

"I know," I said, nodding my head. "But I honestly feel like I can get through to her. She just needs a friend more than anything."

"Be careful. Reopening old wounds with unstable patients is not only highly ineffective but also risky. "I never pry too far. I let her guide me there." I stopped him to defend myself.

"I hear you. But remember, most patients in her condition do not have the coping skills to handle the reemergence of suppressed emotions that therapy will inevitably demand they uncover." Now, he sounded like one of my old textbooks. It wasn't that I didn't agree with him. Jane was not a case study in a textbook or a liability like my mom believed. She was my friend. I couldn't abandon her. Why did she have to be unstable? She had denied any suicidal ideation for months. She was wearing makeup again, and she was slowly finding things to occupy her time that she enjoyed.

"She listens to me. And she trusts me. A lot of the time if I make something seem like it's her idea, she's more inclined to do it. She wasn't going to Bingo until I suggested it. It just took a while for her to open up to the idea."

"I trust you'll figure out the right thing to do."

"Thank you. But I'll reconsider if things don't seem to get any better. I promise." I said.

"Just remember, wasted time is not something you can buy back." He said, uncrossing his legs and standing up. I wasn't sure if that was shade or not, but I was definitely rethinking how I was handling Jane.

"Now, I know someone else who needs a friend." He stood over me for a second, his crotch inches away from my face. Leaning over, he lifted my chin gently with his finger and with one look, demanded my eyes surrender to the desire I was hiding behind them. His actions were mannish, but his touch was tender. He read my body for signs of approval, and I read his. A sly smile, a lick of the lips, his hand on my head, and my face to his crotch, was all it took. I couldn't fight it. Hell, I didn't want to. He bent me over the chair and climbed my back.

Blatant disregard for professional lines… I knew it was wrong, but I didn't care. From the grunts and breathy moans Dr. LeRoy was releasing behind my ears as he bit down on his tie, he didn't care either. Professor. Student. Supervisor. Ex-boyfriend… Married. Whatever. Why miss out on perfectly good dick, because of a label?

Bad Decisions

Never have I everrr…had sex in a graveyard. Okay, I'm lying, but hear me out. Jackd had become a parasite in my life. When sex is easy, and at your fingertips, it can be hard to resist for someone like me who is driven by his desires. There is no satisfaction greater than tasting the fruits of instant gratification. It can become a cycle.

Meet on Jackd, exchange pics, send freaky texts, hookup, then ghost them until your itch needs to be scratched by the same dick again. Eventually, you fall off and both move on to another fuck buddy. In this lifestyle, you become numb to the cycle. The quick fucks, sexting, and the occasional party drug start to feel normal. Before you know it, you're an addict. An addict to a cycle that does little to improve your ability to connect and share true intimacy.

I was deep in the hookup cycle. The release I got from an orgasm was the only time I could guarantee sleep at night. Thoughts about my dead father and Jane made sleeping that much harder. I couldn't help but think that my inability to help Jane through such a bleak moment in her life, had everything to do with my lack of experience and know-how. It was embarrassing. I'm ashamed to say that the embarrassment spawned resentment toward my parents. None of the work I was doing was the fruition of my ambition. Hell, I still don't know what they are to this day, but after "The Closet," I would spend the rest of my days feeling obligated to make up for my shortcomings—Feeling as if I owed my mom for having embarrassed her and maybe even breaking her heart.

One night, I was underneath my black mink blanket trying to close my eyes and hoping not to dream. It was pointless. 10-minutes in, and I was back in the same wrecked car. This time, watching from behind a shattered windshield that was speckled with blood. A man hollered for help from the driver's seat of his smashed pick-up truck in the distance. The whole front end looked like it had been pummeled with Thor's mighty hammer. The car was engrossed in a violent flame and as it grew bigger, so did the man's cries

"Heeeelp! God, please! Heeel—" The truck burst into flaming metal pieces that flew into the air before they sprawled all over the road. I hear one final hysterical cry for help. The smoke chokes me as it invades my lungs and it's as if the man's pain is mine. The desperate whimpers of a child echoes in my mind. When the pain became so sharp that I felt as if I had been impaled with an arrow to the gut, my arms curled over my knees and my eyes sprung open. Sweating and hyperventilating. When I reached for my phone, I couldn't hold it steady. I glared at the clock and held my stomach as I leaned over the edge of the bed white-girl wasted style, anticipating seeing my dinner a second time. This time, splattered all over my bedroom floor. It was half past midnight and I had yet to get any sleep.

I stayed there until my racing thoughts and rapid heartbeat became overwhelming. I was forced to find a temporary solution. Well, distraction. I hooked up with a guy who went by the screen name J-long on Jackd. I just called him Jay. He was mixed with black and Asian. Stood about 6-feet tall and liked to play in his parent's garage when nobody was home. 37 years old and no place to call his own and still calling himself the plug. Not suitable for dating, but he was a lot of fun for 8-minutes. One and done. Nothing more. I returned home around 3 a.m. and slept for 3-hours before it was time for me to get ready for work.

The next day after work, I had another session with Dr. LeRoy in his office. Later that evening, I met Mark. Mark was a chocolate snack, barely taller than me but had the body of a ball a football player to make up for it. His idea of a "date" was atop a hill in a graveyard hidden deep in the backwoods of Willis Texas. The first time we hooked up, I drove 40-minutes into the country and parked my car at some old church in the woods. He pulled up next to me in an old white Dodge Durango. His face was damp and his shirt was stuck to his skin. After a quick exchange of glances to make sure we matched our profile photos,

"Get in!" He said. Something told me to run, but I also knew what I came for and suddenly danger didn't exist.

"The church?" I asked, as I open the squeaky door and abandoned my car to hop in a complete stranger's truck in the middle of nowhere. As soon as the door slammed, I knew why his face was damp…The fuckin' AC didn't work! We rode in silence for about 5-minutes. There wasn't much to see but a bunch of trees, grassy hills, ditches, dirt, and a few junkyards. I couldn't shake the frown from my face when I noticed a sea of tombstones lining a dirt road getting closer and closer. We passed by a fence on the way in that wasn't keeping anything in or out because it was hanging off its hinges and covered in overgrown weeds and dirt clumps. The potholes, rocks, and snapped tree branches jerked my neck and shoulders back and forth as he sped over them with confidence. He must have noticed I was having a miserable time because he leaned over and placed a firm grip on my shoulders to hold me still. "That's why I had you park your car, bro." He said. "That Benz couldn't handle all this."

"Why here? We could have at least done this in the church, and it would've been just as hot."

"Nah, bro. I go to that church." I didn't know what to say. Apparently, sex around a bunch of dead people was better than sex in a church. The graves sites were blotchy and more than half of them were cracked or covered in weeds and ant piles. We drove over two hills before the truck finally came to a slow and squeaky stop underneath a large weeping willow tree in the back corner about a quarter mile away from the busted gate. The path was worn with tire tracks like he had been there many times. I ignored that part. Beyond the tree was nothing but deep woods for miles and in the other direction, well I tried not to think about it. Nothing but dead grandparents and beloved ancestors. He propped me on the truck bed and took my shirt off. No formalities. He didn't bother to ask if I was okay with hooking up in a graveyard, or anything. It was as if he knew I was not about to put up much of a protest.

After a grope here and there, heavy kissing, and nipple play, I succumbed to my arousal and we rocked the graves of someone's Christian grandparents. I'm sure of it. I knew it was wrong, but it was exhilarating, so I went back for more. After our third hookup that week, it became a thing and by the end of the month, we had defiled the graves of an entire family tree. It was all hot and exciting, until the day he decided it would be fun to do something different. After the first hookup that morning, he told me he had to take his kids to school, and I had to run off to work. I drove almost an hour to the office, saw only four patients, and I was back at the church by 6 that evening.

I had just parked my car and was struggling to hold a cell signal while I browsed Jackd to see who else was around when he pulled up. This time, when I was getting out of the car, he rushed to open the door for me. He was wearing red basketball shorts and a torn wife-beater. His dick was already semi-hard and he smelled like sweat and Irish Spring bar soap. "Um... Thanks?" I said, trying not to be obvious with my side-eye. Controlling my facial expressions has not always been my strong suit. He opened the passenger door for me to get in his truck, which I tried to ignore as well. Hookups are not a time for 100 questions. Was he catching feelings? I figured I was probably over thinking, again and brushed it off. As we drove down a winding back road, I didn't see any of the junkyards I had gotten used to seeing on the way to the graveyard. I use to imagine us doing it at one junkyard that had BMW M3 parked in a rundown shed, every time we rode past it. So, when I didn't see it, thought maybe I should start asking questions. I was confused and a little worried. I had already started thinking about whether I needed to tuck and roll or wait until the car came to a stop and sprint like a runaway slave as soon as the opportunity presented itself.

I was in the backwoods, with little to no survival skills because I was never a boy scout, and I was back there without access to my car. Suddenly, I realized just how dangerous this whole arrangement had been. Granted, he never gave me any reason to think he was a serial killer or something, but sex in taboo areas of the woods could have been part of his M.O. for all I knew. Maybe the time for him to gut me and sell it to some deranged cannibal on Craigslist had finally arrived.

"Where are we going?" I asked.

"I wanted to do something different today." He said.

"I hate surprises. Is this a new route to the graveyard?"

"You're one of those controls freaks aren't ya?"

"What's that supposed to mean?"

"Nothing bad. Just something I picked up on when we're having sex."

"I let you bring me back here in these sticks," I said, pointing out the window at the miles of trees and an old rusty truck passing by us with all the windows rolled down. "If I had my way, we'd be in a nice hotel with a view."

"Nah, that just means you a freak." He licked his lips like he was LL Cool-J or somebody, but I was low-key intrigued by how blunt he was about everything. I see how you like to pin my arms down while you ride me, and you like to do all the work. "

"Okay, and? It feels good to me that way."

"You get off to pleasing and control. You like that shit." He licked his lips again and this time it was kinda cute. He had a nice body and a scruffy beard, things I typically gravitate towards depending on my mood.

But, I had no idea that I'd find his ashy black snake boots, and backwoods accent attractive. "Well, I like that shit, that's for sure." He said, with a grin that suggested he was thinking nasty thoughts. I turned away to smile and that's when I saw us approaching a lake. For a moment, I thought maybe he planned to tie an anchor to my legs and dump me in the lake.

"The lake?" I asked, trying not to look nervous. He nudged my shoulder and grabbed his dick.

"I got a boat, I thought it would be fun if we fucked on the water."

"Do you have something against beds?"

"Nah, but I've been making plans. Besides, you have to admit this is a lot more exciting than a bedroom." I started to get optimistic as I looked around at all the shiny white yachts and their white captains. It was short-lived. When he walked me over to the bank ushered me into an old John boat that could barely hold two people and a picnic basket without tipping over from one too many sudden movements.

"I appreciate the thought. And I might be a size queen for this, but this boat is too small for what you have planned."

"Trust me, it's not."

"And, I'm not trying to be in the water. I'm not the best swimmer in anything where I can't touch the ground." The thought of it made my neck stiff and my fingers fidgety. "Don't worry. I got you. Have I let you down yet?" It was a fair question. I had never left without an orgasm when I was with him, and there have been times when I had been stuck with a two-pump-chump, no orgasm, and a face full of disappointment.

I hopped in and he rowed the boat to an unoccupied pocket on the lake that had access to a small patch of land. He jumped out of the boat, fed some rope around a moss-covered tree stump, and tied it, so that part of the boat was in the water and the other half was on land. It was like he was Tarzan and I was turned on by it. "What is the point of all of this?" I asked, swatting at the flies above my head.

"I wanted to do something special for you."

"Why? What we've been doing is fine."

"Yeah, but I want you to be my dude." I didn't see that one coming. Hell, I barely remembered his name. It wasn't relevant to what we were doing. All I knew was that what we had going was working and I didn't want to ruin it by asking real questions or throwing feelings in the mix. At least not with him.

"Is this a joke? I saw the tire tracks in the graveyard, I'm not the only one you're bringing out there."

"Nah. But, you are the only one I've ever brought to this spot. You my Lil freak. I want to freak you all the time." That backwoods appeal was tainted at that point. How could he think we would make a good couple based on me being his "Lil freak?" Aside from, are you a top, bottom, or verse, we had never really had a real conversation. The whole excursion was a new development and I didn't have time for it. Plus, I had no desire to be a stepdad. I also didn't want to piss him off and find myself dead in a ditch. So, I responded with a few slow kisses on his lips, looked him in his eyes like I loved him, dropped my pants, got on my knees inside the boat, and told him to come get it. The man knew how to please, me no strings attached. That's what I came for and I was not about to leave without achieving an orgasm.

When it was all over, he drove me back to my car. He talked about me coming by his house sometime when his roommate wasn't home, and I entertained it. "How long have y'all been roommates?"

"About 5 years. She's my ex-wife. We didn't want to shock the kids like that."

"Oh. I see. Well, does she know you're gay?"

"Yeah, she get down too." I didn't want to find out exactly how down she was, so I just smiled and nodded."

"That's wassup. Well, let me know. I'll be around." Before I got out, he kissed me goodbye and told me he'd call me later to make sure I made it home safely. I nodded and kissed him back. "See you later," I said. As soon as I made it out of the woods and back to suburbia, I blocked him on Jackd and blocked his phone number.

Two days later, I met Twuan while I was browsing the men's sneaker collection at Neiman Marcus in the Galleria mall. I wasn't cruising for a date this time, but I also was not opposed to the idea. A pair of black and gold Giuseppe sneakers caught my eye and I decided I had to have them. Twuan was standing behind me but I didn't notice until his bright and fresh aroma made my nostrils flare with curiosity. I turned to face him, pleased to find him wearing a full suit. His hair was taper-faded, and he wore Prada eyeglasses with bold red frames. I quickly turned my attention back to the wall of sneakers, thinking he would walk away but he didn't.

When he leaned over to ask if I needed any help finding anything, his lips were so close they almost grazed the tip of my earlobe. I smiled uncomfortably and took a slight step in the opposite direction. I read his badge and tried to find a reason why the Credit Manager, would be on the floor asking me if I needed help. Why wasn't he behind a desk running numbers?

Yes, thank you." I said. "Do you have these in a size 42?

"Yes, sir. I believe we do. I'll check on that for you." He pulled a pair from the back and returned with a stunning shoe box the color of storm clouds in his hands and handed it to me.

"Would you like to try them on?" He asked. His eyes traveled down the seam in my black jeans and stopped at my ankles. I returned the favor, but my eyes stopped at his crotch.

"Of course," I said, sitting down in a nearby accent chair. He got on his knees and removed one shoe from the box. Slowly, he slid my pant legs up and I could feel the slightest graze from his fingertips tickle me just above my ankles. It made my eyebrow twitch. "How does that feel?" He asked after guiding my foot inside the insole.

"Feels good." They were even more beautiful now that they were on my feet. The light hit the gold accents and the bling dazzled me. Twuan was smiling too. "Perfect fit," he said.

"I'll take em!" After checking out, I barely made it out the door before I got a message on Jackd. It was him. His screen name was *MinajaTwuan*. He sent a few tempting photos, showcasing exactly what was underneath that designer suit. One bad decision after another, and I turned back around and found myself on my knees under his desk…Slurping.

When I got home, I crawled into bed and was relieved that my eyelids were heavy. I was having a lot of sex but I still couldn't shake the feeling that something was missing. I would look around at all my blessings. Luxuries of which I believed myself unworthy. Material wealth, a promising future, and a family who loved me despite all my bad decisions and self-inflicted trauma that influenced my ongoing path to emotional distress. Something...was missing.

I had been afforded every advantage in life, except skin color. A social challenge I have been sheltered from my whole life. I am as they say, "woke." But merely in the textbook scope of things. It brings shame to not intimately know the struggles of my people, to not know the blatant discrimination of which I am well aware still passes through the veins giving life to this country, as my own experience. Somehow it makes me feel like an alien. I hear about innocent brown faces being hunted like prey on the African Safari and gunned down like targets at a Texas shooting range. I am woke in the sense that I can see the legacy of slavery continue to be a catalyst for racial tensions, but the more I hear about these events, the more it makes me acknowledge my privilege. That acknowledgment carries a sense of guilt and a struggle to know myself outside a family who has paved an even path over all the ugly truths of the world so that I might walk it, unscathed—has told me who I am to be.

Designer clothes, sneakers with shiny gold accents, and a Benz parked in the garage patiently awaiting my coachman-ship, still, something was missing. Everything around me glistened and sparkled with privilege. And so, I found the thickest and blackest, mink blanket I owned and wrapped myself inside, and hide there until morning. Even though my eyelids were closed, my mind was racing with thoughts about how to help Jane. Maybe she was a liability. But I refused to acknowledge her in that way. I thought about my mom and the risk I was taking disobeying her wishes, and the anticipation of the inevitable nightmare to come, had me losing a battle with a cold sweat. I was somewhere in between a catnap and a daydream when my mom called. I didn't answer, at the risk of not being able to go back to sleep. She called again. This time, I answered. She told me she was cooking Sunday dinner and that I had better be there since I hadn't been to one in 3-months.

I knew I was home when I walked in the door. Seasoned chicken, smothered in homemade gravy and steamed veggies, kissed my nose. I thought I entered unnoticed as I tiptoed up the spiral staircase. The familiar shrill of my mother's voice called out to me from the opposite wing of the house and demanded I take the trash out to the curb. Such a simple request, but one I hated when I was a kid. It reminded me of a simpler time. I laughed under my breath and did as I was told. When I walked outside to the back of the house, I found my stepdad, Lee, laying on his side, with two old couch cushions placed under his shoulder and hip, as he polished his white salt-water boat with a coat of Turtle Wax.

I hesitated before proceeding with caution. I was afraid he might ask me for help. I took a step back under the covered patio. The cool breeze from the ceiling fan was swooshing across my forehead. "Valair, is that you? Can you bring me a glass of water?"

"Nah, pops. It's just me." He maneuvered his bald head from underneath the belly of the boat and wiped a bead of sweat away from his forehead with a damp rag. He just sort of glared at me for a moment, as if to wonder where he had gone wrong.

"What brings you by, Khai?"

"Just missed home, I guess. Need a fresh towel?"

"Nah. I'm good."

"Shouldn't be sweating like that, dad. It's not even that hot outside." He must have been working hard because it was a cool 67 degrees.

"Son, when you get to be as old as me, everything makes you sweat."

"Nah. You're just fat."

"Fuck you. This what you got to look forward to in about 20 years."

"Doubt it," I said with a smug look on my face. I hoped to run so much that I'd never gain weight.

"Sooo, you finally decided to come on home, huh?" He said. "Things that bad?"

"It's only been 3-months. Besides, it's not like I don't see you guys every day at the office." He shook his head.

"Sunday dinner. And one game of Phase 10 with the family. That's all your mom asks of you. You can at least show up to those." Knowing the great lengths they had gone through for me, I knew he was right.

It's just I've always felt my dark cloud was a mood killer and tried not to bring that energy around my family. Unfortunately, that distance made my parents think I resented them for a reason undisclosed. My misery did not like company. That's all there was to it. "Need some help?" I asked.

"Yeah. Finish taking that garbage out for your mother and then come help me clean all this shit up."

"Yes sir." I dropped the trash off at the end of the driveway and we worked together to put all the supplies he used to spit-shine his beloved boat into the garage. He did all the talking and I mostly nodded and said yes sir. Conversations between Lee and I always seemed to be surface-level. He, like my biological father, felt like a stranger to me. My mom never really talked much about my dad after he died. She said it was an accident, but that's all she would give me, and couldn't remember our last days together.

At the time, all I had to work with was the memory of waking up in the hospital and being told he died in a crash. When I asked about him, she just said he had a thing for his cars and used to let me ride in his lap when I was small. She insisted that's where I got my love for cars from. She made him sound like a good man, but something in her eyes always suggested she was protecting me from something. They would wiggle ever so slightly as though she was fighting tears whenever I asked about him. I never wanted to make my mother cry, so I tried not to pry.

Lee had been around ever since. He retired from the military and I think it fucked him up. He just always seemed a little off his rocker. He was the kind of guy who would cuss you out one minute, only to turn around and act like your best friend an hour later. Maybe he just overreacted to things, I don't know. After my mom told him I was gay, he barely spoke to me for a year. He eventually came around and we were able to be cordial. We didn't know how to interact with each other. His interests were more hunting, fishing, the NBA draft, and fantasy football or—whatever.

Still, I learned to respect him. He made my mom happy and he taught me a lot of things, ranging from laying tile to changing a flat. My interests were always a bit more, Cosmopolitan, Shonda Rhimes, HGTV, Sex and the City, expensive cars, and Mariah Carey. We mostly joked around and talked trash to one another. And we both were pleased with things that way. Sometimes, per my mother's tactful nagging, he would lecture me about my more questionable life decisions. Namely, my shameless promiscuity, and the very real threat of HIV in the gay community, as if it only exists there. I always nodded and said, yes sir until he shut up about it. My brother was the one sleeping with any and everything. A case of the clap never stopped him and it's why he had a kid so damn early. But he was sort of applauded in a way I would never understand. I guess that's what boys are supposed to do. "Procreate."

He asked me how work was going. I lied and said it was fine even though I had a lot of pent-up anxiety about Jane and I longed to quit. The mental health path just seemed to place too much weight on my little shoulders. It was like constant sadness and tragedy every day, without a moment of relief. "I'm surprised you stuck around after graduating. Your mom and I believed you would leave and never come home. Not even for Thanksgiving."

"You two always think the worst of me. I'm not going anywhere. I'll be around. Besides, I still can't cook. Where else am I going to get a free home-cooked meal?" He laughed so purely that I was envious but glad to see that I was able to put a smile on his face.

"Are you staying for lunch and dinner? I think your brother will be by later." I hadn't slept well in days. I couldn't very well say that I was teetering on the edge of delirium. I couldn't tell him I had been having nightmares and cold sweats. Mom would worry and I kept telling myself I could handle things on my own. "Yes sir." I finally said. He dabbed his head and neck with the dirty towel again and ushered me inside the house. My mom was standing in the kitchen, setting the table. I walked in and she gave me the sharpest look. I don't know if it's a Gemini thing, but my mother has many faces. Some are more friendly than others. "You take that trash out?" She immediately asked.

"Yes ma'am."

"Thank you. Make sure you wash your hands. Don't be bringing germs into my kitchen." I washed my hands in the downstairs restroom and sat down to eat. She made me wait until Lee got out of the shower and we ate lunch together. I was feeling a little weak and drowsy as I was sitting at the table. My blinks were getting slower and heavier. I was cutting my chicken into small strips before giving up and leaving the rest of it whole. When I failed to neatly group them into a designated corner of my plate, as usual, my mom caught on to it.

"You been sleeping?" She asked.

"Yes. As much as one can get in this business." She looked at me as if she were waiting for more. Perhaps the truth. How she managed to separate the tragedies of her patients and not be affected mentally, fascinated me. It was a skill that I had yet to adopt.

"You sure?"

"Yes, ma'am. I'm managing."

"Good. Just want to make sure you're taking care of yourself. Have you given any more thought about law school down the line? I still think it would be good for the practice if we had you in our corner as the family lawyer. Plus, your background in psych would make you a force." Instantly, I felt this weight on my chest. I was still trying to figure myself out. I shrugged my shoulders and told her I was taking it one day at a time. I had no intention of going back to school anytime soon.

"Well, considering you're still seeing Jane after I told you not to, it may behoove you to become more familiar with the law."

"Mom. Can we not do this? I told you I can handle it."

"She refuses to take her meds. And, she's a high suicide-risk patient! She's a liability and you need to be careful. If she doesn't come to her next appointment, you will discharge her and I don't want to hear anything else about it."

"I know, I knowww. I have been working on that. She seems to be coming around. Slowly."

"Khai, do you really believe a little cognitive behavioral therapy is enough to treat someone with a long history of Depression and suicide attempts? You and I both know you know better!"

"No, but I also don't believe in twisting her arm to take medications."

"She's had 3 suicide attempts in the past before I took over her care. I'm not giving her options."

"Not all patients need medications, mom. Some just have to learn to develop better-coping skills with the grief in their lives."

"Oh, yeah? How's that working out for you?"

"She's still alive," I said. She cleared her throat and shook her head as if she knew it was one of those lessons her child would have to learn the hard way. "I'm telling you, it's a bad decision. You need to reconsider. And that's all I'm going to say about it."

The front door opened and shut with a heavy thud and everyone paused to listen. "Just me!" A husky and goofy-sounding voice called from around the corner. My brother, Jordan, walked in smelling like he had tried to mask the smell of weed with cologne. He was wearing ripped jeans with a red sweater that draped past his knees and his wife, Erica, was on his clinging to his arm. She wore blue sweats with a hot pink sweater. Her hair was slicked back in a ponytail, revealing a constellation of small diamonds on her neck. One of my nephews, Kevin, was tugging at her pockets with his green Fun-Dipped fingers. When his eyes met mine, he ran towards me and hugged my knees. "Uncle Khai! Uncle Khai! You gotta come go ice skating with us? Pleeeeezzee!"

"Ice skating? Do you know how to skate?" Erica nodded for him.

"We got em signed up for lessons today at the Galleria," she said.

"Oh, okay. That's a good idea. It should help with all that hyperactivity. Is his brother coming too?"

"No, his daddy, won't let him yet. He said it was too girly for his son." I was trying to avoid Kevin's question, so I kept grilling Erica, but Kevin wasn't having it.

"Uncle Khai! Uncle Khai! Are you gonna come? Pleeeeaseeeee" Erica gripped his wrist and commanded him to sit down. "Stop all that yelling and sit down and eat your carrots!" I laughed uncomfortably under my breath and looked around the room before catching my brother's judgmental gaze.

He had grown his hair out in an attempt to grow dreads. It looked like wool. Only, it was sandy brown, like my mom's when she doesn't dye her hair black. He was the only one in the family to not have finished college and had the unpolished and scruffy look to show it. He opted to join the Masons and worked at a tattoo shop, selling weed on the side. In fact, the weed is what got him banned from the family business.

Lee had given up hope for him and my mom got tired of defending him. "He'll never do right." he'd always say. Jordan was waiting for my inevitable excuse. My mom looked down at her plate I got new skates and everything!" Kevin said, with a mouthful of mushy carrots. He was still smiling at me and breathing heavily with excitement, waiting for an answer. The word no was building up inside me like tea in a squealing kettle. Jordan grunted and rolled his eyes because he knew what was on my mind. I've never been fond of children. They ask too many questions, and they have way too much energy for me. All that excitement makes my nerves bad. Plus, I don't know how to interact with them. I tend to talk to them like they are adults. Jordan never let me forget the time I told Kevin and his little brother, Raj, that reindeer don't fly, Rudolf isn't real, and that Mariah Carey is Mrs. Clause as far as I was concerned.

"Sup half-pint? What brings ya?" I wished he'd quit asking me that, but he never did.

"My free will," I said.

"Still an asshole I see."

"Not so sure your judgment is reliable, with your eyes looking like you been swimming in chlorine."

"Don't start!" My mom ordered. I knew I hardly came around outside the office, but I didn't need to be constantly reminded of it when I did show up. Honestly, that was part of my flawed reasoning for not coming around for more Sunday dinners. Why can't people just let things be? Not everything that is clearly understood needs to be spoken. I had no problem remaining silent when there was an elephant in the room. However, this is a skill my family deliberately chose not to utilize. They said what they were thinking and whatever was said, you can guarantee they meant it, whether it was nice or not.

"We can all ride to the mall together after we eat" My mom ordered. "Sounds good to me. I don't feel like driving." Erica said. Her voice was hoarse and slightly raspy from years of smoking. Not quite Fran Dresser, but getting there for sure. My mom looked her up and down and rolled her eyes. "You can sit at the end of the table, smelling like a damn walking ashtray." Erica put her head down and fake smiled.

"Whatever you say, Dr. Allen." She said. My mom was not the one. Erica knew that. And she should have known not to come in there smelling like that. My brother nodded in agreement and looked at me. His bug-brown eyes were just waiting for my response. There is a certain degree of control you have to relinquish when you decide to ride in a car with someone, even though you are perfectly capable of driving there yourself. I didn't like the idea of not being able to leave on my own time. The thought of it made me feel stranded, held hostage even.

“I can drive myself. I’ll follow you guys there.” I said. Lee finished chewing his chicken and swallowed loudly in the awkward silence. “No. You will do what your mom told you to do. That’s your problem. You’re hardheaded.” At that point, I knew it was not up for debate. I glanced at my brother who was smirking at me. “It’s rude to stare,” I said.

“It’s rude not to listen to ya momma.” He sassed back at me.

“You’re one to talk. Pick up any degrees lately? Walking around here looking like a runaway slave!” My mom cleared her throat again to interrupt.

“How about you both shut the fuck up and eat before I reach around this table and slap the taste out both of ya mouths.”

We did exactly that and there was no more discussion about it. After lunch, headed out to the mall. When we arrived, it was crowded as usual. It took us 15-minutes to find a suitable handicapped spot that wasn't taken before my mom decided to valet. She deliberately parked on the opposite end of the mall, away from the Neiman Marcus entrance, because, she knew I wouldn't have made it out of there without buying something.

When we walked up to the ice-skating rink, Kevin started jumping up and down. "Hurry up, mom! They are gonna start without me!"

My parents had gotten softer in their older age. I remember when I did that, I got pinched in my side and told a stern, "NO. Put your hands in your pockets and touch a damn thing!" My mom just smiled and admired him. The next thing I knew, we were in line to rent skates. My thumbs were fidgety and I was getting warm, even though we were surrounded by a chilly ice rink. The sugar-high children skating around with Kool-Aid stains on their shirts with the scent of hotdogs and Gatorade lingering like a dense fog was unsettling.

Slow down, Jimmy! You're going to hurt someone!" I heard one worried mom call from the bleachers. I looked over to see which kid was hers but instead found my eyes drawn to an Asian girl in a tiffany blue jacket with faux fur cuffs. She was ass-first on the ice, crying and making a scene. Jimmy must have knocked her down because she was pointing and yelling across the ice at a little white boy wearing a loud orange Astros hoody and black and red hockey skates. Kevin ran over to the bleachers and hurried to put on his skates. Jordan was wrestling with his feet, trying to help him put them on, but Kevin wouldn't sit still long enough. Everything grabbed his attention.

"Look, Uncle Khai! I've got Spiderman socks! Look, uncle Khai! That's where we put our stuff!" He looked like one of those aircraft Marshalls with his arms shooting across his body to point at the red wall lockers. Finally, after about 10-minutes, Kevin and Erica were out on the ice. Meanwhile, my brother stayed behind. His prosthetic leg did not agree with ice skates or any skates for that matter. The rest of us retreated into the stands. My mother insisted we sit as close to the rink as possible. I was already uncomfortable. Strangers coming left and right flashed fake smiles at me as they made their way up and down the steps. I needed something to keep my hands busy. After about 15-minutes, I excused myself and wondered about the mall and into Neiman Marcus. Part of me was curious about whether or not I would run into Twuan.

I made the mistake of going to the fragrance department. I had convinced myself I needed something new. I arrived at the counter where there was a sales associate spraying cologne onto a sampler sheet for a man that was standing in front of her browsing the selection in the glass casing. He had broad shoulders and a silver band on his finger that was familiar. Immediately, I wanted to turn around. It was Terrence. He was wearing a tight red V-neck from Armani, and black jeans.

I tried to turn around, thinking he wouldn't notice me, but those green eyes would not fail him as I had hoped. I was trapped. That's when I realized, I should have stayed my ass home. I wonder how different things would be if I did. Would I be sitting here, writing any of this at all?

"Oh, so I see you one of thooose people." I heard someone say. I turned to face him as he was approaching me from behind. He scowled at me, making it clear that he was talking to me.

"Excuse me?"

"You know exactly what I mean." He said.

"What brings you out?" I asked, trying to change the subject.

"My daughter begged me to go skating and I needed to shop. Everybody wins." He said, directing his head towards the 5 shopping bags sitting on the ground next to his black and red Jordan Retros.

"So, you have a daughter and a son…Noted." I said, with a firm yes motion with my head.

"Yep. I'm fertile!" He said.

"Oh. I see. Is her mother with her?" I wasn't sure that was even the appropriate question to ask, but I found it hard to believe he had left her alone.

"I raised her to be independent. She's fine." From what I saw back at the hotel, I found that statement confusing. Didn't look like he did much raising of anything except what was between his legs, but I rolled with it.

“That’s good to hear,” I said. The sales associate was just standing there with a forced smile. “Are you looking for a new fragrance as well, sir?” She asked.

“Sure,” I said. “Chanel Eau de Toilette.” Terrence looked at me and smiled.

“Mmm. My favorite.” He towered over me, smelling like something out of GQ. Why did he make me nervous? Maybe it was because smelled so good. Fresh. Crisp. Sexy. Or maybe it was his eyes, but I had to get away from him. Can I try something else? I feel like the Chanel is too…common.”

“Oh, so you got jokes,” Terrence said, laughing.

“I’ll try the Creed Aventus.” The lady pulled it from behind the glass and handed sprayed some on a sampler sheet. “Let my friennnnd here smell it,” I said. She wafted it across his nose. He raised his eyebrows and nodded with approval.

“It’s a little pricy. Dontcha think?”

“I’ll take both of them.”

“Will that be all for you, sir?” I was about to respond when Terrence interrupted me and hit me with what he liked to call “the headliner.”

“I’m sorry.” He said. I stopped dead in my tracks. It was hardly the time for an apology. But I guess he did that intentionally. I should have ignored him, but those words were like the fries at Mcdonald's. I had to have more. He had me stuck.

“Will that be all for you today?” The lady repeated.

“Yes. Thank you.” I finished paying for both and started walking away. I was in such a hurry to get away from Terrence, I forgot my bag. “Sir, don’t forget about your parfum!” The lady called from behind the counter. I turned to face her as she was dangling a black bag in my face.

"Thank you!" I said. I grabbed my bag and made a b-line for the exit. Terrence followed me.

"I'm sorry." He said again.

"What do you mean?"

"For everything. I ruined our date."

"Date? Is that what you're calling it?" He smiled as if he had said nothing wrong.

"Well, I'd like to make it up to you."

"No thanks. I am not in the business of screwing married men anymore. Especially married men with custody issues. I thought it wasn't relevant to what we were trying to do, but Nah. I'm good."

"How bout you come over and let me cook you dinner? I used to be a chef ya know. I make a meeaannn shrimp étouffée!"

"Nah. I'm good. That Creole stuff is too spicy for me anyways."

"Oh yeah? Well, how bout you try my roast beef?" He said, with a grin, looking me up and down as if he knew I was lusting.

"No thanks." I left him standing there with his brow raised. I was sure he was not the kind of guy who knew rejection all that well, so I understood his confusion. What I didn't know, is exactly what the word no, meant to him. It was simply a delay in the inevitable.

The Warning

I don't have many friends. I have fuck buddies that I enjoy conversations with from time to time. And most of those conversations veer into sex or plans for sex. If I'm being perfectly honest, I would say Jane was, at the time, the closest person to a friend that I had.

Fall, 2016. Jane called me around 11:00 one morning. She said she had something really important to tell me. It could not have come at a better time. I looked forward to our Starbucks and dog-watching. Plus, I needed to get my mind off Terrence. I had been with 4 other partners since the Terrence episode. And thanks to the Jackd, I had another 4 lined up in my inbox, waiting for their 15-minutes of fame. None of them measured up to the anticipation and curiosity I had for Terrence. Yet, I wasn't taking his calls or responding to his texts. Every time he called, I couldn't help but be reminded of how much of a disaster our last encounter was. Everything in my mind was telling me to stay away.

I was itching to tell Jane about him. I knew she would keep it real with me since I was having a hard time convincing myself to leave him alone. I thought it might even make her laugh. Usually, Jane did most of the sharing, but when I did spare a few details here and there about my weekend jogs, and bad decisions, it was nice to have someone to talk to that I knew wouldn't judge me. That job was once my mother's but over time, she became so consumed with the stress of running a 7-figure family practice, that she struggled to turn off Dr. Allen and just be what I needed her to be…mommy. I needed her to be the same mom that used to run my tepid bath water when I had a fever, the same mom who cleaned my ears because I was too afraid to use q-tips, and the same mom that held me until it felt silly to cry any longer when Rick broke my heart and when my dad died.

The whole ride to the shelter, I was trying my best to be optimistic, so I toyed with the idea that Jane might have been good news about Steve's return. When I arrived, caramel macchiato and raspberry passion tea in hand, she looked up at me with the saddest brown eyes. Something wasn't right. She wasn't wearing her blue contacts or one of her colorful French Berets. She never left the house without one. Even in the summer months. I just knew she was about to tell me he was dead in a ditch somewhere.

"What's with the puppy eyes? Everything alright?" I knew very well that things were not alright. The Jane I knew, would have sassed me for such a stupid ass question. I will never forget the first time she sat on my couch a year ago. I asked her that very same question when she teared up about Steve not wanting kids.

"Don't be fake with me, hun. You know damn well if everything was alright, I wouldn't be sittin' here in your office, now would I?" She was my first patient when I started working in my mom's clinic. I was nervous and for someone trying to be a therapist, I never cared for talking to strangers. Something about small talk felt, well...fake. It makes me cringe which is probably why she read me the way she did.

This time when I said it, however, she did not respond. Instead, she just angled her head down at the old dusty wooden bench. That was my cue to sit down. Today was not the day for jokes. "It's time for me to be honest with you, Khai." I couldn't imagine what Jane had to be dishonest about. I wanted to say, well, it's about damn time, but I refrained from being childish and told her to take all the time she needed. You could have told me she swallowed cotton that day and I would have believed it because the moment she opened her mouth in an attempt to pull that skeleton out of her closet, she choked on her tears so hard I felt a lump in my throat for her. After a few minutes of deep breathing and holding my hand, she finally pulled out the skeleton.

"Steve didn't leave for work. Steve left because of me. We've been unhappy for months, hun."

"What do you mean he left because of something you did?" She nodded.

"No matter how many hormones shots I got, no matter how fabulous my ensembles were, and no matter how much makeup, wigs, and weave I wore, I felt incomplete."

"Incomplete in what way?" With the cuff of her pink cardigan, she wiped her tears and then her runny nose. I offered her a tissue and she blew her snot into it.

The wind was harsher as the dry September air swept dust across my sneakers.

"I spent my whole life playing dress up." She began. "That's what it felt like every time I looked in the mirror and removed the makeup, the wigs, and weaves dresses, and gowns. I would see it hanging there in between my legs and cry."

"What about seeing it made you cry?" Frustration, confusion, and anger. When every fiber in your soul is telling you who you are inside, but everyone around you is constantly telling you that you're something else…It eats away at you until there's nothing left. It eats away at you until you become an empty vessel for people to fill with their desires and opinions about who you are."

I wanted to turn away before my eyes watered. I wished I knew who I was, at least that way I had something to fight for. "I've always wanted to be a mother." She said as she took a gaze at the dogs running around and playing in the shelter's backyard park.

"I suggested that we do it the traditional way before I got my surgery, which made Steve uncomfortable. He did not want to carry the baby. And that devastated us." Her voice cracked, so she paused for a moment to swallow but she might as well have been swallowing peanut butter with no milk because it got stuck and she had to massage her throat with the tips of her fingers until the pain passed.

"Steve left because I asked him to use the very thing that defied who he was, and the thing that tormented him in the way that mine tortured me…"

"Jane! You didn't!" I gasped.

"I did! I did! Oh. My god, I hate myself, but I did!" She was shaking her head no repeatedly. "I ask him to carry the baby! How much more disrespectful could I have been?!"

"I can see how that could go wrong, but love, real love should concur matters of the ego. Right?"

"It's different for men and women like us. We spend our whole lives having our manhood or womanhood challenged by a society that hates us. To do it to one another is another level of disrespect."

"Even love has its limits." She said. Her face was aimed at the concrete now and she was clenching her eyelids together.

"What did you do?" Still looking at the ground, she said, "For a while, silence. And then I realized that for once in my life, I had to choose me and went through with my transition."

"Was he around for the surgery?"

"No. But he did stick around for me during the healing process. He was there but he was also cold."

"What about kids? Did you still want them?"

"Yeah. Of course. I thought that maybe we get a surrogate or even adopt, but it didn't matter. Steve had already tossed me out of his heart. A few months after the surgery, he was around a lot less. We hadn't been sleeping together because I no longer had anything he wanted down there. When I finally swallowed my pride and asked why he wouldn't touch me, he told me I was selfish and left in the middle of the night and hasn't been back since."

"How long has it been?" She chuckled a little between her tears. I knew it was to keep her from crying.

"6-months, maybe longer. Honestly, he's been gone so long, I've resorted to sleeping in bed with some of his dirty laundry, just to feel closer to him at night." I gripped her hands tight, and through my teary eyes, I looked into hers.

"I know it's too late for me, but I want you to promise me something." She looked up and into my eyes. After a few sniffs, she said, "Promise me when you find love, you won't lose yourself in him. If you don't honor who you truly are, you will live in regret for the rest of your life." It was the kind of thing that was easier said than done, but if it gave her peace of mind and stopped her tears, I figured I give her that. "I promise," I said.

My mom called as I was leaving to see if I was on my way back from lunch. "Hey, you busy?"

"Just running a few errands."

"Oh, Okay. I was thinking we could make some coffee and look over some numbers after work. We're making more money than ever these past few months!" I could tell she was excited because she sounded like my mother again. Warm, inviting, uplifting and loving.

I used to hang around after hours with her and talk about a whole bunch of nothing but after a while, it seemed I never knew what side of her I was going to get. She had been so mean and cutthroat at work, I didn't recognize her sometimes. We would never see eye-to-eye on Jane and that had made things more uncomfortable because I wanted to help her but my mom had pretty much washed her hands with her like a bad habit.

"Maybe later, mom. I have a date."

"Oh… Okay. Maybe tomorrow after work?"

"Maybe," I said.

"Well, you need to getcho ass back here on time today, Khai. I'm not playing with you. I will dock your pay."

"I am, mom. I'm headed back now." I said, having barely put the car in drive.

"That's your problem, Khai. You're spoiled. How many therapists do you know getting paid a six-figure salary fresh out of school?" I had no response.

"Anyways, I need you to meet with Mr. Robinson. He's a recovering cocaine addict and part of his treatment will be weekly psychotherapy. He's on your schedule for 4:00 this afternoon."

"No problem."

"Khai, I need you to be paying attention. If you suspect he isn't taking his meds, I expect to know about it. These cocaine addicts will tell you anything."

"Yes ma'am," I said.

"And what time is your little date, because there are still some things I need you to do after work."

"Like what, mom? It can't wait?"

"I'm just saying your priority needs to be helping me run my practice." This is why I hated telling her about my relationships. She swore throughout high school and most of my college career that she accepted it and that it was I who needed to quit overthinking things. And maybe she was right, but something about what I perceived her true feelings to be about my past relationships, or attempts at relationships, seemed veiled in subtle undertones that suggested they made her uncomfortable.

Every now and again when I'd mention I was out with a "friend," both in high school to present, she would say something like "Oh…" and after a long pause, she'd say, "Okay." She would say it through the lump in her throat like it pained her to visualize me with another man. She used to try and redirect me by offering alternative things to do with my time. She even took me to church one summer after my sophomore year in high school. After a sermon about homosexuality being, in so many words, a perverted deviation from Christ, she asked me if I was sure about being gay. She looked me in the eyes and gripped my wrist like a child being told to behave in a grocery store, and said something I will never forget:

"It's not that I feel you're perverted or dammed to hell, Khai, but there are people out in this world who will kill you solely because you are black and gay in America." I appreciated her concern to some degree, but the fact that she said it like being gay was something I could just change like a bad outfit, or a low credit score, was what made her words that much harder to hear. I knew I couldn't change it, and I had no desire to do so.

From that day on, I believed that as long as I identified as a gay man, I would continue to bring a great deal of anxiety to my mom's heart that she refused to admit was there. That was the hardest pill to swallow. Lee, on the other hand, seemed indifferent. If my mom was happy, he was happy. They were just that simple, and I mean that in the best of ways. I longed for a relationship like theirs. And as for my biological father, I guess I'll never know how he felt about it.

In the meantime, I had a fix to chase. After work, I headed down to the park for a run. I liked to build up tension before sex. It intensified my orgasms and also help me keep my body nice and tight. I used to frequent Buffalo Bayou Park. It was my favorite spot to run in Houston. I had no idea at the time, that Harvey would later fuck that up for everybody for a while. Going running at Buffalo Bayou was out of the way for me because I lived about 30 to 40-minutes north, but the scenery and all the muscled and sweaty eye candy made it worth the hassle. 30-minutes into my run, I had 20 messages from guys nearby who were looking to play. I parked my ass on a concrete bench in this little shaded rest area, right next to a giant metal statue that spelled out, "REFLECT".

In a chatroom room full of dogs, I was looking for my pick of the litter. I settled for a Latin homo-thug whose screen name was *Dom-Culo*. I liked his body tats, and tan skin, and imagined him with a sexy Latino accent. I hurried home to shower and douche because I already understood based on the nudes we were swapping back and forth that this was about to be a versatile encounter. Those guys were the most fun because I was the type of guy who not only liked to have his cake and eat it. I wanted to indulge and not get fat doing it. Best of both worlds was for amateurs. At the time, it was my goal to have a different man for all my fantasies. I also wanted something consistent with no commitment. At least that way I could cut down on my number of partners and still be guaranteed my daily fix. The poison of hookup culture was deeply injected into my mind.

Dom-Culo not only claimed to be DL, but he also turned out to have a job in construction, so when he told me to meet him at a developing suburban neighborhood on the west side of Houston where several new homes weren't much more than sticks and sheetrock, I didn't think anything of it. He led me into the garage of one that was mostly finished but had yet to be painted. It had that new house smell. No furniture or family photos, just marble, granite, stainless steel, and floor-to-ceiling windows. I followed him to the master bedroom. My jaw dropped as he stood in front of the entryway of the closet. The hue of the lights looked like champagne and the floors had a white and black checkerboard pattern. It looked like a department store, and all we did was smudge the marble with ass cheeks, sweat, lube, and handprints. The disrespect of it all was what made it so hot.

After, I went home, showered, and got in bed. I had 2 missed calls and a voicemail from my mom telling me to call her back. It was late, around 11 going on 12. Why was she up? I thought it was strange because all my life I had known her to be in bed by 9:00. Plus, I did not hear Lee snoring in the background, so I thought something was wrong, but it would have to wait because she gave me an earful about calling her so late. "Go yo ass to bed, boy! It's late as hell and I got an 8:00 new patient tomorrow! Have you lost your mind?" She was laughing when she said it, but it sounded like she was sleeping or crying because her voice was a little horse and shaky. I laughed and told her I'll call her in the morning, and as soon as I hung up the phone and plugged it into the charger, Terrence called… I didn't answer the first time. Then he sent me a text.

TERRENCE: Hey, WYD?

ME: With a patient

TERRENCE: I wanna see u 😈

ME: Oh, baby mama let you out to play?
TERRENCE: Something like that.

ME: What about shiny shoes?

TERRENCE: Man, do you want this dick or Nah?

The phone rang again.

"Hello," I said.

"Hey, you busy?" He said through the phone. "Yeah. Just about to head to bed."

"That's what's up. I'm about to do the same myself unless you tryna come over and take dis dick. You done ignoring me? I know you want it." I did. But, considering how complicated things were the last time, I was still on the fence. "Boy, please. You can hop on Jackd and get you some easily. Plenty of ass out there."

"Yeah, I can have anyone I want. But, I want some of youuurrrr booty." Why did my cheeks pull back into a slight smile? Why was I flattered? Still, I played it off.

"Good night, Terrence. Find somebody else to play with tonight."

"Bet. So, I can fuck you later?" His voice was enticing. I had a semi going from the tenderness in his tone and flashbacks of Palace Inn before his baby mama and kid showed up and showed out. I was sure it was good. Better than good. Fantasy fulfilling. "Bye, Terrence. I'm hanging up."

"That wasn't a no. And I see you remember my name. It must be on your mind." Without another word, I hung up the phone.

As I lay in bed, I imagined laying on his chest. I wondered if it would be worth the trouble. My mind was telling me, no, but my flesh was telling me to get my ass up, shower, and go ride it to kingdom cum. The trap was set, and he knew it. That's why he was so smug about it. Still, I was determined to make him work a little harder. And if he was the adonis I believed him to be, then he might appreciate the chase.

The Agreement

I was being as Wendy Williams would say: "Less than smart." Maybe I was blinded by lust and hormones, but Terrence was physically everything I had been looking for in a partner. And after many calls, texts, and voicemails begging me to allow him to explain, I finally decided to meet with him.

He told me to meet him on the Buffalo Bayou bridge at 8 that evening. 7:30 rolled around and I would find myself well on my way to the Bayou. The commute would be about 30-minutes from the office and about 40 in traffic. It was out of the way but it was my favorite place to run in Houston. There is more than one bridge at that park. How could I possibly know which one he was talking about? I sent him a text:

ME: 👋 Hey, I'm On my way! Which bridge?

TERRENCE: Bet. 👍
ME: 😨 Could you try to be a bit more specific?
TERRENCE:😈 Best view in the city.

I was in the parking lot of this place called Spott's Park, overlooking the intersecting highways that towered above Allen Pkwy for a few minutes, trying to figure out which bridge I would most likely find Terrence. I stopped to admire some of the guys running up and down the outdoor basketball court and wondered which one of them was on Jackd. DL status. I had a thing for that type too. It was a cool fall evening. The sun had gone down and the steady wind only made it feel colder.

Being outdoors for an extended period with merely a black Calvin Klein V-neck, with white Dolce and Gabbana jeans that clung to my legs for dear life, and my favorite red Giuseppe sneakers did not seem to be the best outfit for the occasion. The idea that he might offer me a jacket excited me for some reason. I looked at the text one more time before exiting the car. All I could do was guess and I decided to go with my favorite spot on the bayou. For my Houston natives: it's the bridge that crosses over Allen Parkway. It is lined with white lights and overlooks the bayou. Across from it, you can see a maze of blue lights outlining a path to one of my favorite brunch spots, Kitchen at the Dunlavy, a brunch spot that sits on the bayou. I arrived at the entrance to the bridge with my arms folded tight and my chin tucked in my shirt.

The wind was drying my eyes out, so I was having a hard time seeing anything beyond my feet. After a few hard blinks, I finally spotted Terrence tapping the center of his cigarette with one finger to dump the ash onto the cherry-colored wood. My eyes followed the ash to the ground, where I spotted two Panda Express takeout bags dangling just above his ankles.

"Hey." He said softly. His eyes met mine and he extended his arms out to me. I was surprised to see him being openly affectionate. He said a lot without having to say anything at all. One of my questions had already been answered before I could ask. The question being: *are you comfortable with public displays of affection?* I walked into his arms and rested my ears on his chest, welcoming the much-needed warmth. He smelled like cigarettes and cologne. I knew the sweet scent well: it was that damn Chanel, to be exact. He uttered a deep "How are you, love?" A soothing hum cast a wave of vibrations on the back of my neck, making me feel like I was home bundled up in an oversized sweater and sipping eggnog.

"I'm alright. A little cold."

"Don't worry. You can wear my jacket." He removed his black leather jacket and draped it over my shoulders. After a deep breath, I let the warmth sink in, "Thank you. I needed that."

"Anytime, love. I see you found me pretty quickly. How'd you know which bridge?" He was in better condition than how I remembered him from the day at the hotel. Sober was a much better look for him. He smiled and I tried not to look at him. I couldn't have been the only one who remembered the events of our last encounter. But the way his face lit up, you would have thought I had offered to give him head on the spot.

"Lucky guess," I said. "This is the best view the bayou has to offer in my opinion, where else would you be?" He smiled and nodded.

"What's with the bag?" I looked down at my Coach crossbody bag resting on my thigh. I was so used to carrying it, I hardly noticed it anymore.

"Oh, just a few things… lotion, mints, deodorant, and all the essentials. I like to be prepared."

"What are you preparing for?" I couldn't very well tell him that this was my hoe-bag, fully stocked with condoms, travel-sized lube, scented wipes, and most importantly an emergency douche. Instead, I pulled out my hand sanitizer and offered him some.

"Oh, I see," he said. "You like to stay clean."

"Ehh… Something like that." Without saying anything else, we both took a minute to admire the metropolitan architecture towering above us and the browning greenery mother nature created below us. Either the whooshing of tires rolling over the concrete road as traffic sped by was oddly soothing, or I just liked being in Terrence's arms. It all was synonymous with the prolonged and airy whistle of the wind rustling between the trees. It was almost romantic. "You hungry?" He asked, holding up the Panda Express bags.

"Yeah," I said. "For answers." I was willing to eat anything he was serving, but I was still playing hard to get.

He looked at me like I was some sort of challenge. Considering the circumstances and my need to not feel like a homewrecker, the undeniable temptation to jump his bones was outweighed. He grabbed my hands, instantly engulfing them in heat and told me to walk with him. We walked down the paved trail, and I pointed at all the dying foliage. I remembered what they looked like when I jogged passed the same plants in the springtime. Bright, and colorful. Being there with Terrence, however, gave me a similar feeling and I didn't know what to make of it. No butterflies fluttered about and no bees were out pollinating the flowers, but I felt the warm buzz and the butterflies in my stomach.

He led me to the courtyard in front of the Dunlavy. We sat down at one of the tables and I stopped eyeing Terrence down for a minute to admire the bayou and watch all the runners, walkers, and cyclers pass by. I wanted to join them. "It's beautiful, isn't it?" He asked. I turned to face him and that smug expression he often wore when he was being charming. I could tell he was pleased with himself. I rolled my eyes and shrugged my shoulders.

"You're ruining it for me to be honest," I said.

"Ha-ha! Oh, so you one of thoooose people?"

"What does that even mean?" I asked.

"One of those people that always has something smart and sarcastic to say."

"I missed the part where intelligence was a bad thing."

"It is when you use it to block your blessings."

"Excuse me?" I rolled my eyes so hard it damn near gave me a headache. I was pretty sure he was calling me bitter and deeming himself as a blessing to my otherwise insignificant life or some shit.

"Miss me with the undergrad psych, please. And let's start with the part about you being married."

"What you want to know, playa?"

"What should I know? Or rather, what should I have known the first time we met?" I said, taking a sip of my sweet tea that wasn't at all sweet enough. Just when I was about to complain, he pulled out a packet of sugar and passed it to me.

"I gotchu, love," he said, as he dumped 3 packets of sugar in his.

"So, about your wife?"

"Well, before I met my wife, I used to be an escort." He said it with little to no hesitance and his head held high, either because he was not ashamed of it, or because he had several years to make peace with it. My interest peaked, I raised one brow and I stopped mid-sip. With the rim of my glass slicing my view of his face in half, I looked at him with curious eyes and nodded, cueing him to continue.

"My wife was a regular client of mine before we married. What made her different than the rest, was that she fell in love with me, I guess. Though I can't say she was the first to fall for me, she was the first to offer me financial support in exchange, for me leaving that lifestyle behind. That was the agreement."

"How'd that pan out?" I asked.

"Ehhhh…I guess it worked out alright. We have been married for 8-years." That wasn't the answer I was expecting. I took a sip of my sweet tea and in the process, I looked around as I considered all the different excuses I could come up with to leave."

I'm not sure I follow. I mean, because we're both sitting here having this conversation…" I said. "Do you love her?"

"Very much. Just—not in that way. I like to believe she knows that, which is why we are in the middle of a separation."

"…Oh, okay…" I convinced myself that I knew exactly what he meant. *I love her, just not in that way*. How could he say some shit like that and make it sound like it was okay, like some sort of honest mistake? "So, you married for money, knowing you were gay? Or, are you even gay?" He opened his mouth to speak, but I interrupted. "Don't give me that sexuality is not black and white crap either. You strike me as the kind of guy who knows what he wants."

I was a bit insensitive; I'll admit, but I had to ask. "Weeell, I do know what I want. And, I always get it. So, let me hit you with that headliner first, playa." The sly grin fell off his face the moment he got a glimpse of my eyes rolling. "Now, you and I both know in this lifestyle sexuality is not black and white." He said. "But in my case, playa, I will never be able to love a woman in the same way that I want to love a man."

His face was straight and he looked into my eyes as though asking me to find the lie. "I hear you," I said.

"Now, that's not to say I am incapable of loving and appreciating a beautiful woman and for the right piece of change, I would." I fiddled around with my fork over my Lo-Mein noodles for a few seconds before winding the noodles around its teeth.

"So that's over now? Right?"

"Most definitely. You heard it yourself. She's taking my son back home to Chicago."

"Noted," I said. "You're not going to go after your son?"

"She'll be back, and he will too."

"What makes you say that?"

"Experience." He said. "So, wassup? We doing this or what?" I looked into his eyes. It was as though I had been caught in a blinding beam of sea-green hues and levitated in the sky towards the sun. His grin was devilish and persuasive and peered through the clouds to smile at me as though they knew my desires even more so than I did. Suddenly, I wanted to say yes to everything.

I thought about Jane and how highly she spoke of love. I allowed myself to imagine that happy ending with Terrence. Maybe I found the perfect guy in the most morally challenging of circumstances. He reached under the table, grabbed my hand, and made me grope his crotch. His firmness made my eyebrow raise and he nodded his head yes for me. Not that he had to. Aroused, I told him I had to get home soon.

"Meet me in the parking lot." He ordered. There was no desire in my body wanted to say no. I knew he came with a lot of baggage, but with all his cards on the table, I couldn't help but be intrigued. Does sharing your baggage set you free or make you vulnerable? It seemed to work for Terrence because I still wanted him. It may not have been the perfect fairytale romance if I was to imagine one, but at least I knew exactly what I was getting into and didn't have to decipher mixed signals and lies to find out what a man's true intentions are. And for that reason, I found myself legs-up on the backseat of his old Impala. I was unsure whether I was predator or prey, but from that day on, the trap was set, and I would find myself legs up in the backseat of his car many, many more times after that.

Triggered

I've never had good luck in the rain. For me, rain is an unwanted reminder of a tragedy.

Embarrassed by what to most people would seem like an irrational fear, I never shared it with anyone until Terrence gave me a reason to.

After our little agreement, Terrence and I had been hooking up on the regular at the same nasty hotel and in the backseat of his Impala almost every day. It started every Tuesday and Thursday after we both were off from work. Sometimes, when he was really feeling freaky and couldn't wait, I'd come to see him on my lunch break. He worked at a box-printing factory in the Warehouse District of Houston, so we would fuck around underneath one of the loading docks, usually right at dusk. He'd pin me up against the wall of one of the truck beds, I'd wrap my legs around his waist, and for what would always feel like seven minutes in heaven, he'd stroke me into a state of ecstasy.

I had done frisky things before with other guys. I mean, nothing topped the graveyard moment. But something about being with Terrance made anything sexual feel like a fantasy fully realized. I used to think it was because he was an exceptional lover, but nowadays I'm not convinced. It had to be something more. I wondered if it had anything to do with the fact that he was my…prototype. You know, the kind of guy you imagine when you lay in bed at night with your eyes closed and picture your Prince Charming. Everything he did or said, was electric because aesthetically, he was all I had ever dreamed of. I was a sucker for a big dick, pretty eyes, a gym body, and a smile. The man was fine. Nobody can take that away from him, except maybe, death. Beyond that, I was fascinated with how much more was behind all that body, someone troubled, resilient, a little angry, but deeply passionate in his own right.

When he encircled his strong arms around me and flexed, I felt safe, even though I could feel karma's patient and savage gaze stalking us like blind prey. He was still very much married and I was a glorified side-chick. It didn't matter to me much. I was patient. The thrill was addicting. He was addicting. I found myself wanting more and more of him.

In a month, we graduated from just the Tuesday and Thursday evening quickies to Monday evenings, Tuesday mornings, Wednesday evenings, Thursday mornings, and both Tuesday and Thursday evenings. If I wasn't stuck in Houston traffic on my way home from the office on Fridays, I'd get to see him for about an hour. It always meant more to me to see him on Fridays because that's when he went home to his wife. It made me feel closer to him. After hunching me, he'd leave right at 7 p.m. to go home. Meanwhile, I lingered around and cleaned his apartment. That's when things sucked the most. So much of my time had become complacent around his schedule, I hardly made time to do anything else. I wasn't running at the park nearly as much and I was skipping meetings with Jane to see him.

I imagined us going on dates and having outings with other couples, but that was my problem. Terrence never gave me any other indication that we were beyond sex at that point. After sex, he would get up to pee, and then we would lay there together in bed and just talk. We talked a lot. We would talk on his lunch breaks at work, we talked while I was in-between patients, while we were on our way to meet up after work, and most importantly, to me, first thing in the morning.

I liked to listen to him. He had a lot of stories about things I could never imagine happening to me. We talked a lot about his kids and all the things he wanted to buy for them. We talked about some of his wildest sexual encounters in history as an escort, and at least once a day he would complain about how he hated his job because there was no air conditioning and only one bathroom in his department. For a man that seemed to have the bladder of a 5-year-old, I could understand his frustration. We seemed to be in a honeymoon phase. We had no reason to argue, the sex was hot, and we were always laughing. That was until the day I called myself avoiding him because of my little problem with the rain.

It was Tuesday, which meant I was supposed to meet him in his garage before he went to work. He liked it that way because he could just grab a few wipes from his stash in the glove compartment, wipe off, and go straight to work. It was convenient for him, but I had to wake up

2-hours early to douche and clean up, and still had to turn around and be at work by 8:30. It was raining that morning, and I had been ignoring his calls and text.

```
TERRENCE: 😡 I won't call
again!!

ME: Sorry. I was sleeping 😓

TERRENCE: WTF you mean you
sleeping?! That's bullshit!
```

It was around 5:30 when he called and I was in my best shit, trying to avoid conflict. I knew what he was calling about, but I had not the gall to explain to him why I would not make it to our regularly scheduled Tuesday morning booty call.

After mauling it over for a few minutes, I realized I wanted him to stick around. I was surprised he picked up when I called him back. I had no idea what I would say but hoped that my calling would be enough to salvage the situation. "What the fuck is the matter with you? How many times I gotta call? You got me here waitin' like a damn fool!"

"I'm sorry. I—I was sleeping."

"Bullshit! I know you saw me callin'. What the hell is goin' on?" A crack of thunder rattled my collection of framed Mariah Carey records mounted on the walls in my bedroom, each in individual glass casings with gold trim. My heart skipped a beat and I clenched my fist together 3-times to release the sudden tension in my neck and back. The blinds were closed, but my imagination still visualized the downpour behind my eyelids against my will.

"I honestly didn't hear it." I insisted.

"Nigga, it's raining like hell out here and I know you sleep with your phone under your pillow every night. There is no fuckin' way you didn't hear me calling." I didn't know what to say. The truth would sound like a lie, so I continued to scan my brain for a plausible explanation. The whooshing of the slanted rain was distracting. It was throwing me off my game. "You're avoiding me." He said, interrupting the silence. "I know you want this dick. Everybody wants this dick, so what the fuck is the problem?" He was stern as if he were giving me a warning. I read in-between the lines and it sounded something like: *If you don't, someone else will.*

I don't know why the thought of him with someone else bothered me a little. Initially, I just brushed it off as my ego that needed to be checked, but it would later prove to be a little something more. "Helloooo? You there?" I racked my brain. What do I do? What do I say? I didn't want him to think of me as a liar. Suddenly, I couldn't figure out why I cared what he thought of me and what the hell that was supposed to mean. And then, as Cady Heron would say… word vomit.

"I can't drive in the rain!" I would say I ripped the band-aid off, but the sting lingered a few seconds too long. I had snatched gorilla tape off of a nasty scab and it was starting to bleed.

After a long sigh, "Why didn't you just tell me that? We could have worked something out." He made it sound so easy, but how could I tell him that the harder the rain fell, the louder the wailing truck horn honking in my head grew? How could I tell him it was worse when I got behind the wheel? Would he look at me the same if I had told him that every time it rained, I had vivid illusions of headlights peering through the grey of a storm and tires skidding across the road? "It's not something I care to talk about," I said.

"Relax. It's not that deep. All you had to do was invite me over there for a change." It's not that deep? I was a little offended. Had he just belittled my fear? Deemed it irrational? Now, I was embarrassed. And what does one do when they feel embarrassed? Flee the scene. Meaning, I hung up in his face. 10-minutes later, he sent me a text:

TERRENCE: I'm sorry… Please, let me explain

TERRENCE: Where are you? I'll come to you.

I contemplated for a minute about whether or not it was appropriate for me to share my address with him. I had always thought the guy I brought into my home would be my future husband. I always did my dirt away from home. Those were my rules, and I followed them. He called me and I lost my nerve when he said these 7 deadly words. "Let me make it up to you."

He said it softly, but from his chest, so it carried weight. Ugh! He was good at that. It made him seem sincere, and the next thing I knew, I was texting him my address. I didn't hear from him for 30-minutes and then, my phone rang with a call from the front gate. I buzzed him in and a few minutes later, when I opened the door, he was standing before me, damp and smiling slightly.

He gripped a large red umbrella down by his side and shook the droplets onto the hallway floor. The navy-blue button-up he was wearing was unbuttoned at the top, allowing his golden chest to bulge through. He wore it well. I felt like Paulette in Legally Blonde. I was ready to bend and snap and do whatever else it took to have him undress me. My tongue played behind my lips as I eyed the rain droplets trickling down his chest. I followed them until they were hidden behind buttons and fabric that dared you to take a peep. My mind could still imagine them as they traveled further down his stomach and soaked into the band of his white Calvin Klein boxers. I peeped down the hall to see if anyone else was coming before I let him in.

"What? You embarrassed of me or something, playa?" Hints of spice, damp wood, and jasmine floated in the air. It was divine. He walked forward without my concession and I just stepped aside and let him in. He embraced my eager body. The heat emitting from his arms and chest cast invisible steam around my neck and relaxed me.

With a firm yet careful tug at the back of my neck, he pulled me away from his lips and stared into my soul. And then, with a warm sigh, he said, "I wasn't laughing at you, baby. I was just trying to understand you." I looked into those alluring eyes and my knees turned to putty. He took off his Steel-toe boots and walked over to the window in the back of the living room. Its view stretched from the floor to the ceiling and overlooked suburban townhome rooftops. The diagonal lines stretch toward the horizon and fade into a sea of oak treetops with brown leaves and a splash of the sky. His silhouette made the view that much more captivating. The rain clouds faded, but rain still tap-danced on my foggy window panes without a care in the world.

"So, tell me what scares you about driving in the rain, baby?" I was intrigued. No man had ever said anything like that to me before. I took a deep breath and thought carefully about how I would explain it.

"That's when my anxiety is the highest," I said. "It triggers this awful accident in my mind. It becomes so real, I feel like I'm there. My heart races, I break out into a cold sweat and my hands shake uncontrollably. And if I don't pull over to calm myself, I blackout." Hearing it out loud made it sound ridiculous. I was too embarrassed to say anything else, so I avoided eye contact. I had never shared that with anyone.

"Damn, playa you a lil high-strung, aren't you?"

"Something like that. I don't like to talk about it because I usually have it under control."

"It was raining the night my mom died." He said.

"Oh, man! I'm sorry to hear that."

"Don't be. She lived in a raggedy old house in Acres Homes. There was a bad tropical storm. I rushed to her house that night because I didn't want her to be alone. When I got there, she wasn't answering the door. I was too late. I found her face-first on the floor in the kitchen with a mop bucket tipped over at her ankles. The ceiling was leaking. Blood was everywhere. I wasn't about to wait for an ambulance to pull up in the hood in the middle of a storm. Plus, we didn't have insurance at the time. So, I tried to rush her to the emergency room myself. We made it but she ended up having a heart attack in the ER and died."

He didn't tear up like I thought he would. He said it with a heavy heart, but with a calmness that said he had made his peace. "You don't have to worry about that anymore." He said. "I know how to drive in rain…" He placed one hand on my shoulder and used the other to reach into his pocket. He pulled out two small blue pills. "This should help with all of that. And, when I get in that booty, I promise you gone feel a whole lot better."

"What is that?" I knew what it was, I just couldn't believe my eyes. It was the same pills I had locked up in my cabinet.

"Where did you get that?"

"On the street, playa. Where the hell else?"

"I dunno, a doctor?"

"Not everybody has access to medications like you do. Some of us have to do what we can."

"You want some"

"No. Thank you. I've seen patients get dependent on that stuff. No!"

"Khai. Calm down." He was reaching for my hands and I was trying to pull away.

"Answer me this. Have you tried it before?"

"No."

"Then, how do you know it won't help."

"I never said that it wouldn't help. Dependency and ineffectiveness are two different things."

"Look, playa. You got problems relaxing when it rains. You don't think that warrants some kind of intervention?" It was a fair question. I looked out the window at the downpour and imagined what it would be like not to be afraid anymore. When I turned back to face Terrence, he had already popped one on his Tonge.

"Give me a kiss." He said. Just like that, I kissed him. For once, I had someone I could confide in. He carried me out onto the balcony and pinned my back against the rails. Gripping my waist firmly, he pulled my hips to his and kissed me all in one motion. The slanted rain soaked my back and dripped from his scalp and onto my nipples. My arousal intensified. And there, in front of a picturesque view of my backyard in the suburban forest that is The Woodlands, I stumbled into deeper waters, dangerous waters. Also known as feelings.

I had a man who knew how to drive in the rain so that I didn't have to. His grip overtook my jumpiness and nervous hands. A nibble on my lips relaxed tension I didn't know I had, and the cool water drenched my neck and trickled down to the arch in my back as we played in the rain. Whether we had an audience or not, I didn't care, because for once, the downpour did not trigger sounds of skidding tires and echoes from a single gunshot. I wanted that feeling to stay. I wanted it more than anything because... it made the nightmares go away.

When it was all over, Terrence passed out on the couch, snoring. I was shaking the hell out of him when my mom called.

"Khai, are you alright?"

"Yes. I was—"

"Waiting for the rain to stop. I know." She interrupted. "...but the rain stopped over an hour ago. What were you doing?"

"I fell asleep."

"Well, get yo ass to work. I don't want to hear excuses. I'm docking your pay if you're not here by 10:30." I looked at my phone and it was 9:45. Then I glanced over at Terrence, who was still out cold. There was no time.

"Yes, ma'am," I said, and hung up the phone. I shook, tickled, and even slapped Terrence, but he didn't wake up. His snoring only grew louder. I was forced to make a hard decision. Leave my house with a former ex-con inside, or risk pissing my mom off and getting my pay docked. I decided that not seeing the disappointment in my mom's eyes was worth the risk of coming home to an empty house, or a dead man.

When I looked at Terrence as he was laid out on the couch with his mouth wide open and his pants wrapped around his ankles, I was glad to not have tried that pill. I cut off all the lights, locked all the doors, crossed my fingers, and sped off to work.

Terrence ended up calling me around 3:00 that evening to tell me that he didn't make it to work until after 1:00 and needed a doctor's excuse. After the morning we had, I had no reservations about drafting up one with my mom's official letterhead and stamping it with my mom's signature. From that day on, Terrence would have me by the balls, and not in the way that I liked it.

After weeks of badgering me about how I owed him for not buying him anything for his birthday back in September and with Christmas around the corner, Terrence started to lay on the pressure. An unspoken ultimatum. Either I step up my game, or somebody else who was a little bit more generous would step to the plate and bat for me. It was Friday, but I skipped a meeting with Jane again so that I might make it in time to see him before he had to go home to his wife for the weekend.

It was the third time I flaked on Jane. It was slowly becoming a habit that would eventually ruin me. I was more determined to get there more than usual because just the day before, he asked me not to come by because his older brother would be spending the night there.

"Get here in the next 30-minutes or not at all, love. My wife and I have plans and I can't be late." I wanted to know what plans exactly because I believed them to not be on the best of terms, but I had no place to ask. We were spending almost every day together. Prematurely, I was imagining a life together. A white picket fence, a small dog, and a large home in the suburbs. You know, all the domestic shit. I was willing to bend my grip on reality for a little wishful thinking if that meant I got to hold on to the dream a little longer. And that is where the problem lay.

A 40-minute drive from southwest Houston to the north, became a 20-minute drive instead thanks to the Toll Road I had no business using without an EZ-Tag. They will send the ticket in the mail. No biggie. I still spared a few minutes to stop and get him something to eat. Panda Express was his favorite. It took 10-minutes too long because somebody fucked up the order by giving me white rice instead of fried rice. I could have had that time with Terrence before I had to go home and be alone. When I arrived, the door was unlocked for me as usual while he was in the shower. I entered and got to work cleaning up the apartment. He was a creature of habit, so he would always leave the clothes he wore to work that day draping over the counter in the bathroom, waiting for me to retrieve them and put them in the washing machine as soon as I walked in. He worked in a warehouse, so the shit was rank! Stunk like outside, ball sweat, urine, and Old Spice.

He washed his socks separately because, for some reason, they were always covered in black ink dust from his machine at work. His bath towels were not to be in on the same load as the kitchen towels and he liked his underwear rolled like tootsie rolls and placed in the dresser by the window, the third drawer down. I was careful to hang the shirts that he liked to wear out, in the closet, and tucked away the shirts he wore around the house in the second drawer down. Sometimes, it was hard for me to tell the difference. Everything was designer and looked like something I'd wear… in a smaller size. It was a little more work than my basic whites from colored, and weekly trips to the dry cleaner's routine. I was sitting on the couch rolling his underwear when he peeped his head out the bathroom door. He wore nothing but a smile and a damp bath towel around his waist that showed his print.

"Heyyy, boo. Or whateva!" He said, with a grin and a raised eyebrow.

"I need to be compensated," I said as I rolled his favorite pair of briefs. They were all black with a gold band with Versace's signature print and logo.

"And I need a new TV." He said.

"And people in hell want ice water."

"Ima make you a good man for somebody."

"I'm trying to be that for you."

"Well, you're gonna have to do more than that."

"What do you mean?"

"I mean, you ain't even get me anything for my birthday."

"I didn't know we were at the point where we were exchanging gifts. How is that fair?"

"Well, alright. I'm just saying even some of my Instagram followers sent me a gift. Hell, even some of my exes. None of them gettin my dick. But the one that's gettin my dick, didn't buy me shit. Now, that's fucked up. Dontcha think?" When he put it like that, I kind of felt like an ass.

"I'ma finish taking my shower. Come in here and keep me company." I listened to him as he sang horribly for a few seconds before I decided to interrupt. "Hey, Mr. How was your day?" I said from behind the curtain.

"It was hell! I barely gotta lunch and I got ink all over my fucking uniform because I still haven't figured out how to work this new machine they got for printing. Then, I forgot to take my boots off when I walked in, and some of the shit was on the carpet." I grabbed his clothes off the counter and as I was walking toward the door when I dropped one of his socks that was splattered with black ink. It fell next to the wastebasket that was right by the door.

I kneeled to pick it up and a shiny gold wrapper caught my eye. It was distinct and hard to miss. Small and square, with a little round indent in its wrapping that had been torn right through the top right corner... Something unfortunately familiar, and something I am ashamed to admit we did not use. My skin got hot and all I could hear was the sound of my heart pounding like that white boy from "Drum-Line" when he beat the hell out of that bass drum to get his spot back on the field. Instantly, I had this overwhelming feeling as if I had plummeted down the steepest hill on a roller coaster at Six Flags.

I rushed out of the bathroom without a word and started throwing his clothes in the wash. Still doing so in the manner he liked and I managed to scrub that ink out of the carpet before the shower stopped running. Something told me to bleach everything in his closet and throw them over the balcony, but I wanted to wait for an explanation. The washing machine rattled but I could hear him calling my name from the bathroom loud and clear. "Did you get my food?"

"Peppered Steak, and Kung Pow chicken, with fried rice? Yeah, it's on the counter." Fucking Panda Express. He never ordered anything different. I couldn't believe I had worked myself up about some damn fried rice for a mothafucka who was fuckin around behind my back. It was confusing.

"Of course," I said through the lump in my throat. When he stepped out of the bathroom, still wearing nothing but that red bath towel around his waist. Small droplets of water dripped down his chest. That damn pull in my gut flared up again. Envy. Anger. Disappointment. I'm not sure what offset it, but it ached and made it almost impossible to speak without my voice cracking. I was afraid. When I felt that pull in my gut, I knew I had little to no control over my response. Playing it cool and casually asking questions was not a skill set I had developed yet.

"Thank you, baby." He said it so easily, it made me cringe and the weight tied to my gut tugged even harder.

"You're wel—come." I almost choked. The rattling from the washing machine became rhythmic, like a steady kick, kick—kicking on the walls of a trunk lid from a desperate kidnapped victim.

"You okay? You seem distracted." He stroked his goatee and nodded his head as if he understood my frustrations.

"What makes you say that?" Because you look like you're in a daze. Plus, your forehead all twisted up like you got something on your mind."

"I'm fine," I said. "Just have some patients on my mind that have me a little worried. I don't know how I'm going to get through it. Everything seems so... pointless."

"You know, Khai, if you are that unhappy with your job, maybe you are studying in the wrong field." It was perhaps one of the most important things he had ever said to me, but I didn't at all hear it. Not at that moment. It was nor the time nor place for me to hear it as I should have. All I could hear was the sound of him tearing that gold Magnum wrapper, while I was away at work thinking about his ass and neglecting patients to see him. I was disgusted with myself. He wasn't even worth it! My imagination ran wild with all the nasty things he did with that used condom. It was like one of those movies with split screens to show two scenes simultaneously happening at the same time. It just looped in my mind.

My eyes beamed down at him stabbing the chopped pieces of steak with one of those pathetic plastic forks. With every stab, I winced. Stab and scrape. Stab and scrape. Stab and scrape. I grew more and more irritated. Finally, I stood up from the table, walked to the bathroom, pulled the wrapper out of the trash, and threw it on top of his food.

"What the fuck is this!" He stopped dead in his tracks and looked at me with a look I would not only never forget, but a look that would re-occur more often than I should have allowed. He looked right through me.

"You must be crazy, throwing that shit in my food! I ought to beat yo ass! Why the hell are you going through my fuckin trash?"

"I wasn't snooping. I found it! Who was it for, because we don't use them, Terrence!" It was a dumb question, but I guess I needed confirmation. I wanted to be wrong. I wanted him to tell me he hadn't slept with someone else, but I was wishfully thinking again.

"I used that for my wife." He looked me straight in my eyes as if he was appalled at my audacity to question him as if I was the one in the wrong. I knew it was a lie. It had to be because he made it a priority to reiterate how he no longer slept with his wife. And there he was, saying it so casually as if I was supposed to have known all along that he had been sleeping with her. I had no place to question him about his marriage. I had no right to expect him not to sleep with his spouse. My only thing was, I didn't want him to lie to me about it. It wasn't the sort of thing I thought one should have to lie about in our particular relationship.

Rather than beat a dead horse, I walked out. Leaving him standing there with big eyes and a greasy condom on in his cheap-ass Panda Express noodles. I had every intention to leave and never look back. I sat in the car outside his complex for a few minutes. Contemplating. After ignoring 5 of his calls, I finally made a decision.

"I'm sorry you had to see that, love." He said as I stood in his doorway. He had been standing there waiting because he knew I would come back. He knew from experience just as he said before. With a tilt of the head and eyes that comforted me with false sincerity, he pulled me back into the doorway and hugged me like it was the last time we'd have this moment. It gave me hope that maybe I would be the one to change him. I wanted to keep him. I wanted to do the impossible. Make him mine and only mine. No matter what, or how long it would take. My ego couldn't handle the idea that he might be losing interest, or maybe he required a little more attention than I was capable of giving. There was something that made me feel connected to him. Something familiar. Something I had to discover. If I was going to see this story to the end, I had to step up my game.

After makeup sex, we laid in bed talking as if nothing had ever happened. He lit a blunt and chased down two of the same blue pills. I wanted to say something but was afraid of starting another argument.

"What do you want for your birthday?" I asked.

"I'm not that hard to please, love." He took another puff of his blunt and blew it in my face. "A watch, some cologne, or some Jordans would be just fine." An hour later he was snoring the paint off the walls. Still triggered by the images of him in the very bed we shared, I wanted some insurance. While he slept, I unlocked his phone and enabled his location to be shared with me, using the month and day he was born. He wouldn't be able to go to Panda Express or meet up with anybody he met online, or take a piss without me knowing about it.

One week shy of the condom fiasco, I came bearing belated birthday gifts. A gold Gucci watch, his favorite Chanel cologne, lavender-scented candles, and massage oil, for the late-night treat I had planned. I knew better than to try and buy a man's affection, but I was triggered by envy and logic was not a player in this love game.

Instagram Flexxx

I don't know if it was all the Disney movies I watched as a kid, but I believed in true love's kiss and happily ever after. You would think that with the number of men I've slept with, reality would have slapped my ass in the face a long time ago. I used to call it optimism. When I told my mom that I really believed Rick would wait for me to graduate high school so that we could be together, my mom called it…wishful thinking. She also called it wishful thinking when I told her I believed I could still help Jane even though she was off her meds. I guess the lesson didn't quite stick.

Halloween of 2016. Spoiler, it sucked. With my relationship with my mother on the rocks, I was motivated to put more effort into my relationship with Terrence. I decided to be a sexy male nurse. Original, I know… It was more of a statement if anything, having been forced into nursing school for my first few years in college. It made sense at the time. I also hoped it would get Terrence's attention, given all the half-naked fuckery flooding his Instagram feed.

To say he was a socialite would be a gross understatement. Sometimes I thought life would be easier if he were a regular celebrity. He was one of those sex symbols on social media that everyone including straight women, gay women, gay men, curious straight men, and everything in between lusted after. It was like being around someone with a superpower he had no control over. God granted him the gift of attraction. It's one of those things you're born with, or you're not.

He said it was mostly due to his days as an escort and dancer back in the day, but I knew it had everything to do with him being an infamous thirst-trapper on Instagram, a "former" escort, and a known playboy in Houston. I knew this about him but I had fooled myself into believing that I didn't care and that maybe he wasn't whom he portrayed himself to be on the internet. The benefit of the doubt? Maybe. Wishful thinking? More likely. Instagram and Snapchat were his main stomping grounds when we first met.

All the attention he got on Instagram added significantly to what attracted me to him. Call me shallow, but I liked the idea of having someone that everybody wanted. It did a number on my self-esteem. To be an object of his desire gave me a weird sense of confidence I didn't know I lacked. The confidence wouldn't last long though. It was about two weeks before Halloween. Terrence and I sat on the patio together.

He had his cigarette in one hand while the other one scrolled through his Instagram timeline. I was going on about possible costume ideas, trying to see which one would pique his interest. I was better off talking to myself. He was more interested in all the attention he was getting on Instagram. "Damn! that one only got 5,000 likes in an hour. I'ma have to take it down." I looked at him frowning at his screen. He was so fixated on his photos that he couldn't even look me in the eyes.

"You're quite the socialite," I said, twisting my lips and rolling my eyes. It made him grin.

"Yeah, everybody wants some of Terrence's dick, baby! You thought I was joking when I told you they loooovee ya boy on the Gram?" He motioned for me to come close and look at what was pulled up on his phone. He showed me all the thirsty ass comments under his photos and the unsolicited nudes he got in his DM's from both men and women. There had to be over hundreds of messages coming in just that sitting. The man was in high demand. But as much as it bothered me, I had it in my head that he was mine.

He was just smiling and showing me all the guys he thought had nice asses when a message from Snapchat popped up in his notification bar. I didn't think anything of it. Given he was showing me all the fans he had, I was sure that was another one. This one made him tense up. He swiped it away so fast, I had no choice but to think he had something to hide.

"Who's Ivan?" I asked.

"Oh, that's just some guy from Atlanta that has been trying to talk to me for almost two years now."

"Oh, okay. What you got on Snapchat that has him in your inbox?" Without batting an eye, he pulled up his Snapchat story. It was a video of him in the shower, panning the camera down to the suds dripping off the shaft of his dick. Before the whole thing was revealed, the video abruptly ended and went on to the next post, which was a selfie of him posing in front of the mirror holding a bath towel over his dick. "Ah, just a little sample." He said.

"Looks like the whole damn treat to me!" I backed away and sat in the chair opposite of him. "Aw, don't be jealous, baby. I'm just teasing these hoes. You getting the real deal." I gave him a nasty side-eye. Why when he said that it made me feel a little better? It validated me somehow. I mean, I was the one who was always in bed with him, and I was the one sitting on the balcony with him.

"How am I supposed to know you're saying no to everybody that slides into your inbox? I didn't major in math, but..."

"What is that supposed to mean?" He eyed me down like I disrespected him.

"I mean, I'm sure there's people sending you messages that you wanna fuck. You telling me you're saying no to all 1,000 people that have slipped a nude in your inbox within the last 5-minutes, just for me?"

"What? You think I don't have self-control or something?"

"I don't know what to think."

"Look, this is just fun to me. I'm not entertaining any of these people. I don't have the time for it." I thought to myself how he had the time for me when we first met. How was this any different?

"What about Ivan? Y'all still keeping in touch? For what? Just in case an opportunity presents itself or some shit? What are Y'all? Friends? Or, do you have something you wanna tell me?"

"You need to chill out with all these damn questions. I am still married at the end of the day. Ivan had a bad accident a year ago. He had to go through extensive physical therapy because he couldn't walk. Now, he's walking again and looks good. I just respect his struggle." To me, it sounded like they had gotten to know each other with Terrence knowing all of that.

They had a connection I couldn't relate to. He showed me his photos and sure enough, he looked like he lived in the gym and drank Creatine for breakfast. I was to believe he was saying no to that?

"You don't have nothing to worry about, baby. For one, he lives in Atlanta. And two, if I wanted him, I could have him. I'm here with you. Now, leave it alone" That's just what I was afraid of. Just because he was there with me, didn't necessarily mean that's where he wanted to be. I nodded and made up an excuse to go to the bathroom. As I looked in the mirror and stared at the reflection of my shaking hands as if I had the power to make them stop. I thought that maybe I was overreacting. It was just social media. Even I was guilty of posting the occasional thirst trap on Instagram and flirting in the comments and DM's.

It was fun. Empowering. Who doesn't like to be admired? Sure, maybe Terrence enjoyed it a lot more than most people, he seemed to feed on it. But who was I to judge? On the flip side, I knew flirting on social media often led to me rolling around in someone's sheets. Was it wrong to assume that everyone was guilty of the same sins as me? That may have been my experience with Jackd, Instagram, and Snapchat, but that doesn't mean it was his. Yep, that's the dumb shit I convinced myself. The fans may not have been ideal, but I liked the idea of being the only one far better than whatever the reality was.

No more than 10-minutes later, I was in his bed on all fours with an arched back and something to prove. A couple of days later, I was busy cleaning the kitchen while Terrence was walking around the living room in a red bath towel, gripping his junk, and scrolling on Instagram as usual. I knew something was wrong when I saw him frowning at the screen. "Some hater flagged all my photos!" He finally said as he stood up to come show me.

"Damn? Really? Who would do that? I thought all your followers followed you just to see you half-naked."

"Some of them be getting mad when I turn them down. Happens all the time." He shook his head and chuckled slightly.

"So what? Did they ban your account?"

"Yeah. Says I'm on a 7-day probation or some shit. I'm tired of it happening. Plenty of people be on there showing way more than I do, but they don't get flagged.

"I know, right? I be seeing people butt-ass naked and showing dick prints all the time. Doesn't seem like they be getting reported." I was feeding into it, but I wasn't that upset by the news at all. I know what you're probably thinking, I did this. It's awfully convenient, right? If you are thinking that, you're right. I did do it.

"Man, they about to make me get on Tumblr and really show out!" That one caught me off guard. I had no idea he even knew about Tumblr with him being in his early 40s. I thought his crowd mostly lingered around on Facebook. But I guess I shouldn't have been too surprised since he was popular on Snapchat and Instagram.

"All I see on Tumblr is porn."

"Which means I can post what the hell I want. I'm tired of people hatin' on me." He sounded like a child.

"So what now?" I asked.

I was drying off the last of the dirty plates when he shot me a serious look, one that told me he was only going to say this once. "You're gonna make me an account on Tumblr."

"For what!"

"Because I don't want nobody thinking that they got the best of Terrence, baby. They will not win."

"I mean they ran you off of Instagram. I'd say they won, babe."

"...The battle. Not the war." I couldn't even hold the phone steady when he handed it to me.

"You alright?"

"Yeah, just need to eat. You know I've been on my bottom diet." It was the truth, just not the whole truth. I figured it wasn't the time to mention that rain isn't the only thing that gives me the shakes. Usually, it was crowded events, public transportation, small talk, cops, uncertain futures, and hunger. I had skipped breakfast and lunch. The only thing I had eaten that day was water, a handful of Ritz crackers, and some mints. Nobody likes a messy bottom. I was determined to get some because of it.

I couldn't risk looking suspicious and I didn't want to seem insensitive or judgmental, so I helped him make it. When it was done, he uploaded the same group of pictures I reported on Instagram and after a quick announcement on Snapchat, he had hundreds of followers within the hour. I laid in bed with him that night, nervously running the tips of my fingers over the top of my nails, back and forth until the anxiety passed. Why did it matter? He baffled me. How was it that this 40-something-year-old man cared more about his fame on social media more than I did? I'm pretty sure I was the only millennial in that relationship.

Maybe I was a hater, but I didn't like the idea of all the competition. Looking at all the fans in his inbox made me insecure. A lot of them looked like fitness models, or they were professional Instagram-thirst-trappers who also got a lot of attention from people that just wanted to get them in bed. How could I, the "slim-fit" schoolboy with a runner's body compete with all of those people? The odds were simply not in my favor. I knew that, but instead of backing down, I reported all of his pictures. Was it petty? Yes. Did I care? Nope. Would I do it again? Probably not, because it backfired.

Tumblr started to consume him. Within a week, he had posted over a dozen nudes and had gained over 10k followers on Tumblr and I would be the one behind the camera making him look good, not that it was hard to do. It was a turn-on to watch him flex in front of the camera. After we got the perfect shot, I'd be on my knees pleasing my man.

Halloween finally rolled around. I rushed to Adam and Eve on Westheimer Road in Montrose (or, the "Gayborhood" as some like to call it). I needed to pick up my costume and a few bags of candy. This was the first Halloween that I got to share with a guy, so I was a little excited. I timed everything, accounting for 5:00 traffic so that I would be walking in just after he had finished showering. He smelled like ink, cardboard, and Old Spice when he was fresh off of work. I didn't mind it, but the ink would get everywhere and I'd be stuck cleaning the carpet and washing it out of the sheets.

I wore my old lab coat and stethoscope. It was unbuttoned, showing my chest. Years of track and field did wonders for my body. I was proud of that. But I just didn't seem to catch his eye like before, when he would undress me with a sultry stare and a head nod. He was out on the patio smoking a cigarette and scrolling on Instagram. I walked out to join him, my body glistening from Johnson and Johnson and generous kisses from the sun's rays. The wind was chilly and his cigarette smoke blew in my face. I did my best to pretend like I wasn't the least bit phased.

His eyes traveled down to my skimpy crimson-red jockstrap and back up. Raising one brow, he said,

"That's supposed to be your costume?" I looked around. I was uncomfortable as hell at that point.

"Yeah," I said.

"First of all, you're late. My bathroom needs cleanin' and my neighbors could have seen you! That's embarrassin' as fuck!" My head hung low and I apologized. I had never felt so rejected in my life. He looked into my eyes, but he did not see me. "Go inside before somebody sees you." I buttoned up my coat and did as I was told. After cleaning up, I refilled his candy dish. He laid in bed with his shirt off, rubbing on his dick and scrolling through porn on Tumblr.

My feelings were so hurt, I made an excuse to leave. I told him I had forgotten I had some unfinished progress notes to do and that I left my laptop at home. Without flinching "Get it done." He said and sent me on my merry way. When I got home that evening, I stalked his social media only to see him liking photos of guys wearing a lot less than me on Instagram and Tumblr. What the fuck? Was I invisible? That's when reality hit me. To believe Terrence would be faithful to me was naive. Cue the insecurities and endless comparisons to other men.

It's amazing how the lack of your man's affection can make you feel like the dirt underneath his fingernails, and yet, you cannot shake the almost instinctive desire to reclaim a dying passion that was never meant to last or be rekindled. I don't know why but I decided to play a little game. If thirst-trappers were what he was into, then that's exactly what I would be. I stood in the bathroom, making sure the lighting was right. Click, click, click, annnnd… post. Seconds later, me and my skimpy nurse costume were on Instagram. Hell, the thought that someone would appreciate it, motivated me more. The caption was iconic!

"Halloween is the one day a year when a gay man can dress up like a total slut and no other gays can say anything else about it."

Within an hour, the floodgates opened. Unsolicited dick and ass photos in my inbox than I could keep up with. I can't lie, the attention felt good. Still, it slightly re-boosted confidence that was slowly dwindling the more time I spent with Terrence. About two hours after I posted the photos, I got a call from him."Wassup with the pics?" Suddenly, I was visible again.

"I dunno. Was feeling myself, I guess." More like, you hurt my feelings, but I'm damn sure not about to tell you.

"Well, you look a mess." He was laughing, so I figured he was being sarcastic.

"If you say so. Don't come for me because you're old and tired."

"I thought you had work to do."

"I was taking a break."

"Well take another one. I wanna see you." At that point, I was feeling very Mariah Carey Shake it off, but failed to execute.

"Nah, probably not," I said. "It'll be too late to drive."

"Look, I just took my feel-goods and I'm horny, baby. You not gone come take care of that for me?"

"By feel goods you mean, Xanax and poppers."

"And your point?"

"You need to lay off of those."

"You need to get over here and ride my dick before I fall asleep." Maybe it was paranoia, but I read that as *If you don't one of these fans on Instagram or Tumblr will.* I didn't want any of the guys that were suddenly interested in me now that they had seen me half-naked on Instagram, so I got my ass in the car and went to please my man. That's whose attention I wanted. When I got there, the door was unlocked so I walked right in. The shower was running and Anita Baker's "Sweet Love" was playing in the background. I turned the corner to the bathroom to find him in a pair of soaking-wet Calvin Klein briefs and standing in the shower. The briefs were white, so I could see the skin and shape of his dick head teasing me through the fabric. He looked down at it and made it jump, then looked at me. "Close the door, and get in."

The steam fogged the mirrors and stuck to my skin. I was about to slide off my jockstrap and hop in when he stopped me and told me to get in just like that. "Jock and all." His kisses put me under a spell and I completely surrendered. He pressed his middle finger against my lips and I sucked on it while he looked me in my hungry eyes with a sexy grin that promised to satisfy my cravings. The pad of his soapy fingers tickled a little but it relaxed me. He massaged his warm finger into my yearning walls and held pressure in a spot that turned me into putty. His touch had the power to silence insecurity. After a deep exhale through my nose as he continued to kiss me and fondle the walls between my cheeks. In one smooth motion, he pulled me so close I could taste the salt on his chest. It deceived me into believing that I belonged to him, as he joined our hips.

The water drenched us as we massaged our heads together with slow, passionate grinding. My body tingled with goosebumps as our shafts kiss each other, and I feel the weight of my anxiety float away in the steam. The heat magnified the smell of his Chanel.

My vision was cloudy, but that must have heightened my sense of touch because with every bulge, every ridge, and with every flex in his dick against mine, the tingling that danced all over my neck, back, and shoulders, intensified. My nails dug into his back as my thighs quivered with anticipation. I could feel myself getting close. I could feel him getting close. He bit his lip and clenched his eyelids together. His grip on my ass grew firmer and more aggressive. Time stood still for what felt like hours of edging to near climax. Carefully, we both slid down to the floor, water still cascading on our sweaty bodies and rinsing the sticky mess away.

My thirst, quenched. A wave of possibilities flooded my mind. I could see it all. The happy ending. A warm body to cuddle with every night, couple-photos for Instagram, and sex on the regular with a man that everybody lusted after. It was a race and I felt like I had my trophy. Two slow kisses on my neck and back, and he hit me with a headliner. "I want you to love me." He said. I turned to look him in his eyes.

"I love you," I said. Instantly regretting it, I tried to get my ass up in a hurry, but he pulled me back and in my ear, he said…

"I love you too."

Nothing can describe the pure exhilaration and ultimate satisfaction of it all. It had me speechless. I felt like I had won the lotto. Those 3 little words were powerful to me in that moment.

After that night, every time he was ready to post a photo, he would get all dressed up as though he was going to some posh event as usual. The only difference was, he would have me take the photos. All of them, half-naked and of him grabbing his crotch to show everybody he's hung like a horse in some way shape, or form. Nothing had changed! He was still thirst-trapping. He captioned his photos with shit like–*Like if you'd let me fuck*, and bragged about how big his dick is.

When I told him I didn't like it, and that it made me look stupid to everybody, he told me, "You should be proud to show people what they can't have!"

The worst part about the situation was that I wasn't in any of the photos he uploaded on his page, but he was all in mine! The whole situation was fraud in retrospect. He was a fraud. Every time he got paid, he'd go to the mall. If he had anything left after child support, and after pulling himself out of the negative with his bank account, he'd blow all of it! Boasting diamonds, gold watches, and designer clothes as if he had all this money when in reality, everything he wore was either something he had blown his whole check to get or something someone else bought for him. Namely, me, his wife, or "former clients", and his social media "fans" as he called them. Truth is, he was struggling to pay his bills with the $1,200 a month he was getting from working at a local box printing factory.

None of that seemed to matter to him. It was all in the name of appearances, likes, and comments. He was a textbook Instagram-flexer. I wanted to expose him, but I loved him. Light skin with tattoos, wealthy, grown and sexy, masculine, and most importantly, a sex symbol who wasn't just a tease. For the right price, you and everybody could suck his dick too! That's pretty much how he advertised it. Blind followers believed him to be the total package. The dream… the prototype.

Part of me was envious. Everyone seemed to have his attention except for me. At least not in the way that I wanted it. I knew the reality. With all the attention he got from both men and women, there was no way he'd be saying no to all of them just for me. Instagram models, porn stars, soccer moms, other married men, teens, grandpas, you name it. They were all lusting after him. Who could blame them? I lusted for his body like everyone else and I guess that may have been part of the problem. Maybe he just didn't take me seriously? I had to set myself apart, so I started buying him shoes and clothes whenever he asked for them and sometimes, just because he was more affectionate after having received a gift or anything that required money to be spent on his behalf. He'd cook for me and fuck me good and tell me how much he loved me.

Money was his love language and I learned to speak it. Before long, I was paying his cell phone bill, cable bill, and light bill and funding his trips to the mall. But I didn't mind. I had something shiny and gold that everybody wanted. I don't know why that was so important, but it made me want to do whatever I needed to do to keep him around.

I continued thirst-trapping more frequently on Instagram. My following went up and I was getting a lot of the wrong attention. But it seemed to keep Terrence interested. Every time I posted something sexy online, he'd want to be all over me. I don't know whether it was optimism or wishful thinking, but somehow I convinced myself that mind games and manipulative antics were more like playful banter and foreplay, rather than the early signs of a toxic relationship.

Man's Best Friend

It was another Friday at the office. After finishing up a diagnosis letter for my last patient, I planned to meet up with Jane at the shelter. Then stop by for a meeting with Dr. LeRoy. I was sitting at my desk texting Terrence when my mom walked in.

TERRENCE: Hey, baby. You busy? ••

ME: Not really. Just waiting on my next patient. She's running late AF .If she thinks I am going to cut my lunch short so she can get a full session, she thought wrong!

TERRENCE: Cool. Ima call you in a few minutes when I take my lunch

ME: Okay!

"Khai, get off that damn phone." I knew she was annoyed because of the way she slightly tilted her head and angled her nose down at me to force eye contact. I put it on the desk and looked up to see her squinting her eyes. "Your dates with Jane need to stop. Now!"

"What? Why?" I asked like I had no idea that Jane was not taking her meds. What was I supposed to do?

Force it down her throat? I still wanted to be there for her. Medications or not but I was starting to reconsider.

"Told you I'd give her one more chance, and she didn't show up. Discharge. Period."

"I'm sure there's an explanation."

"Where is your head? What's the policy?"

"If a patient cancels 3 or more appointments consecutively, they are to be discharged, unless there are extenuating circumstances." I recited. " I know, I know, I knowwww."

"Good. Make it happen." She tasked me with drafting up the discharge letters and contacting the patient to inform them that they would no longer be a patient of the clinic. She said it was part of grooming me for the harsh realities of the field, but it always made me feel like shit. At the end of the day, business is business, and my mom has a license to protect.

"I'm sorry, mom. I—." My phone was buzzing with a message from Terrence, I couldn't help but read it out of the corner of my eye.

"Dr. Allen." She corrected me. I was too busy trying to make out the message to look back at her.

TERRENCE: I'm starving…

ME:?

TERRENCE: I don't have money for lunch… Had to buy my daughter some shoes for Christmas.

TERRENCE: ???

TERRENCE: I want pizza. You got me?

TERRENCE: 😬 HELLO!?

"And, look at me when I'm talking to you!" She closed the door behind her and I turned to face her glaring at me. "How'd you let this happen? I will not lose my reputation, the reputation of this clinic, or lose my license to practice because you want to be defiant."

"I'm not being defiant. Jane is my friend."

"Khai, these patients are not your friend. How many times do I have to keep telling you that? They are your responsibility."

"I'll take care of it, mom," I said, not wanting to continue the conversation any longer. She put her hands on her hips and shook her head.

"If I go down, we all go down!"

"I know, mom. I'll get on it." I thought that would shut her up but she loved to elaborate.

"You like driving that Benz you got parked outside. Dontcha?"

"Very much."

"That's what I thought. Stop trying to be everybody's friend for once, and do what we have to do to protect our livelihood and your pampered lifestyle. These patients are not your friends."

"But Jane is—" she wouldn't let me finish.

"Jane is non-compliant with meds and inconsistent with follow-ups. She's a liability at this point as far as I'm concerned. Handle it. Now!"

"Yes, ma'am." Her face didn't budge and her glare dared me to disobey her. It was in elementary school all over again. After a quick zhushing of her blazer, she abruptly exited the room. After she left, I got to work writing Jane's discharge letter for my mom when Terrence called.

"I know you seen me texting you."

"Yeah, I'm sorry. Was talking to my mom.

"Oh, okay. Tell mommy dearest I said heyyyy or whateva."

"Boy, anyways. What else is going on?"

"You got me for lunch, baby, or what?" The thought crossed my mind to ask why he couldn't afford to buy himself lunch if he could afford to buy a pair of shoes for his daughter, but it was out of bounds. Besides, it was just lunch. I could at least do that for him. I thought maybe this little favor would show him that I cared about him.

"Yeah, I got you. What kind of pizza do you want?"

"Just get me a 5-Meat-Feast from Little Caesars with ranch on the side. Oh, and add a liter of Coke."

"Aren't you a diabetic?"

"Mannn, just get the pizza, baby. Please. I got that under control." That's all it took. I was on the phone with Little Caesars less than 2-minutes after that. After I placed the order, I got a call from Jane. She told me she'd be running a little late because there were some things she had to get in order before coming. It ended up working out because I had an impulse to get her a gift. With Steve still missing, I struggled to find the words to comfort her, so this time when we met up, I would have a surprise for her. Something to help with the loneliness. At least, I hoped it would. Plus, I was feeling generous, because Terrence and I had been hooking up regularly which meant I was fueled by plenty of orgasms and a meal now and again.

It had been weeks since she'd heard from Steve and months since she'd last seen him in the flesh. Unlike Jane, I was expecting the worst, but I wouldn't very well tell her that. I arrived outside at the shelter half past noon. When I walked inside, I was overwhelmed by the obnoxious barking and meowing that ricocheted off every wall. The chaos gave me a headache and it reeked of wet dog and urine.

The harsh fluorescent lights hurt my eyes and had me seeing spots. I must have walked past 2-dozen dogs and cats. All of them were afraid for their lives and either whimpering or barking. Initially, I found myself thinking that there was nothing to suggest that any of these four-legged carriers of ruckus and feces wouldn't cause Jane unnecessary stress. That was until I spotted a small white and black raccoon-looking thing, all bundled up in a cage. Alone. Silent, and shaking. He was the same feisty one Jane and I watched give the dog-catcher hell a while back. Can't say I was surprised to see him there because unlike some of the other more social and vocal dogs, he didn't exactly bark, *adopt me, please,* or even, *help me!*

His eyes were closed but it was clear he was not sleeping well. Looking cute and flashing puppy eyes was not a skill he cared to master, even though it was vital for any dog looking to escape the pound. He was a misfit. I don't know if it was because his hopeless appearance was familiar, but I gravitated toward him. For several minutes, I sat in front of his cage in Indian style and waited for him to notice me. He ignored me for at least 5-minutes. I was just about to stand up when he finally approached me and sniffed my kneecaps through the openings in the cage door.

"Oh! Wow! Cade never comes to annnybody! He must really like you!" One of the employees said. She had big brown eyes and her dirty blonde hair was in a messy bun. She was full of shit. At least, that's what I initially thought. Then, she went on to tell me how Cade had been with multiple fosters who all brought him back because he wasn't kid-friendly. "Yeah, he's a real snappy one, and a bit of an escape artist too—ran away from two of his homes." She said to me as I stood up to greet her. She had to be from Cleveland Texas with a backwoods accent as thick as that.

"I'm sure I can handle that." I extended my hand out to shake hers. "Cathy," she said, "But people usually just call me Cate. She shook my hand with a half-firm grip. "Glad ya came in."

"I'm Khai, and he's adorable."

"Yeah, he's got a lot of personality. Is he for yooou?"

"No. A friend."

"Weeeell, he ain't got much time. They gone be puttin' him down at the end of the week."

"Oh, man… Why?"

"We run on donations and we don't aaaalways have the funds or the means to take care of all of 'em. Sometimes there's just too many."

"So what does that mean?" She tilted her head and rubbed her freckle-covered neck. "It meannnns, every animal that comes in is given 60-days to be adopted, or else we gotta put 'em down to make room for the others."

TERRENCE: Thanks for lunch, baby. Wyd?

ME: Out grabbing a gift for a patient. Wby?

TERRENCE: You got time to come through on my next break? I want some 🍑

ME: Yeah. 🤭 If I end the session early.

TERRENCE Bet! 😈🍆💦

"Oh, man. I'm sorry. It must be hard to see this every day."

"Yeah, you get used to it. The older onnnnes, we usually just put down immediately. Not many people want an ole stray." She reminded me of my mom when she said that. She said the same thing about working with mental health patients and hearing all the trauma that people have experienced. You get used to it. I looked at Cade. His muzzle had a few grays. The way his ears drooped melted my heart. He just looked tired and scared to me. I nodded.

"I can see that being true."

"If you want him, he's free, to a good home." It was a shame how she had pretty much deemed him worthless because he was old and antisocial.

"Make it $1,500 and I'll take him," I said.

"Wow! You sure bout that?" If I could spend that on a pair of Giuseppes, surely this dog was worth that much.

"Absolutely." She pulled open the kennel door and as soon as she did, Cade scurried to the back corner. He was shaking like a leaf on a tree during a hurricane. The closer she got, he started to growl. I told her to allow me to give it a try. She placed her hands on her hips. Her khaki shorts were stained with God knows what animal juices.

"Have at it." She said as she backed out of the kennel. I walked in, closed the door behind me, and sat on the floor as I had before. Part of me was second-guessing the whole thing. He could have tried to rip me to shreds.

Would I have been so bold with a larger dog? Probably not. Cade stared at me for what had to be another 5-minutes before approaching. This time, he crawled on top of my lap and sniffed from my crotch up to my lips before finally licking me on the nose. His breath stunk like tuna. I held my arms out, and timidly, he slid in between them. His coat was dry and scruffy, in need of some TLC before he would be at all presentable to Jane. There was no time.

Jane was sitting on the bench reading a book when I walked up to her with Cade in my arms. "Well, how about that! You took my advice after all, hun. Good for you!" She said as she stood up from the bench. She wore a maroon trench coat and a black French beret. She loved those things and wore one every time I saw her.

"Actually…" Buyer's remorse kicked in and it was all starting to seem like a massive mistake. It was too late to turn back though. "I got him for you." Her eyes grew big and just as she was reaching out to rub his head, she stopped and took a few steps back.

"You did what now!"

"Think of it as an early Christmas gift. You said you wanted something small."

"I was speaking generally, hun. I am in no condition to take care of a dog." She was still clenching onto Steve's black silk tie and stroking the tip with her thumb, no signs of letting go anytime soon. "Awww! Look!" I said. "He's not even growling at you. Must mean he likes you." Now, I was the white girl from the shelter. Some nerve I had.

"No, dear. I think he likes you."

"Come on, Jane. Try. For me. Pleeeease!" I gave her my best puppy eyes and puckered out my bottom lip. She looked me up and down with her ice-grey contacts and then glared at Cade. Seconds later she burst out into tears. At first, I didn't understand why. But then I remembered.

"Any news on Steve?" She looked at me through her watery eyes and shook her head.

"His phone just goes straight to voicemail." I wanted to ask her if she was prepared to deal with things in the event of Steve's death, but I figured it was a bad time to bring it up. And honestly, the answer scared me because I knew it was, no. Then again, there never is a good time to discuss the possible death of someone's spouse.

"I've been praying," she said, wiping her tears. "But I've gotten so used to his absence, I'm not sure I can tell the difference these days, whether he's dead or not." I wasn't sure if I agreed. Knowing he was dead with no possibility of return would surely spawn a different breed of loneliness and grief, rather than if he had simply just missed his flight home and would eventually turn up.

"Good. I'm sure there's a good explanation for this. Has to be." I broke another rule there. I was taught not to give patients false reassurance. It's just as bad as lying. But what could I say? I didn't have all the details of their separation, to begin with. Jane was holding back. I was just waiting for the subject to change.

"Well, whatcha name him?" She asked as she wiped her tears with Steve's tie. I sat down on the bench next to her. The wooden slates were so cold, I had to squeeze my butt cheeks together. The wind would have made my hands numb had it not been for the hairball I was holding like a newborn. "Lady inside called him Cade."

"Hmm. Interestin' choice. I kinda like it." She said.

"Me too. It's a strong name for such a little guy. Wanna hold him?"

"Sure, hun." She said, holding out her arms. I handed him to her, but he started to growl. "No worries." She said, reaching into her black leather purse. She pulled out a small rectangular box that was wrapped in a red silk bow. I recognized the black cursive script on top of the glossy white box.

"I planned to give these to you before you left, but now is as good a time as any I guess." She handed me the box and I slid the cover off. Inside, were 3 red-velvet French macarons, two strawberries in the middle, and one raspberry. My favorite!

"Aww, Jane! You didn't have to—"

"Hush, hun. Of course, I did. You have been a tremendous help in my life and I just wanted to show my appreciation for your time. I know Dr. Allen doesn't approve of our relationship." My eyes drifted to the side. There was that pesky Discharge Letter I was incapable of telling her about. She pulled out the only raspberry macaron in the box and wafted it in the air like she was at a showroom ball. Cade's big pointy ears perked up and he was sniffing the air with excitement.

"Aw, looks like you both have the same taste in pastries." She said. I smiled and shook my head.

"Dogs shouldn't be eating pastries. Whatcha tryin to do? Give him diabetes before he gets the chance to piss on your carpet?"

"You looooove being theatrical. Dontcha?"

"Shade much?" I said.

"Call it what you like, hun. But let's not forget how you called the Harris County Non-Emergency line and demanded a deputy be dispatched to my house for a wellness check."

"First of all, I swear I don't remember you telling me you had an appointment with your Cardiologist," I said, laughing. I stopped to read a text from Terrence.

```
TERRENCE: Taking my break at
3:30, so you need to be on your
way.

ME: Okay. I will leave as soon
as I can. Something just came
up.

TERRENCE: You need to leave
now! I DON'T HAVE TIME!
And you got
```

"Hun, I told you two days in advance. Isn't that what Dr. Allen's cancellation policy requires?" She was rolling her neck and waving her finger in the air at me. "48 hours in advance. I know. I knowww!" She said playfully, bumped her shoulder against mine, and smiled.

"You know I love you, Khai. You are like family to me.

"I love you too, Jane."

"Alright." She said, sniffing. "Enough of the mushy shit. What are your plans for New Years?"

"Uh, probably just sit at home and take a bubble bath. I found these cute little red bath bombs from the Lush off of Westheimer Road." She said.

"A little R&R. Sounds long overdue. Light some candles around the tub and enjoy a little music while you're at it. I recommended lavender scents. Good for promoting relaxation." She looked at me and smiled.

TERRENCE: If you gonna be flakey, let me know, bruh so I can stop wasting my time.

ME: I didn't say I wasn't coming. I just need a lil more time than anticipated.

TERRENCE: Get here, or lose my number. 👌

"Yeah, yeah. I hear you, schoolboy. What about you? Any Plans?" When she said that, I started to panic a little on the inside. Terrence had given me an ultimatum and I had every intention of doing what I could to get to him faster. I had to think of something quick, so I stole the opportunity to bring him up.

"Fireworks at Hermann Park with my new friend," I said.

"Oh, hun! That's wonderful! What's his name?"

"Terrence," I said, with my head slightly tilted up. "In fact, I've actually gotta run and meet him for a bite to eat in a few." She paused to look down at Cade and then looked around the area. I knew I had made her a little uncomfortable. At least that's just how I read it.

"Just remember to enjoy yourself. Find love and be high on life! I will die happy knowing that there is someone in your life bringing a smile like that to that handsome face of yours."

"Eh, we'll see."

"Why you saying it like you're not sure?"

"I dunno. I'm starting to wonder if we are on the same page."

"Oh, hun!" She said as she reached out to grab my hand. "That's ya problem. You too damn cute and patient. He must be fine as hell?"

"Very!" I said proudly.

"Yep, that'll cloud your judgment real fast." She said, giggling. Her eyes rolled back like she was remembering a different time. When she finally refocused them on me, she said something I'll never forget.

"Promise me you will be careful, hun. These men are hurting in silence out here. Just because it isn't visible at a glance, or sitting on your couch asking for help, doesn't mean the pain isn't there. And we all know what hurt people do to others."

"I promise." She teared up slightly after I said it, so I hugged her and told her that I would smile every day if it would make her happy.

"I just don't wanna see you get caught up in the wrong lifestyle, Khai. It's easy when you're cute and in shape, hun. Too easy. Before you know it, you're fuckin every Tom, Dick, and Harry with a stiff dick and a pulse."

"I hear you, but I don't think Terrence is like that." She squeezed my back harder and told me to go before she started crying. Cade was in her lap trying not to get smooshed in-between us and stood up to sniff my face.

"Take care of him," I said. "You know I don't mind babysitting either if you find yourself having a bad day or another episode."

"Just go, hun! We'll be fine. Don't worrrrrry. You just worry about keeping that smile. It's more valuable than Red Bottoms and Giuseppes." Cade had given me hope. I couldn't make Jane happy. It was something she would have to find within herself, but if a smile from me, a skittish dog, and me going on a date with Terrence was a step in the right direction, then so be it. I hadn't even noticed I was smiling before she mentioned it. Hell, I was trying not to, but that's the thing about body language. It's a terrible liar.

I was kind of proud to have had a real date planned for once. One outside the bedroom and the graveyard for that matter. Maybe I did have something to smile about. I had hoped that maybe I could find someone who would love me as much as Jane loved Steve. Even though I was skipping my meeting with Dr. LeRoy so that I could make it to a booty call, I was starry-eyed about the idea of Terrence and I spending New Years together. Before taking off down the road, I change into a blue wife-beater and grey sweats. No underwear for easy access. The speed limit was 65, but I was doing 85 all the way to Terrence's job.

I pulled up next to a massive tractor-trailer underneath a loading dock. There were about 5 loading stations, each with a truck waiting to be loaded with boxes. Workers were spread out between the first 3 stations. Terrence met me at the dock closest to the back of the lot, with nothing but a truck bed and the cover of dusk to hide us. He had his ink-stained work shirt unbuttoned and his hands in his jeans.

"Bout time you made it. I been wantin' some of that booty all day."

I barely closed the door to my car before he put his hands around my waist and pulled my hips against his. I was looking around to see if anybody was passing by when I felt his bulge press against my ass with a firmness that commanded my attention. Audience or not, it no longer mattered. He was breathing down my neck as he spun me around and pinned my hands up against the truck bed. It was cool to touch and dusty.

"Thank you for the pizza, baby. I was hungry as hell." I liked how he smelled like sweat and cigarettes. It made me eager. With the side of his face resting in the groove between my shoulder and neck, he slid down my pants. Lube in hand, his knuckles beat against the back of my bare thighs as he stroked his shaft. His throbbing stretched and sucked the wind out of me as he put it in. The press of his lips behind my ear released the tension in my legs and thighs. Only then, was I able to exhale and welcome him in deeper. Feet shuffled in the distance, and metal machinery squeaked. At any moment, any one of his coworkers could have walked by and Terrence would have been out of a job.

I was biting my bottom lip and trying not to moan as he stroked, but they felt so good I couldn't contain myself. It was chilly outside but the joining of our body heat made it feel like a warm spring night. His grunting became more rapid as he got close. A rush of adrenaline and hormones that yearned to taste him, overtook my body. It was all a thrill. His dirty nails dug into my hips and the sweat from his chest dripped down the curve in my back. Our hearts pounding and the wind blowing, I was high and he was the coke. Caught up in fantasy, I was high on his touch, high on his kiss, high on his words—high on his stroke.

Breakfast at Denny's, his vanilla cream drizzled down my pancakes. Trying to catch his breath, his eyes rolled back in his head, and he gripped my ass like handlebars. I got on my knees and cleaned him up. No warm towel needed. Lips, tongue, and the warmth of my mouth were more than enough. A little sweet and salty, I wanted to taste him all the time. He kissed me goodbye and promised to call me when he got off. My ass was wet and my mouth was sticky, but I wore a smile all the way home.

Ghostin

I guess it was my turn to be ignored. During a time when everyone is usually coming together, the fall vibe was starting to feel lonely. I woke up one morning for the first time in weeks without a single good morning text or call from Terrence. We were supposed to link up for our morning quickie.

We had settled into a routine. He'd called every morning around 5:30 to ask if I was on my way to meet him in his garage. After, he would leave for work and talk to me on the phone the whole ride there. Like clockwork, he'd call me a little before noon, around 11:45. That's when he took his 30-minute break. At 3:00, he took a 15-minute break and normally called me then too. Around 5:45, he'd call and talk to me on his way back to his apartment. It got to the point that I no longer needed to set an alarm in the morning. I knew Terrence would be my wake-up call. Call me a hopeless romantic, but I looked forward to hearing my man's voice first thing in the morning.

Hell, the excitement and anticipation of his phone call would have me up and moving early before the phone even rang. No big deal. I thought. I'd just call him first for once. We normally did things on his time because he was the one with the marriage issue. I tried to be a good mistress…well, manstress, and not call his phone unless he gave me the okay. One could easily mistake my lack of calling for a lack of interest, so I thought maybe he wanted me to show a little more effort. But when I called, he didn't answer. I called again. It went straight to voicemail. Instead of assuming that he overslept, my first instinct after two failed phone calls was to log in to Jackd and check his most recent activity.

I mean, what else would you expect from a guy you met on a hookup app? That was the cultural norm. Meet someone, swap pics, fuck around, thank you, next. If the sex was good, you might even hookup more than once. That's when things can get complicated. If you're not careful, eventually one of you will catch feelings and start looking for more. Some guys will be brutally honest and tell you they just wanted to fuck, some will stroke you like they love you only to block you the next day, some guys will have you taking a trip to the clinic, and some will string you along for the sake of keeping a good piece of ass in their list of contacts. Those guys are a special kind of evil. They get off on deceit and will say all the right things to keep you around. They'll have you living in a whole fantasy world of bullshit and lies. Meanwhile, he's out doing whomever he wants and you're standing around with a wet ass looking foolish.

Which guy was Terrence? I was still on the fence. How could I have expected to keep his attention after revealing that driving in rain gives me the shakes? Talk about a turnoff. It would have been nice for him to just say he was no longer interested instead of dickin' me down like he cared about me, only to ghost me in true thank-u-next fashion. My heart stopped pounding when I saw that he was the usual 11.5 miles away from my place. He hadn't blocked me on Jackd and my messages were still blue, so I knew he was getting my texts.

Maybe I assumed that he would do those things because that's what I would have done if I had been weirded out by a guy, or if the sex was trash. It was easy for me to move on to the next with little to no explanation to the poor sucker who was foolish enough to be interested in me. Maybe there was hope and maybe I was overthinking things. After my shower, I turned on the tv to watch reruns of Wendy Williams on Youtube while I sipped tea from my favorite red mug with the letters MC engraved on it, and mentally prepared for a day at the office. Waiting by the phone through all of "Hot Topics," I was unable to focus on the fact that I was running late for my first appointment at the office. It was going on 7:45 when I finally hit the road, and still no call from Terrence.

The lobby was full when I walked in 10-minutes late. I thought I was sneaking in, but my mom was sitting in my office behind my desk. Waiting. I thought she was about to jump down my throat, but she smiled. "Don't make a habit of being late, Khai. You've been doing good getting here on time."

"I'm not. Just got stuck in some traffic."

"Mhmm. Whatever you say. You have to be careful. You know you tend to be habit-forming, and tardiness is not a good one to have." The only thing tardy was my good morning call from Terrence. What the fuck was he doing? I dropped my bags on the sofa and slumped down on the cushions.

"I like how you've taken over my desk."

"I own the motha-fuckin' practice. This is my desk." She said. Pleased with her comeback, she giggled under her breath playfully and smiled at me. "Anyways." She said. "I've been waiting to talk to you about your brother."

"What about him?"

"I want him to join the practice, and have him work in the billing office as the supervisor."

"Have you talked to him about it?"

"Yeah. He said he'd come on part-time to do the billing Tuesdays, Thursdays, and Fridays."

"Is he going to have the time? He is pretty booked at his shop."

"He could use the extra cash. Let's just say that."

"Oh, so he's still throwing his money away on those damn Cryptocurrency stocks, huh?"

"Ha-ha! That's your brother. Always looking for a get-rich-quick scheme. What else is new?"

"He's got a family now. He can't be doing that."

"Yeah, I think joining the practice will be good for him. Better environment and I can monitor his pay and spending. What do you think?"

"He's better with numbers than I am, and he used to do your billing before the practice grew like it did. I'm sure he'll be fine. Question is, what does Lee think?"

"He's not feeling it at all. You know he thinks your brother is a fuck-up and just won't do right."

"Jordan can be lazy, but he gets the job done. He needs to quit that."

"Well, we aren't really talking much these days ever since I brought it up. I figured I'd get your opinion."

"It's supposed to be a family business. He's family. Period."

"That's what I'm saying. I built this for you two so that long after your dad and I are gone, my boys would have something!" She started choking up after that, but she cleared her throat and got herself together. Where did that pain come from?

"You okay, mom?"

"I'm fine. Just a little stressed out. You know Lee can be a little mean when he gets upset."

"What did he say?"

"Nothing. I just don't understand what his problem is with your brother. It's like he likes to see him fail these days for the sake of being right."

"He's just insecure because you're the breadwinner. It's sad to see a century-old way of thinking can still survive in a world of Black Girl Magic."

"He's always supported me. But nowadays, he's just vindictive and mean for no reason. He needs some Melatonin."

"Well, maybe he's just salty that you reduced your work hours even though he told you not to."

"Khai, I had to. I've got to take care of myself. I'm finally getting my diabetes under control."

"Yeah, and you're slimming down."

"I knowwww! I've lost 30-pounds. Can you believe it!"

"You look great, mom. Can you get out of my office now? I've got work to do."

"I was just checking on you. You know when you start breaking habits, I know something's going on."

"Mom, I'm fine. Don't worry." The only person that needed to worry, was Terrence. As the day went on without a single call or text, the humiliation I was feeling, turned to anger. The raging bull that lived inside me was blowing steam. I got up to crank the A/C down, but the cold sweat lingered for over an hour. As soon as the bell dinged at the lobby door as my last patient walked out, I snatched my things in a hurry and made a B-line for the door.

Who was he with? Why would he bother wasting both of our time? I was just fine with a quick fuck before he came along. I could go back to that life easily. But, I didn't want to. My mind was racing. The more I thought about what I could be doing and who I could be doing it with, the more I lusted for Terrence. On the last quarter mile to his apartment, I gripped the steering wheel as if for a race and mashed the gas to a mean 90mph in a 30-zone. Clammy hands, and twitchy eyebrows, all I saw was red.

Tasting my own medicine did not sit well in my stomach. This was the type of stunt I was used to pulling on guys. It was better on the other side. That's for sure. I wanted to knock on the door, but I was afraid of what was on the other side, and I didn't want to look like a crazy person. Part of me was concerned that he might be hurt or something, but not very much of it.

The idea that he might be with someone else after being turned off by my moment of vulnerability, is what put me in front of his door. Uninvited and unannounced, again. The déjà vu of it all…The door's cool surface touched my ear as I leaned in to listen. All I could hear was what sounded like gay porn buffering and playing over and over again. Enraged, I struggled to swallow. My skin was clammy and my hands balled into a fist. It was Rick all over again. There was a chance that I was tripping and nothing was going on. I told myself that I needed to find out who else was in there without causing a scene or ruining my chances with Terrence by looking like some lunatic that likes to show up unannounced and cause drama. Something told me to kick the door, and so I kicked it like I was trying to kick it down. Still no response! It made me frantic, so I kicked harder. One of his neighbors peeped out their door and yelled at me.

"Kick it again, and I'm callin' the fucking cops! Get out of here, ass hole!" He was a middle-aged white man with a hairy chest. "Fuck off and mind your own damn business!" I wasn't thinking straight. All I could see was what my imagination created on the other side of Terrence's door. "You're going to jail, bud. You just keep doin whatcha doin." He threatened. I kicked and kicked until the approaching footsteps down the hall startled me. The crispy clicks that followed each step, told me that they were walking with a purpose. I scurried to the other end of the hall and peeped around the corner.

It was Jarvis and his sparkly Christian Louboutin loafers. I snatched my head back so fast you would have thought it was Friday the 13th and I was hiding from Jason. He didn't even knock on the door. He shoved a key in the lock and opened it like he owned the place. No announcement or anything. At first, I thought that maybe because Jarvis was there that Terrence wasn't doing what I suspected him to be doing, but then I remembered how we met.

My face boiled with envy. I had half a mind to run and catch the door before Jarvis could lock it. I would have been the new Jasmine, but I didn't think it was worth it… Not yet. I decided to wait and see who came out of the apartment. The sex with Terrence had certainly worked to make me jealous and territorial, but also calm and slightly more rational because I feared pushing him away.

I waited a few minutes before approaching the door again. I could barely make out all the mumbling over the sound of my heart beating and the porn. There was nowhere to go if Jarvis, Terrence, or whomever the hell else might have been in there, suddenly decided to storm out for whatever reason. They'd run smack into me eavesdropping. The moaning from the porn finally stopped.

"Terrence, I'm sick of this shit! You can't keep doing this to yourself and expecting me to come save you all the damn time!" He sounded like he was trying not to cry. "How long have you been here?" He asked.

I waited for a response from Terrence, but there was none. Something sharp scraped a glass surface, a toilet flushed and the shower was turned on. Whatever the fuck was going on, I couldn't stick around to find out. My mom called as I was standing outside the door. The fact that my mom needed me to stay later to run some numbers completely slipped my mind.

"Khai! I thought I told you I needed you to stay! How you just gonna walk out like that!"

"I'm sorry, mom. I forgot. I was on my way to the park, but I'm turning back around now."

"Don't even worry about it. I'll take care of it myself."

"Mom, I'm not that far. I can be there in 20-minutes."

"No. Go run. We can do it another day." The disappointment in her tone made me feel like an asshole.

"I'm sorry, mom."

"I'll see you tomorrow, Khai. Be on time. Bye." When she hung up, I checked my messages to see if I had any from Terrence. Nothing. My shoulders fell into a slump as I drove to the park. I couldn't enjoy my run because I was still anxious about not hearing from Terrence and jealous that Jarvis was the one he called in a time of need. I couldn't help but wonder if there was more to Jarvis's label than, sponsor. Longing for a distraction, I decided that I was not about to be the guy who sat around waiting to hear from another mothafucka to call or text me. Suddenly, I was glamorizing my old hoe-life and it made me feel empowered. The next thing I knew, I was on Jackd again.

After scrolling through profiles for an hour, I stumbled upon a guy named Andre. He was shorter than what I normally aimed for but he had the body of a gymnast, so I was able to overlook it. He told me to meet him at his place downtown. I cleaned up and drove straight there. He lived in this old brick house that you could see right through the front to the back. It smelled like wood rot from the aged and creaky wood floors in the living room. He was standing in front of a brown rocker chair, biting his lips and checking me out. I was staring at the small fish tank behind him that sat on an end table next to the rocker when he decided to break the silence.

"Wuz good?" He asked as he smoked a cigarette. I hated the smell, but I found it oddly attractive.

"You tell me," I said, glancing at my phone to see if I missed a text from Terrence. Still nothing.

"You clean?"

"Yeah."

"You positive?"

"No."

"Cool, because I'm out of condoms." He abruptly dropped his pants, revealing a solid 8. "Bring yo fine ass over here and put that phone down." I looked down at him, wishing he were Terrence instead. I was on my knees about to suck when he pulled out a small glass bottle and snorted it like it was cocaine. "Want some? It'll rave you feelin' right." I held the bottle up to my nose and paused. What was I doing there? I was feeling disgusted with myself. Looking around the room to avoid eye contact, I spotted a bottle of Imodium on the nightstand.

"Excuse me," I said. "Can I use your restroom? I have to pee." He grabbed his junk and slapped me in the face with it.

"Yeah, just hurry up." Normally, that sorta thing would have turned me on, but it just made me feel sick to my stomach. I was in the bathroom sitting on the edge of the tub, staring up at the ceiling. After checking my phone one more time only to be disappointed again, I started to wonder about why he would have diarrhea and decided to check his medicine cabinet. I quietly went through all the usual pain pills and antibiotics on the shelf until I found exactly what I was looking for. Hidden behind the Tylenol PM, a white pill bottle labeled Emtriva caught my eye. I twisted the cap open and poured a few of the little blue and white capsules into my hand.

Was this the lifestyle Jane warned me about? Drugs, sex, and disease?

I gathered what was left of my dignity, barged out of the restroom, and threw all the pills and the bottle at his head. "Mothafucka! Are you crazy? You would really try and fuck me raw, knowing damn well you're positive!" His face was stuck on stupid and his dick deflated.

"I–I–" He stuttered.

"You, nothing!" I wanted to wring his neck, but he kept apologizing. Not that it was enough, but I had nobody to blame but myself. I stormed out of the living room and headed to the front door when a destructive impulse overtook me, and I started breaking shit. The coffee table flipped, fish tank shattered. He ran after me and I sprinted out the door to my car. I pulled off as he ran behind me, banging his fists on my trunk lid until he couldn't keep up anymore. Halfway down the road, I broke down in tears. Humiliated and still being ghosted by Terrence. How could I have allowed myself to be so desperate? My hunger for sex therapy was out of control, and my desire for Terrence's attention had me questioning my feelings for him.

The Widow

Not everyone responds to trauma the same. Some people respond with Aggression, some people respond with Repression, and some people respond with—Depression.

December 1, 2016: 7:00 a.m. I arrived at the office that day an hour early before anybody got there. I didn't have to worry about my hookup with Terrence, because I still had yet to hear from him in over two weeks. Jane called and begged to see me in the office. I knew I couldn't allow her to be seen in my office. My mom would surely have my head. But this was an odd request from her. Something had to be wrong. Otherwise, she would have wanted to meet at the shelter as usual. She sat on the chaise lounge across from me for the first time in almost a year, with a dirty handkerchief to her nose. She blew her snot into it and changed the surface. Blew some more and repeated it until she was ready to speak. She's always been a sad woman. But that day, she was different. Exceptionally sad. She had spent most of her time in my office, in an agonizing crying spell. "I can't believe it! I can't! I can't!" She cried. I knew something was wrong when he didn't even call! I should have said something right then!" She uttered it all through several brief moments of hyperventilation. She had been torturing herself, holding on to this.

I was empathetic, but it was early, and I had barely gotten any rest. 2-hours to be exact. My ego struggled to shake the sudden absence of Terrence in my life at night. I wished she had asked me to meet her at our usual spot. Both of us could have used the fresh air. Besides, it suited the supposedly casual relationship between us considering she was technically discharged. The office made it more formal and likely to put me at risk should anything happen to her.

Time was ticking and we had barely gotten to the nature of her unexpected visit. The last thing I wanted to do was get caught defying my mother. I glanced at the mirrored clock mounted on the wall behind her disheveled hair. It was taunting me. Jane's repetitive snot bombs into her handkerchief which by then, had surely run out of clean surfaces became rusty nails on a chalkboard to my ears. She was usually one of my easier clients. She mostly just wanted to talk and I listened. She did not want my advice or silly self-improvement homework. I resisted my urge to rush her and just waited for her to tell me. For 10 more minutes, she just cried. I got up from behind my desk and sat next to her. I figured it would calm her. She looked into my eyes and I looked into hers. I nodded, cueing her that I was ready to hear what she had to say.

Her tears slowly traveled over the earned wrinkles on her cheeks like cars over speed bumps.

"He's dead..." she finally said. "They say he died in a crash." She buried her head in my chest and screamed so loud, my ear started ringing for a bit. I could feel the loss impale her heart and twist at her gut as if it were my own.

"Where was he?"

"In Vegas! He had a whole other family. Engaged and everything."

"How long have you known?"

"About 3 weeks, more or less." She said, sniffling. "His grieving widow reached out to me because she thought I deserved to know, so she called me from his new phone. Yet, she didn't think I deserved to know she was playing house with my husband!"

"Oh, my! Jane, I'm so sorry to hear that!"

"It's fine. I'm sorry I took so long to tell you about this. I just needed time to process it on my own. Plus, you've been busy doing exactly what I wanted for you. Enjoying your life."

Little did she know, I was just as miserable as she was. "How'd you take the news?"

"Initially, I cried as soon as I hung up the phone with that...that, bitch! But I realized he might as well have been dead to me all this time. Now, I just feel... lost. Not sure what to do. How to go on." In-between one of her blows into her handkerchief, I slipped in a simple question, that I feared may have rubbed her the wrong way. Still, I was curious to observe her response.

"Jane," I began. "If you were to die today, what would your epitaph say?" Her blue eyes shifted from side to side. "I'm not sure I follow." She said softly.

"The inscription on your tombstone. What would it say? Something that perhaps defined you and the life you lived?"

"I'm sorry?" She said.

"Can you name one or more things that you loved to do, but could not do while you were married?" She looked at me, puzzled. The kind of look you give, when you are unsure whether someone has disrespected you or not. "Close your eyes," I said. She leaned back in the plush lavender recliner and followed my instructions. "I want you to allow your mind to travel back to a time before Steve. Dig deep. I want you to find yourself in your happy place. Whenever and wherever that was for you before you met him."

In all honesty, I was more curious than she was. I tried this many, many times and failed to find myself in such a utopia. Perhaps, she would have better luck. Or, maybe escapism wasn't the answer. I got up from my chair, switched off the strategically dimmed lights, and played a few instrumentals from some of her favorite songs we discussed in previous sessions. She would hear the sounds of familiar country tunes and fill in the lyrics herself as she listened and drifted.

I had hoped the music, with its power to enter eager ears and transport its listeners to another place in time, would help her begin her journey back. Make her lose herself in a musical narrative that would inspire imagination and nostalgia. I let her sit with her eyes closed for several minutes, not speaking a word. I wanted her to forget where she was. Allow her mind to truly travel back in time. Whether she spoke another word for the remainder of our time together, was irrelevant.

After about 20-minutes, she spoke with a slight smile through her drying tears.

"I liked to read. A lot."

"Liked?" She wiped her eyes and blew a final bomb into her damp handkerchief.

"I guess it became one of those things I was convinced I didn't have time for. You know? I met Steve back when I used to work in the University library Downtown. He came in looking for some references for his graduate dissertation. It was my job to help and the rest became a series of dates and hardships that would eventually lead to a 23-year marriage."

"What is it that you loved about reading?"

"Hmph," she said, smiling slightly. Her eyes closed once again. I knew she was remembering something. "I'm not special. I grew up in a time when getting married was the career path of choice for most women. Reading was a luxury and it allowed me not only to keep a sharp mind but live in a temporary fantasy." I knew what she meant. I understood the lure. Only, she had found a healthy avenue to fall victim to her wildest desires.

"Well, Jane, I might actually have homework for you this time." She sat up straight and stared at me sharply.

"That is not how this goes. You know that, dear." I ignored her comment.

"I want you to read one book of your choice, before your next visit in two weeks." In a world where she had been consumed by the loss of one love, I wanted her to find utopia by resurrecting an old one.

"I think I can do that. But let's not make this homework thing a habit, hun. I'm knocking on 70. My eyes ain't what they used to be."

"I promise. If you'd like, we have about 10-minutes left of our session. We can both close our eyes and enjoy Ms. Ross together.

She smiled and laid back down, her emerald-colored balloon-sleeved blouse failed to completely cover the family of used tissues stuffed in her slightly exposed bra. She did not have on her French beret. Said it brought back too many memories. It was 8:00, which meant we only had 30-minutes before my mom walked through the door and put my head on a platter for Sunday dinner. "Alright, hun." She said, "I'll get out of your hair. Don't wanna get you in trouble. Thanks for listening as usual. You're the best."

She didn't even look me in the eyes. I did not see it then, but Jane would be a lesson for me, one I would not learn until the damage was already done. After the workday, I called Jane again and again around 5 p.m., but no answer. A rush of heat crept up my spine as I sat at my desk scratching my head. My mom barged in, asking if I had finished my progress notes for the day, my mind silenced everything around me like a vacuum. The heat turned into a flame. I knew this flame all too well. It was the same flame that compelled me to trash Andre's house and murder his pet fish. My awareness of its presence troubled me because I knew I had little to no control over what I would do next. "Khai! Do you hear me talking to you?" My mom quizzed.

"I've got to go, mom. It's an emergency."

"What kind!" My stomach turned at the idea of fessing up to seeing Jane this morning. It was as if I blinked and the next thing I knew, I ran past my mom in the doorway and was in the car heading to Jane's house. She lived in the back of Kingwood with a house that sat on the San Jacinto River. There is only one way in and one way out of Kingwood, so traffic jams happen easily. The threat of the rain made my hands unsteady with anticipation as I gripped the wheel.

I wouldn't let that stop me. Something else had taken the wheel and I was merely a vessel for something far more powerful than I and beyond my comprehension. Something, determined. It was the most peculiar feeling. I was driving, but I wasn't driving. As I was speeding down the road noticing the clouds become a deep grayish purple, I kept calling, but no answer. It took me 20 minutes too long to get to her house. It was white like her car but from the lack of maintenance it had become quite dingy and the grass was overgrown with weeds and ant piles.

I was in such a hurry when I got out of the car, I left it running with the door open. The air smelled like mud, and a cool wind rustled the trees. I looked up to find thick clouds brewing a storm. It started to drizzle. My leather seats would surely get wet, but I did not care. I sprinted to the front door. Bang, bang, banging on its solid wood surface and hollering, "Jane! Jane! Jane!" There was no answer.

My heart was jumping out of my chest and slamming back in with every rapid beat. The drizzle was cold, but my flame burned hotter as I worried my worst fear would soon be realized. I ran around to the side of the house and clawed my way through some healthy hedges. That's when I saw her. I was— I was too late.

She was there, hanging by the grip of Steve's silk tie in front of the window she often spoke of gazing out of as she hoped for Steve's return. Her body was swaying ever-so-slightly back and forth, her gray hair covered her face and her chin was dipped into her chest. The flame inside me became an aggressive blaze as I stepped away from the window two stories up and paced uncontrollably back and forth. My hands were clammy again, and my head was throbbing. Suddenly there was this overwhelming feeling as if I needed to vomit. It compelled me to hurl a stone through one of the windows on the first floor and climb in. Alarms sounded and lights flashed in every direction in the yard.

I rushed to her aid, her neck was black and blue, and her tongue protruded through her teeth. It was a ghastly blurple color. I wanted to ball up and cry for her but that would have to wait. I had to get her down. Cade was curled up in a ball underneath her dangling feet and growled as I approached. I moved her recliner under her feet and cade took off down the stairs to hide. I followed behind him and scrambled around the kitchen for something to cut the tie.

It took another 20-minutes too long for the sirens to whale their tune down the streets, accompanied by their red white, and blue lights flashing in the windows. They rushed in and pried her from my arms, as I lay there rocking back and forth in the chair, her fragile still body clinging to my chest. Images of her frail hands with purple paint on her nails, clenching that black silk tie on the couch in my office, on the bench in front of the animal shelter, and dangling from the pocket of her trench coat as she walked to her car, all bombarded my vision with every blink of disbelief.

I inhaled but I couldn't release. I knew the hysterical whimpering it would bring. Instead, my eyes swelled with tears and I covered my mouth. When they carried her body down the stairs and I followed only to stop in the middle of the driveway and collapse to my knees. I was lying on the ground, small rocks left little dents in my arms and cheeks, dirt was in my hair and ants crawled nearby. All I could do to soothe the stabbing pain was hug my knees and clench my teeth. The guilt was stifling.

My clothes were drenched. It was a nightmare. I gazed out over the roofs of the wet dodge chargers, Crown Vics, and the ambulance and watched the lightning illuminate the sky. A crack of thunder soon followed that rumbled my paralyzed body. My tears mixed with the chilling rainwater and debris on my face, as the ABC 13 news team stood a few feet away from her house, getting their story.

"67-year-old Kingwood resident, Jane Mallard found dead in her home. Sources ruling it a suicide!" My flame sizzled to steam as the water came down heavier and heavier and I began to shiver. I found myself in the back of an ambulance, again, sooner than I would have ever expected. The officers asked way too many questions, all of which began to run together. I was a bit disoriented and couldn't speak clearly. They must have sensed it because they left me alone after a while. Flashing lights blinded me as they sped off into the storm and the ambulance doors slammed in my face. The whole ride to the coroners, I sought comfort from someone.

My instinct was to open Jack'd, the devil app I attempted to hide from myself in my phone, but not yet trashed. But for the first time in a long time, I wanted nothing to do with that rabbit hole of no strings attached. I wanted, not sex. Not solitude. But perhaps something with more—sustenance.

Later that night, I was feeling broken. No place to go. And so like any wounded child, I ran home to mommy. I barged in the door and fell to my knees at the bottom of the steps. The cold hardwood pressed against my knees and tears streamed down my cheeks. My clothes were soaked and as a mixture of rainwater and tears dripped from my chin, it pooled atop the bottom step into a small puddle. My mom came rushing to my aid in hysterics.

"Khai! What's the matter!" She cried. My dad was behind her, in his green mink robe, rushing to turn on the lights.

"I'm so sorry, mom. I'm sooo sorry!" I cried."

"Khai! calm down. What's wrong!

"Sh—Sh—She's dead! She's dead! She's dead!"

She grabbed my shoulders from behind and pulled me in closer to her. I could feel her heart pounding against my shoulder blades.

"Who's dead?" She said, trying to hold me still as I was squirming to free myself.

"Jane! She hung herself! And it's all my fault!" I just wanted to curl up in a ball again and hug my knees until the pain stopped. The thunder cracked, triggering my nightmare's return. Kaboom! A flash of purple light behind my eyes and I saw a car crash into a tree. Kaboom! A scruffy beard with blood trickling down in-between the strands of his chin hair. Kaboom! A man's face resembling mine lit up in a shower of purple lights. He glanced over at someone in the passenger seat. I saw him through the passenger's eyes. Looking down at me.

"I love you, son." He uttered just before his head collapsed onto the steering wheel." Kaboom! The sound of a car horn lingered and the innocent high-pitched sounds of a little boy crying, "Daddy! Daddy! Daddy!" repeatedly and desperately shaking the man's still body. The thunder cracks its whip again, hurling my mind back into a loose reality.

"Daaaad! Please! Daaaad! I'm so sorry!" I kept shouting to a dead man. I was kicking and screaming so much I nearly knocked my mom in the head with my elbow. I had no control. Finally, there was a sharp prick in my thigh and everything faded to black. When my eyes opened again, I was in my old bedroom, my mom sitting at the foot of the bed. The door remained off its hinges, and pictures of Mariah Carey were on every wall. All my medals and memorabilia from my track days were in a glass casing that stood about 6-feet tall. It was a time capsule. My mom looked at me, her eyes full of tears.

"I'm so sorry." She said. I couldn't imagine what she had to be sorry about. I was still a little groggy, but I managed to respond.

"Whatcha mean?"

"I think it's time I tell you what really happened to your father."

Stay The Night

A week passed since I received the news about my dad's suicide. I had been cooped up in my room, watching Housewives and eating macarons until my stomach turned. No matter how many times my mom called to check on me, I sent her to voicemail. One night, I was in bed glaring at the ceiling. The clock struck 1:00 a.m. and I was wide awake. Eyes, bone-dry. I was trying to purge my dad's bloody forehead from the forefront of my mind. My sheets were damp with sweat that unfortunately, was not from sex.

I begged for the flood of repressed memories pouring into my mind to retreat to the deepest and darkest corners of wherever the hell their hiding place has been all these years. Desperate for some relief, I got up to search for some eye drops in the bathroom when I caught a glimpse of my scar in the mirror. It's faint and shaped like a janky crescent moon on my jaw. I like the left side of my face better. Nothing there but brown skin.

No matter how hard I clenched my eyes, the images would not go away. They start the same almost every time. A jarring flash of red, then a yellow that spreads in all directions until it's so bright that all I can see is white. When it clears, there's a haunting final glimpse into my father's dark and empty eyes as he looks down at me with trembling lips and a pistol pointed at his head. For a moment, it seems like he's about to apologize, or say I love you, but the thunder crackles, and there's a flash of lightning… Bullet through his temple and out the other side to put a hole in the glass. His lifeless head smashes into the steering wheel. It was on a loop and more aggressive each time that night. I remember all the crying, all the rain, and above all, I remember the blood. My father's blood.

I watched helplessly as it dripped from the steering wheel and pooled beneath the soles of his black steel-toe boots. One foot was still firmly planted on the gas pedal and drove us head-on into a tree trunk. The windshield smashes and I scream until I wake myself up. To now know my scar's true origin had come from such a tragedy, made it harder to look in the mirror every morning. I wished I could talk about it more with my mom, but we were no longer on speaking terms. I didn't know whether to resent her for withholding the truth for as long as she did, or hug her for trying to protect my sanity. Not knowing, tortured me subconsciously. Knowing, tortured me in a way that felt impossible to ignore. Meanwhile, Terrence called again. And again. And again. Any normal person would have blocked his phone number 15-calls ago, but for some reason, I liked the attention. It made me feel, powerful.

Who can resist the thrill of being desired? I went on to lose my battle with my eyes refusing to stay shut for more than 10-minutes at a time. Tossing and turning…Tossing and turning. I thought about Jane and how she was lucky to have loved someone as much as she appeared to have done so. And also how unfortunate it was for her to have allowed it to cripple her when it was lost. The thought of it was a nightmare. It was cold and windy that night. Again, there was that pesky sound of that massive oak tree outside my window scraping against the gutters. I was sweating and in desperate need of water. I peeped at the clock on my phone. It was 2:15 a.m. when my phone rang. "Hello?" I said. It was Terrence. My voice was a bit horse from the impending dehydration from tossing and turning all night.

"What you doin' up this late? Everybody knows the only thing open this late, are legs and mouths." I should have asked him the same thing, but there was a sincerity in his voice that was almost fatherly, yet flirtatious. I felt like I could confide in him, even though I knew it to be a little pathetic.

"Can't sleep," I said.

"What's on your mind?" How he failed to consider that maybe it was his endless phone calls at ungodly hours that was the culprit behind my lack of sleep, was baffling. Maybe the thought did cross his mind, and maybe he didn't care. Or, maybe he was so used to being desired that he couldn't fathom the idea that anybody on the receiving end of one of his calls would feel the least bit inconvenienced. I could picture his green eyes illuminating the walls of my self-imposed black hole—just staring at me with determination to prove I wanted him.

"If I had known you were having trouble sleeping, I would have called more. I am the type of person that always finds a solution." He said. When he laughed, I smiled. I smiled because it was arguably one of the more unattractive qualities about him. It was raspy and nasally at the same time. "Sometimes we all need a little help, playa."

"What do you want, Terrence?"

"A chance to make it up to you."

"You good. Find someone else to lie to."

"Look, I had a little episode like the one I had back at Palace Inn the first time we met. No biggie."

"Oh my god! Are you okay!"

"Yeah. I'm much better. Jarvis took care of everything." I was a little jealous that he called Jarvis and not me, but Jarvis was his sponsor. I had to respect that, I guess.

"Well, call Jarvis. I'm not interested in entertaining married men." I was firm and I thought I meant every word.

"Are you sure? You could have blocked my number hours ago, but here you are. I know your heart's beating fast. You want it." He fell silent, forcing me to listen. I could hear my heart, thump, thump, thumping. Rapidly. My body felt warm with anticipation. "You should let me come stay the night and make it up to you."

"Stay the night? Oh, no. I don't know you to be having you all in my house like that."

"Fine. We can get a hotel. A better one this time. On me." I still don't understand why I had even considered going. I would surely say no, even in my hesitance. But he came in to seal the deal. "I can't," I said. "I have to be up in the morning."

"From what I understand, you need a little help sleeping. Or, am I wrong?" He didn't give me a chance to answer, or maybe my hesitation as I imagined what that would look like, lasted longer than I thought. The word no was on the tip of my tongue, not quite where it needed to be. My phone lit up on my cheek with a text from him. Inside, the address to the famous Marriott Marquise is located in the heart of Houston. The one with the Texas-shaped lazy river on the rooftop and pricy skyline views. "The executive suite is all ours for the night. Your choice. As long as you haven't been fucking anybody else." He said.

"What's that supposed to mean."

"It means I can always tell when another man has fucked my dude."

"How so?"

"That booty be loose. Duh!" There was a beat of silence, then we both burst out laughing.

"So, I'll see you there. I'll bring the wine. I promise you won't regret it. The view is more than enough reason." He said. My bougie eyes were as bright as the jarring white screen on my phone. I had always been curious about that hotel. I could have gone at any time I wanted, but I always imagined I'd go there with someone special. Plus, it was on his dime. Next thing I knew, we were on the elevator headed 23-stories up to a suite he described as "fit for the bad and bougie." He said. The warm and spicy scent of his Versace danced on the walls of the elevator before caressing my nose. It was like foreplay.

"You smell good," I said.

"It's Versace."

"I know."

"Don't worry. You gone get to smell it up close and personal reeeealll soon, playa."

When we arrived at the suite he swung open the heavy cream-colored door for a big reveal. I was immersed in a world graced with all the things I valued in material life: Silk linens, gold finishings, skyline views, city-night lights, and fine wine. My eyes were immediately drawn to the floor-to-ceiling window which was decorated with a glorious backdrop of Downtown Houston and an aerialesque view of the lazy river on the rooftop below. He had impeccable taste. I was pleasantly surprised.

The surrounding buildings reflected the moon and city lights onto the pool water. Vibrant red, yellow, and green hues blended and made the pool glow in the night. "A step up from the Palace Inn, huh?" He said.

"Just a little." He stood in front of the window, completely naked and holding two glasses of Stella Rosa down by each side of his waist. The city lights served as a complementary backlight on his body. It created a soft-glowing outline of his masculine silhouette, reminiscent of something straight out of a film noir. The deep red wine, a stark and sensual pop of color. It was… artistic. This time felt different. This one did not feel like a hookup. It was more like…romance.

Even though he stood in front of me nude, the shadows covering his ankles and up to his thigh, left a journey for my mind to be lost in imagination. He made me want more. Time stood still as I admired God's work. And for once, not only was I not complaining or itching for the hour hand to tick–tick–tick, I lost track of time. Inside the corner of his lips, he held a blunt and talked out the side of his mouth as he eyed me seductively. He summoned me with the lure of his eyes and a head nod. Mentally and physically enticed, I was engulfed in a desire too intense for words. He reached out to offer me a glass. His right hand, still holding the front of his crotch. He was gifted 9-times over, and like a bee to a flower, I was drawn toward him. A natural force beyond my control.

As the wine kissed the tips of my lips and passed through my mouth like silk, I was touched with a rush of heat that would soon slither up my neck and down my back. And he had yet to lay a finger on my eager body. There, in front of the window, he embraced me, his chest and stomach pressed against my back, and a tender kiss upon my neck. Being in his arms was like wearing your boyfriend's jacket in high school. You never want to take it off. You want to flaunt it.

"All you gotta do is say yes." Floetry's harmonies seduced me in the background, had me ready to indulge. As we gazed out over the cityscape and swayed to the rhythm of the music, he whispered in my ear, "Take off your clothes." Again, he gave me no chance to respond, having slid my shirt off and pulled me closer. His bare chest against my bare back (pun intended). I could feel him flexing his pecks against the back of my shoulders. The vibrations were subtle, but the desire they fueled was intense. He Groped my chest firmly and then traced my nipples ever so slightly with his thumbs.

My eyes rolled to the back of my head. My legs and arms succumbed to the tenderness of his touch. I pleaded with them to not fail me now. With one more kiss on my neck as I took another sip of wine, he pulled my hips to his, and I could feel all of him between my thighs. Unable to resist, my hands defied me and copped a feel of his girth. Its abundance excited me like it was the very first time all over again.

He was an artist, having carefully chosen his color palette with my desires as his muse, delicately placing slow calculated strokes with the gentle brush onto a blank canvas. It was clear that he was a visionary. As Carrie Bradshaw would say, he knew exactly how to… *"color"* me. My body was the canvas on which he would paint. His tantalizing fragrance, demeanor, statuesque, all the way down to his choice of wine, was the work of an adonis. He knew exactly what he was doing.

"Do you smoke?" He asked as he flicked on a lighter, igniting a yellow flame that would then turn blue in the reflection of our bodies together in the window. "Nah. Not really. I've tried it once or twice. Didn't do much for me." I said. I watched in the window as he joined the tip of the blunt to the flame.

"You probably wasn't smoking the right shit. I want you to try this. Trust me. You won't regret it." He slowly passed it in front of my face and around to meet his lips so that I could experience a burned earthy aroma that had the smallest hint of floral and citrus notes. After taking a few puffs, he spun me around to face him, pressing his lips against mine. His tongue danced with mine, and he released a slow and steady wave of smoke into my mouth. I was worried I would choke, but he did it so delicately that it felt like I was in control. He pulled away and closed my mouth with his fingertips. As the pads of his fingers graze my lips, I could smell the grape from the cigarillo on them, making me want a taste.

"Hold it." He said. I closed my eyes and submitted to his command. A few seconds passed, and he turned me toward the window. "Now, exhale through your nose." I opened my eyes and released a cloud of smoke into the air, which went on to surround us both. I started coughing so hard my eyes were watering.

"That's what we call a charge." I was still coughing a little and couldn't respond. My throat was on fire. "You want another one?" I was intrigued, so I nodded.

"Are you okay?" He asked. "You're shaking."

"Yeah, it happens sometimes."

"I know you not nervous. This ain't your first rodeo." All I could do was shrug.

"A lot going on outside of this rodeo," I said, briefly thinking about Jane and my dead father.

"Hold on a second." He leaned over, grabbed a small plastic blue box, and pulled out two blue pills.

"Try it. It will help you relax." I hesitated as usual and was prepared to say no. But something in me wanted to feel numb, even if it were just for one night. He placed it on my tongue with a slow kiss and passed me my glass to chase it down with a splash of wine. The reflection in the window made it feel as if I were watching from the outside. But this was no lucid dream.

I was feeling, no, living, every moment of it. Finally, he picked me up and I held onto him like a damsel in distress. My body melted into the cool and airy linens, as he placed me in them with the care of a loving partner. They smelled like lavender and honeysuckle, igniting visions of a lush springtime garden. He had taken me outdoors and into the wonders of nature without ever having to leave the bedroom.

He inched himself on top of me. His warm lips kissed mine. Down to my neck, down, to the tips of my sensitive nipples, and down to the area just above my hips that tickles when it's licked. The wet tingles made my toes curl and my abs flex. My body was begging to squirm, crying out for him as he pinned my arms above my head and whispered in my ear. "Don't fight it. I know you want it." Yeah, I wanted it. Bad. Instinctively, my eyes closed, forcing me to feel his lips as they hovered over my sensitive inner thighs. I could feel his heart thumping as the pulsations traveled from the tips of his fingers and crept up the back of my neck. It was electric.

My head drifted in circles as my body was caressed in a faint breeze that made me feel as though I was levitating. The black behind my eyelids faded into a soft pink, and a blue that was almost green. When they finally meshed together like an abstract masterpiece on a black canvas. I was able to catch my breath. It was like a wet dream. Every touch. Every kiss, every lick, and every stroke was real, yet my mind is lost on a trip.

Every muscle relaxed. As his hips slowly and tentatively stroked between mine, I noticed this feeling was different. For the first time, it didn't feel like I was getting fucked. He was making love to me. It wasn't the pounding I was used to. It was a massage. The subtle fruitiness that the wine left on his breath, lifted my chin to meet his gaze, intently into his eyes. The lustrous pale green gems twinkled under the moon's soft white light, as it cast its erotic shadows of our bodies moving together on the walls.

Sliding his hands underneath my ass, he groped my cheeks and pulled my hips closer. Deeper. While his damp chest kissed mine, my erection glided against the soft, yet defined ridges in his abs. The moist and smooth motions made me quiver for more. Harder. Faster. I reached up to put my arms around his neck and pulled him in for a kiss. Our tongues danced for a moment until his head slowly rolled back and his thrust became more rapid. With his eyes clenched, he gritted his teeth and moaned until a synonymous tingling sensation rushing over our bodies became too much to hold back any longer. Our strong euphoric grunts and rapid breaths spawned vivid illusions of lava. Emblazoned in my mind, it swirled vigorously behind the black of my eyelids until there was an eruption of color. Pastel pinks, blues, vibrant yellows, and mellow oranges, captivated me.

Suddenly, I could taste the honeysuckle and the lightness of the lavender. The heat from his skin against mine hugged me, and an intense release of tension had my toes throwing gang signs! I moaned so loud I could feel the hum in the headboard.

He had me in my head singing like Mariah. *And it's just like honey!* His love was all over me and drizzled like topping on a Starbucks frappe. My mind was blown and thrust into the night sky as a light rain fell. I marveled at his creation, illuminated by stardust. I was his canvas, to be re-imagined when the time would once again stand still and he would once again, ask me to stay the night.

Walk of Shame

For as long as I can remember, I've lived chained to the tick of a clock. Lying awake in my overpriced California King, not sleeping, was my norm. I was able to account for almost every hour that would slowly tick by as I stared at my ceiling which was decorated with a constellation of glowing stars. I would always try to count the little them but I had only ever gotten to 69 before they all ran together and my vision blurred, and I would find myself groggy with a slight headache.

It was the morning after, and for the first time, I woke up next to Terrence. The relaxing hum against my back as he made subtle grunts in his sleep, told me not to move. I couldn't help but wonder if that was what it felt like to actually *sleep* with someone. To be truly intimate. If I had to do the walk of shame and never look back, that was something I would always be grateful to him for. I woke up that day to the ring of my body's natural clock. The sun hid behind the collage of skyscrapers, and the clouds were outlined in a reddish-orange hue that reminded me of a ripe mango.

I remember thinking how pleasant it was to have been welcomed by the absence of that dull morning gray that usually paints the sky between 6 and 7 in the morning. The auburn leaves, twirled in the wind, so slowly and carefree, it was obvious they had no place to be. No one to answer to. And would soon, take solace in the welcoming grassy surface of Discovery Green Park which was drizzled in the morning dew. It was breathtaking. Briefly, I found myself thinking I wanted to wake up to this—to Terrence, every morning. Finally, my eyes rolled over to the clock on the nightstand and I jumped out of bed so fast, I stubbed my big toe on its sharp metal frame. And there, the fantasy ended. Living in the moment: denied.

I hollered 'fuck' so loud the brass lamp on the nightstand vibrated a little. Or, maybe it had been from my big toe disturbing its glossy foundation? I couldn't tell the difference. Terrence rolled over and wiped those gems of his and squinted out at the view, welcoming the same stolen moment I took the time to appreciate just minutes before him.

"What's the hurry, playa? We haven't even ordered breakfast yet." I was scratching my head and hobbling around trying to find my things. He just laid there, the blankets and sheets just barely covering one of his legs, and falling off his shoulder as a few of the sun rays seeped through the glass and kissed his skin. Just beautiful. It was almost unfair.

"I have a life," I said it so harshly, that even I thought it was rude.

"How'd ya sleep?" He looked at me and smiled. So sure of himself. My moment of discombobulation, a trophy for his good work last night. I ignored him. I wouldn't give him the satisfaction of knowing he had been responsible for the best sleep I had that year and arguably, the best sex. Nope. Not a chance.

"Well, at least have a cup of coffee and shower before ya go."

"I don't drink coffee. I am more of a green tea and a splash of almond milk kind of guy. So, I'm gonna have to pass." He rose from the bed and kissed me on the forehead before starting the coffee pot. "You smell like sex. At least take a shower. I'll have it ready when you get out. I have this creamer I think you're going to love." I sniffed my armpits and shoulders. Discreetly, I raised one brow and twisted my lips. Hell, I was almost insulted. Apparently, sex smells like sweat, weed, and a splash of delicious Stella Rosa. I shrugged and figured it unprofessional and downright unthinkable to show up to work with body odor and hopped in the shower.

When I got out and cracked the door to let some cool air in for the fogged-up mirror, the sweetness of salted caramel and hazelnut cut through the steam and danced on my nose hairs. It was divine. I glanced at him sitting by the window in his black briefs, scrolling through his phone and sipping from a porcelain cup.

"You bring that from your wife's house?" He took a moment to look up at me and nodded his head toward the chair next to him, where a cup of salted caramel-flavored coffee was waiting for me. I had about 35-minutes to hit I-45 North from Downtown to Houston's king of bougie suburban living: The Woodlands. Still, I took a seat next to him and sipped the coffee cautiously. I didn't have to say how surprisingly delicious it was because he said it for me.

"I knew you'd like it."

"Whatever."

"Are you always this stubborn?"

"So I've been told. But I've never been inclined to agree." Nodding and taking another sip of his coffee.

"Well, playa, ima break you of that. You can't go through life only ever experiencing the familiar." He said. I looked at him not looking at me. Stifled. How is it he had insulted me, but somehow I felt as though maybe I owed him an apology of some sort for my sass? He was killing me with generosity. Or, I may have been overthinking it. That's always a possibility. It's just the way my anxiety works. "I guess you're right." I finally said, suddenly unmotivated to come up with another snarky response. I took two more sips of my first coffee in 4-years and darted out the door. I think I was about 15-minutes late. I'm not completely sure, but I know I was certainly not on time. When you work in a mental health setting, being late is never a good thing. This particular patient population can be terrifying when they are upset and non-compliant with medication therapies in place by their psychiatrist. The psychiatrist being, my mother.

What was even scarier, was my mom when I pissed her off. I hadn't been home or spoken to my mother since she told me about my dad's suicide. I couldn't fathom how she could keep a secret like that. Still, I had a job to do and so did she. Unfortunately, we had to do that job together. The only way we were able to get through it, was by utilizing the family's best superpower. Suppression. We went along the whole day as if nothing ever happened. It was my responsibility and her responsibility to work through our shit on our own time. That's the tight ship my mother ran. I hadn't even gotten comfortable in my chair before she burst through the door. Her face was stone cold, and her eyes were riddled with worry and disappointment.

"Khai, you know how I feel about having my patients waiting. I don't need a waiting room full of disgruntled patients. I will not stand for it! Especially not at the hand of your bullshit. Pull it together!" She had her hair pulled in a tight shiny bun. Her lips, a soft purple, her favorite color. She pulled back the left sleeve of her tailored light-grey power suit, drawing attention to her purple ruffle collared dress shirt that was blossoming through the pressed lapels. She pointed at her watch. "Did you not see me calling? You do not have the luxury of not checking in like that. Where the hell were you?" She acted like nothing had happened, so that meant I had to do the same. I wasn't too surprised, so I did what we do in my family. Suppressed.

"I'm sorry, mom. My alarm clock didn't go off this morning. Won't happen again. Promise."

"Dr.—Allen." She reminded me.

"We have a problem. Jane's family is trying to sue the practice for negligence and patient abandonment!"

"What? How!"

"I'm not sure. Their lawyers sent over a subpoena for her records and called to say that there was no record of a formal discharge letter in her chart. Which means–"

"You could be held liable for her suicide," I said for her. And right after I said it, my heart dropped. I couldn't remember if I ever sent the email to Jane with the letter attached. All this talk about me needing to forgive her when she was the one who should have been deciding whether or not she was going to forgive me. Fucking Terrence and his fucking pizza! I must have forgotten.

No way I could stomach fessing up to a fuck-up like that. Not when I could have been the very reason my mom lost everything she worked her entire life to build. I had to be sure. "All the records show is extensive documentation that she was non-compliant with meds and a high risk for suicide, and no action was taken, like I just let the woman run around here, just crazy. So anyway, I need you to find the discharge letter you sent, so that we can fax it over to them and put an end to this." She looked at me like she was confident that I sent that letter. With my best poker face, I said, "No problem, I just gotta go through the email and find it."

"Yes, but was she called and informed that there would be a letter coming? She should have been discharged over the phone, Khai. And, a formal letter should have been sent to both her email and certified mail to follow up." I was too chicken-shit to fess up to the possibility that I may have forgotten to send off the letter, so I told her yes.

"Are you going to her funeral this evening?" she asked.

"Oh my god! Is that today?"

"Yes. How could you forget?" I thought about the answer… I was rolling around in bed with a married man meanwhile, back at the office, my mom's life work was in the middle of a crisis as a result of the mess I made with Jane. Sometimes the dead like to play games from beyond the grave. Jane was one of those ghosts. It was the day of Jane's funeral and I wanted to avoid reality. More so, I was avoiding having to bid my final goodbye. Letting go of things has never been my strong suit. I've carried a grudge against a girl named Raven, who teased me in junior high school for being a closet gay. It was like she had a personal vendetta against me. Every time I wanted to join a conversation in class, she'd call me a sissy and even convinced her boyfriend at the time to tell the track coach I hit on him.

Ever since then, I had to change into my track uniform in a restroom on a completely different side of the school and would have to walk at least 5-minutes across campus and onto the track. I would eventually get my revenge Junior year in high school. It was finals season and everyone got the chance to be exempt from 3 of our 5 final exams if our grade average in the class was at least an 85. All we had to do was turn in what my school called, an Exemption application.

We had English together and on the day that the exemption forms were due, she rushed out of class when the bell rang for 3rd period and forgot her form on her desk. I swiped it when no one was looking and tore it to shreds. Long story short, the bitch had to take all her finals. Looking back, I regret nothing, and if I were to see her in the street today, I'd call her a bitch and bust the windows out of her car if the opportunity presented itself.

That said, I could not face my mother, the shame and guilt for having been the reason she had to witness one of her former patients be lowered 6-feet into the ground, knowing her hardheaded son was to blame, would eat me alive. I could not say goodbye to Jane. I just didn't feel ready, not that one can ever be ready to bury someone they loved. I imagined my mom's awkward glances over at me and then back at the casket, then back at me again. A tear emerged from behind her glasses and tricked down her cheek and onto the grass as Jane was lowered into the ground. It would be one of those moments when you wish you had listened to your mother. And so, I refused to attend Jane's funeral because of it.

The painful realization that there would be no more coffee and banter on the bench in front of the animal shelter, no more Diana Ross and Mariah Carey listening parties. I could no longer live vicariously through the stories of her married days that before Steve's disappearance, always sounded like a fairytale. It made me angry, bitter, and confused. I began to wonder why anyone would knowingly bother to love someone so deeply it feels like you can't live without them—only to have them snatched away by death's grip, the wear, and tear of time, or worse… by someone else.

Suddenly, I began questioning every decision I made. I woke up a few mornings later, unable to decide on what to eat for breakfast, so I ate nothing. There were too many options of soap to choose from while I was in the shower, so I just stood under the steaming water, crying for 10-minutes. Finding something to wear usually took me an hour. A closet full of designer clothes, and all I wanted to wear was a pair of grey sweatpants and an old wrinkled white v-neck. I finally got settled in front of the tv with a box of macarons, a glass of Stella Rosa, and a shot of Vodka. It was time to catch up on Housewives.

Problem was, I couldn't bring myself to watch it. Instead, I just laid in bed staring at the wall, daydreaming about the last time I saw Jane alive. I could smell the peppermint. My phone wailed like a siren with a flash-flood alert. That's when I noticed I had missed a call from Terrence. I decided not to call him back right away. More than anything, I wanted comfort but a part of me felt I didn't deserve it. And so, I defaulted to old habits: wallowing alone underneath my dark cloud. And that's exactly what I did until mid-afternoon.

TERRENCE: Hey, I've still us a hotel for a few more hours.

ME: And?

TERRENCE: Come get u some. I know you want it.

I was rolling around in bed with him an hour later.

Baggage

Baggage... It's all the bullshit you carry with you from one relationship to the next. It's the highs, the lows, the memories of betrayal, the hurt feelings, the anger, and the bitterness that fuel it. It's the wasted hope and all of the harsh realities that are dumped on you without mercy when attempting to love. I had gotten so good at carrying my baggage alone, that the idea of unloading it on Terrence, felt both daunting and risky.

Christmas lights were all over the city, but I was just not feeling the festivities at all. A few weeks had passed since Jane's suicide. It felt longer than that. Hours felt like weeks and weeks felt like months. My house smelled like sweat and leftover Lo-Mein noodles. I reeked of something far worse...Guilt. I did, however, manage to make an effort to pull myself together when Terrence called to invite me to dinner one evening. This time, at his place. By his place, I mean the luxury apartment his wife was supposedly paying for.

Initially, I told him I was busy. That was my way of acknowledging that everything about what we had been doing was wrong. Just as I was about to tap that big red button, he hit me with a headliner: "Let me cook you dinner." I was shaking my head no, but I hadn't responded verbally. Why was that so hard? I said nothing.

"I'll take your silence as a yes. Meet me at my place around 8. Bring an appetite, but not *too* much. I still want some of that booty later." He hung up the phone before I could say yes or no or… yes. No man had ever offered to cook for me before. I debated in the mirror for several minutes as I ran the shower in the background. I thought for a moment about our nights at the hotel and grew lustful. I fought the urge to see him for all of 5-minutes. An hour went by and I had managed to manscape, douche, shower, and lather my body in Palmer's Co-Co butter.

As soon as I arrived at his door, I could smell the creole seasoning floating around in the hall. He opened the door in a white chef's apron and nothing else. His chest and arms were bulging out the seams. Damn, he was good at selling a fantasy. It was like he wasn't even trying.

"How are you, my love?" he said, as he shut the door behind me. That was the first time he addressed me like that. I had grown content with, "Playa." It made me raise an eyebrow but it also made me smile. The lights were dim, and steam from the rice boiling put just a hint of warm moisture in the air. It was welcoming. Homey. I remember thinking about how this is exactly what I would have wanted in a husband.

Then I remembered, he was somebody's husband. "I'm alright. But what's not alright, is what we're doing." He tilted his head and frowned.

"Whatchu mean by that?"

"I mean, how's that separation going by the way?" He looked at me sharply and just before he spoke, his lips paused mid-sentence so that he could chuckle under his breath.

"That's why I called you over, boy. When I went home to the big house yesterday, it was empty… He got rid of all my clothes and took the BMW!"

"He?" I asked. He paused and looked to the side.

"Yeah… He." After a long sigh, he dropped a bomb on me. "My husband put me out." My mouth was stuck. "Husband?"

"I haven't been married to a woman in over 10 years." He continued. "My husband's name is Warren. Everything I told you about my wife is true. Just replace that pronoun with him instead of her." I was burning inside.

My theory had been debunked and now I was full of questions. I believed him to have been some cliché closet-case who married a woman not only for money but also because he was still insecure about his homosexuality for whatever reason he had that he wasn't comfortable sharing with me. Either way, he was still an asshole. Suddenly, I was the other man in an embarrassment of gay marriage. It made me feel like the scum of the earth I was. Still, I was curious…

"So, what does this mean?" I asked.

"Means he wants a divorce."

"What about your bills?"

"He transferred $5,000 to my account and said he'd cover my bills for a couple of months until I got on my feet as long as I don't follow him or speak to him again."

I have to admit, it did spark just a little bit of hope. Maybe things might work out after all.

"I can't do this," I said.

"What? You don't wanna see me anymore? I thought you were enjoying yourself if I recall correctly." You know what they say about forbidden sex… Yeah, I was enjoying myself. I wouldn't admit it. Where's the dignity in that?

"Why the hell would you tell me you were married to a woman?" He looked at me with a half-smirk in his eyes.

"Would that have made a difference?" Why did that question make me uncomfortable? Now, I was nervous. The kind of nervous one feels when they're at risk of losing someone. I was stumped. I wanted to think the answer was yes, but for some reason, I wasn't entirely sure. I couldn't make sense of it and still can't. He wasn't the first married man I had slept with, I'm sure. I had a thing for guys older than me. Believe it or not, it comes with the territory. Terrence just happened to be slightly more honest about it. How was it I felt the urge to hold on to someone I knew wasn't minc to keep?

"Why go through all the fuckin' trouble? You could've just told me upfront, especially since you believe it wouldn't have made a difference." I said.

"Trick of the trade, playa. Don't tell all ya business on the first date." Although he wasn't completely honest when we made our initial agreement, the alleged separation seemed to be picking up momentum, so maybe it didn't matter as much. Besides, I couldn't help but wonder what else he was hiding. I was curious in the worst of ways. I wanted to stick around and dig up all his skeletons.

"Well, we are well beyond first dates now," I said, "So maybe now you can tell me what the hell I'm getting myself into?" For a moment, there was no response. Anita Baker's "Sweet Love" played in the background. Finally, he leaned back in his chair, and looked me up and down one good time.

"I went to jail for second-degree murder." My eyes were so big they hurt. "You killed someone!?"

"No. Yes, but…no. When I was living in Chicago, I was coming home from the club one night, drunk and high on coke. I started having chest pain and lost control of the wheel and ended up rear-ending a flatbed truck on the highway… My best friend Hakeem, bled out before the ambulance came." I didn't know what to make of it, why was he telling me this now?

"Long story short, playa. It's a little bit harder for me to hold a job and I need to be kept." Damn, how I managed to go from baby to playa in less than 1-hour, I don't know.

"He came in and offered me a way out, by marrying me and I would have been a fool not to take it. He knew what this was when he married me. He just told me to keep it away from the house."

"So what? You just scroll through Jackd and prey on young dudes who don't ask questions and complicate things?"

"Usually."

"Noted," I said. I swallowed one last forkful of shrimp, gently pushed my plate to the side, and instantly got silent. Maybe he wouldn't be so hard to quit after all.

"I like to pick my affairs wisely." He said. "Keeping multiple partners makes things too complicated. I don't have time for complicated. There are some demons in my past that I don't necessarily need to open the door for again."

"What demons?"

"Stick around and one day, I'll tell you."

"You runnin' game."

"Nah, You got some good ass, I'll admit, but I think there's more to you."

"How did you come up with that, when you found me on Jackd just like every other dick-hungry gay man in Houston with an account on that thing?"

"Well, when you rode with me to the hospital that day, it spoke to me." I'm embarrassed to admit I was flattered he thought so much of me, contrary to my own opinion of myself that day. Imagine having a tendency to focus on all the parts of yourself that are imperfect. I hate that I don't know why my dad left my mom in the way that he did. What was so bad? What pushed him over the edge? Maybe I'm a little melodramatic but for some reason, I always believed it was because of me. And maybe I'm being dramatic when I say I've been living in a never-ending battle within my mind, having to second guess everything I do.

Confidence? Shot… After a while, I just got used to living with a dark cloud looming over my head with a sulk as long and drab as Eeyore in Winnie The Pooh. Never once, had I considered what would truly make me happy. All I could recall was doing things to make other people happy. Hell, I was working in a place where I was constantly surrounded by trauma. Trauma I was not equipped to handle. Still, it made my mom smile to see me there every day. I dunno, it seemed worth it.

When I looked at Terrence with his sly smile and muscles glazed in baby oil, my hands got clammy and I fidgeted in my chair. I felt it, the hunger. And it wasn't for the shrimp étouffée. I tried to ignore it, but the hunger punched harder, this time with flames. "I'm just saying, I'm not trying to be your, mistress…" I said it with forced sternness that didn't convince me nor Terrence for that matter. His knees snapped, crackled, and popped as he stood up from the table and walked into the bedroom.

"You mean, manstress." He called from the closet.

"You think ya' clever, Dontcha?" I was busy sipping the last of my sweet tea when he emerged from the closet and stood in the doorway between the bedroom and the kitchenette. In his hands was a shiny piece of hard clear plastic. At first glance, I thought it was a flashlight. Then I realized it was something far more fun.

"Where'd you get the fleshlight?"

"Jarvis ordered it for my birthday." I rolled my eyes. "What would he order you something like that?"

"Does it matter?" He said smiling at me

"So, wassup?" Terrence nodded and licked his lips.

"We gotta warm it up first." He ran some warm water in the bathroom sink, placed the silicone flesh in, and smiled. Our eyes met and I could feel his gaze undressing me. I couldn't help my temptation and it was okay. He and his husband were separated, right? Sure, he lied about the sex of his spouse, but either way, they weren't together. That made it okay, right?

"Right!" I told myself as he picked me up, carried me to the kitchen, laid me on the center island, and kissed me behind my ears until I couldn't stand it. After about five minutes, he ran back to the restroom to grab the fleshlight. As he pinched my nipples and bit my bottom lip softly, he guided my shaft into the warm silicone hole. The tightness gripped and massaged me damn near to climax. He looked me in the eyes as he stroked me with it.

What felt like steam, drew me closer to him. I wanted to feel him. And just like that, on his granite countertops and with many, many grains of rice stuck to my ass, I let him have me…missionary, doggy, and reverse cowgirl. In every position, he was sure to massage my dick with the fleshlight. It was like being in a threesome without the unwanted extra body stealing some of the attention. I was busy holding my breath and wiping the sweat away from his forehead as he pulled out. And as soon as his dick flopped onto the slippery countertop, his phone rang.

He scurried about to put on his basketball shorts then hurried outside onto the balcony. When I came out to join him, he motioned for me to stay inside. "Eyyy, baby. Whatcha doin!" I went back inside and waited. I couldn't believe how he was just sitting there grinning to himself and cracking jokes on the phone. I wasn't appalled at the fact that he was doing it. More so, I was fascinated that he was convincing. If I hadn't been there to witness it, I would have believed him when he said he had just gotten out of the shower and used all the bar soap to clean the ink under his nails. He hadn't even taken a shower yet and the same filthy nails were digging into my back less than 2-minutes ago.

The more Terrence laughed and talked about how much he missed being at home, the more frustrated I became. I retreated to the bedroom and as I was lying there on his infamous blood-red silk sheets trying to rationalize why I shouldn't walk out there and introduce myself to his soon-to-be ex-husband, or walk out the front door and never look back, he walked in, butt-naked and dropped two slow kisses on my forehead.

"Baby, will you give me a massage before bed? You know I been lifting them heavy ass boxes all day and givin' you the dick. My back is killin' me." His touch was immobilizing and though I yearned for it, it bothered me at the same time. How was he just outside reminiscing and cackling on the phone with his husband when they were supposed to be in the middle of separating? And then, had the audacity to ask me for a motha-fuckin massage?

"Y'all reeeeal chummy for a couple that's about to be divorced." I blurted out. His jaw froze and he glared at me as if I were a stranger in the club who had just stepped on his Jordans.

"Watch ya mouth, boy. You don't know whatchu talkin' bout. The look in his eyes told me not to pry, so I didn't.

"My bad," I said. I didn't want to upset him. I wasn't comfortable with the idea of him asking me to leave.

"You good. At least run me a bubble bath." In true Destiny's Child "Cater to You" fashion, I did as he desired. As the tub began to fill with bubbles and a little steam fogged the mirrors, he turned on some Anita Baker and climbed into the tub.

"You gettin in?" He asked. I admired the baby suds as they trickled down his nipples and couldn't say no. A tingling warmth bathed my skin as the hot water embraced my thighs. He wrapped his arms around me and kissed me on the cheek. "I'm sorry." He said. "I just try to be friendly with him because of the kids. Plus, he's still paying for this place."

I didn't understand why it mattered. He was a working man. I wasn't familiar with what people who worked in a warehouse that printed boxes made on average, but I figured it was enough to rent a decent apartment on the outskirts of Houston.

"No need to apologize. I was out of line." I said. He handed me some Dove bar soap and a teal sponge.

"Since when do I have a sponge?"

"I got it for you on my way home. I figured you could keep it here. That's less you have to carry in that big ass bag of yours."

"It's Coach," I said, sarcastically. Though it was very important to note.

I wasn't a fan of bar soap, but I was grateful to have a sponge in his home. His and His sponges. Call me foolish, but I appreciated little shit like that. "Hey, I like to be prepared," I said, glancing over at my bag sitting on the counter. After our bath, I rubbed him down with lotion and listened to him talk about how his son wanted new shoes that he couldn't afford.

"Makes me feel useless sometimes." He said. "This is why I started escorting. My body never fails me."

"What's that supposed to mean?" I asked.

"It means it's looking like ima have to start escorting again. I have a lifestyle to keep up."

"Why is that the first thing that came to your mind? Why not get a second job?"

"What's with all the questions?"

"Never mind." I smacked my lips, rolled over in bed, and snatched the covers. "How am I supposed to get to know you, if you plan on being so guarded?" He studied my eyes as if debating on whether he should answer the question truthfully or not.

"Well, playa, I've been alive a lot longer than you have. You learn not to tell everybody your business."

"Well, I'm not just anybody."

"Yeah. You and everybody else."

"Sounds like a lonely life you're setting out to live if that's how you feel about opening up to people," I said it as if I was the poster child for transparency.

"Listening to people's stories is what I'm being trained to do. So, try me," I said. He paused to look me in the eyes and then lit a cigarette.

After one puff, "Two of my uncles on my mama side, and one of my aunts, molested me when I was 6... multiple times. When I tried to tell my mom about it, she kicked me out of the house. I had nowhere to go. No money. No education. Nothing. Nothing but my body. That's what people wanted from me. I started to realize people were always fascinated with my appearance. I'm a fantasy for a lot of people, so I used that to my advantage." I remember thinking about how I can see that being true.

It's easy to assume that when someone makes a statement like that, there might be, at the very least, a slight sadness in their eyes. I didn't know what to be more in awe about. His childhood trauma, or the fact that his face was emotionless as if he hadn't said anything at all and we were two strangers passing each other in the street? "Oh, I'm sorry for anything I did that made you feel like you had to tell me that." For some reason, I thought the appropriate response was an apology.

"Don't trip, baby. I want you to know." I had no control over the smile that pulled my cheeks towards my ears. It was the closest thing to intimacy outside the bedroom we had ever been. He wasn't the most sentimental man, and that was part of his appeal. At the same time, I couldn't help but crave to hear him tell me how he felt about me. Foolish, I guess, but it was a part of a fantasy I had concocted in my head about one-night stands becoming happily-ever-afters. Think,

"Knocked Up" meets Whitney Houston and Brandy in "Cinderella."

He took another puff and looked me in the eyes. They were stern, almost threatening, but still alluring. "Listen. I don't want you seeing anyone else." He said. I didn't see that coming. How could I promise to be loyal to someone who had a whole spouse they were never loyal to?

"Are you sure about that?"

"I want you to love me." He said. I guess that's all it took. His cards were on the table. Normally, I played the guessing game with guys. You know, the one where you're trying to figure out if a guy is just saying all the right things to get you naked only to ghost you two weeks later. Or, if he's just trying to hold on to you a little longer while he finds someone new that he's more interested in fucking.

I didn't know his intentions and he came with a lot of baggage, but I fell in love with the fantasy that one day, he would be all mine. The small possibility that he is genuine is what I clung to. He wasn't selling me the fantasy anymore. Either I had bought into it, or I had sold it to myself. "You want a back massage?" I asked. He grinned, gave me a playful old man grunt, and rolled over on his stomach. I was laying on his back, rubbing his neck when he hit me with a headliner: "So, tell me, baby. What's your story?" Story? I wasn't sure I could answer that. The response would have me flooded with unwanted emotions. The last thing I wanted to do was scare him off with all my suppressed feelings. They were just fine lurking in the shadows of my mind.

I could have told him how I watched my dad kill himself. I could have told him that I relived that horrible day almost every night. I could have told him that I may have cost my mom her good name and life's work because I was too selfish to follow protocol. I could have told him that I neglected Jane to chase after him. I could have told him how I was too ashamed to attend my only friend's funeral because I was responsible for her death, but I didn't. It was too heavy, and I had grown accustomed to avoiding uncomfortable conversations about my problems. Hell, it was my job to be in everybody else's business. "What makes you think I have a story worth telling?"

"Because you're here with me." I laughed it off and started kissing from his neck down in-between his legs. My tongue danced around the tip of his dick. That was all it took to shut that conversation down. Afterward, I felt like shit. How could I have expected him to open up to me while I remained a locked diary whose key was buried deeper than the depths of hell? I went to work the next day wondering when it was appropriate to unload all your baggage on your new man. Maybe I wasn't giving him enough credit. He did handle my fear of driving in the rain better than I expected. But he also ghosted me after that. Any chance of opening up further was null and void.

It was time to put up the Christmas tree in the office. That was normally my job. Apparently, being gay automatically qualifies you to decorate Christmas trees. I completely forgot because I was eager to see Terrence. We had big plans. I was just about to head to lunch to meet up with him for a quickie in the backseat of his car when my mom stopped me. "Did you fax off a copy of the Discharge Letter like I told you to? Jane's family's attorney keeps calling the office looking for them." I had done no such thing.

She slammed a packet of papers that were stapled together on my desk. "I'm being summoned to appear in court, Khai. This family is not playing! Follow up with that now!" Her eyes were watering but her face was frigid. I was stuck with no way to talk my way out of dealing with it right then. Right when I thought I was gonna have to confess, there was a knock at the door. It was Rosa, the receptionist.

"There's an emergency on line 4. Oh, and Mister Allen, a package came for you." My mom grabbed the phone and I maneuvered around her to get the package from Rosa. My mom took the phone and Rosa handed me a box wrapped in pink and blue-lined paper. The paper looked like it had come out of a diary because it had small elegant designs in the margins. There was a pink envelope on top that was addressed to me from Jane. My heart stuttered and I could feel the tears coming. After a quick peep over my shoulder to make sure my mom was no longer paying attention, I quickly thanked Rosa for intercepting my package and sped-walked out the door to my car.

I was in such a fog as I was rushing to my car, that it wasn't until Terrence called that I noticed the storm clouds, looming. "Hey, you still coming?"

"I'm not sure."

"I figured you wouldn't want to get caught in the rain, Lil scary ass."

"I'll make it up to you."

"How? Because you got my hopes up for some ass and now you gonna leave me hangin'?

"Excuse me?"

"I'm just saying, you know the rain is a lot more fun with me around."

"Why you gotta go there?"

"Ha-ha! Got em'!" His laughter made me feel a little better and for a moment, I had forgotten why I was sitting in my car being miserable. "We can figure something out for later."

"Cool, just let me know. There's something I have to take care of right now." He told me he'd call me later and hung up the phone. Eyes closed and several minutes of going back and forth about whether or not to do it, I dug deep to find the courage to open Pandora's box. Inside, there were two letters. One was written on pink paper and the other one on blue. The pages had a texture that made it look like they had been aging for decades.

There was also a key, a few photos of Jane and me from our days at the shelter and our occasional trips to the park, a pink diary with a lock, and one of her signature French berets. It was pink with blue with a fluffy pink pom-pom.

I pulled out the first letter and read:

Forgive me, Khai

If you are reading this, hun it must mean that I am gone. I am sorry to have left you so abruptly, I wish I could say something that could help you understand but I don't think there is much to say other than, I love you and only hope that you can forgive me.

I see a lot of myself in you. I see the emptiness that keeps you awake at night. I see your heavy eyes and how they search for relief in all the wrong places.

I know you think you can go it alone. I tried that. And if I may be a testament to the flaw in that logic, hun, please do not make the same mistakes I did.

Find your happiness,
Jane.

My feet were suddenly cold, and I couldn't blink. The sky rumbled and the rain soon followed. I was trapped. The buzz from Terrence calling rescued me from my stupor.

"Hello?" I said.

"Wassup, you busy?" I could feel myself losing my nerve in the sultriness of his voice. I stuttered over my words a little, but his voice was so warm I stopped shivering.

"Nah. I was just leaving the office."

"Oh, okay. How are you? You coming to see me?" He asked. He seemed genuinely happy to hear from me, which was new territory for me. Most guys I was used to dealing with only faked such mundane but important formalities in hopes of getting me in bed. Not to say that I fault all the men in my past who just wanted a quick fix from me. I knew and they knew exactly what sort of encounter we were looking for, whether it was spoken or not.

"I'm okay," I said, even though I was still in shock.

"You sure? I hear the rain hitting the ground and the wind in the speakers. Sounds like it's getting bad over there."

"Oh... right—" I paused to swallow the humiliation. "Well, I wish I could say it came out of nowhere, but I saw this one coming. Just was moving too slow, I guess." I sniffled a bit because my nose was stuffy from crying silently. He must have heard my muffled whimpering because he paused for a minute to listen.

"Hello? You there?" I said.

"Yeah. I just wish you'd talk to me." I was shook. I honestly didn't think he cared that much, so I decided to tell him about what happened with Jane and about the letter. I told him about the coffee and the shelter. I told him about the failed discharge letter and what that may have meant for my mom's clinic. I told him how I wasn't sure if this was Jane's way of haunting me for having not attended her funeral and that this was somehow her way of saying she forgives me. I told him about the guilt keeping me up at night, but I did not tell him about my father. Too much too soon.

"Do you know where she's buried?" He asked.

"Yeah, why?"

"I think there's something you need to do."

"I'm not going anywhere until the rain stops." What to most people sounded like mere patter, to me, sounded like I was surrounded by angry gorillas pummeling my car in all directions.

"Don't worry about it. I'm coming to pick you up when I get off work." When he said that, the pummeling softened and I could catch my breath. He didn't let me answer and hung up the phone. Later that evening, he met me in the parking lot outside my mom's clinic and hopped in the car. "I don't know if I'm ready for this." I said as we rode down the highway." It was nice not having to worry about driving for once.

"There is never going to be a time when you feel like sayin' goodbye to someone you once loved. It's now. Or, you can continue to eat yourself alive inside."

"What do I say?"

"Whatever you wanted to say but never got the chance to."

"If I'm going to do this, I need Starbucks."

After hitting up the drive-thru, we arrived at the cemetery where Jane was buried. For the first time, I carried two hot caramel macchiatos in my hand and stood beside her grave. Terrence by my side. The dirt piled on top of her was deep brown and moist. Atop her little mound in the earth, where there should have been flowers, were a few stray leaves and pinecones wiggling in the wind. I was shaking when Terrence grabbed my hand. “Say what you need to say.” He said.

A little confused, I looked up at his smooth face as the moon’s glow soften the outline of his torso and invited me to hold him. “If we gonna work out, you can’t be walking around here sad and nervous all the time. The baggage you're carrying needs to be buried.” I looked at the dirt beneath my Giuseppe’s then back at Jane’s dirt mound and searched for an excuse to avoid the whole situation.

“Hold this,” Terrence said, handing the umbrella. “If you need me, I’ll be in the car.” I gripped the handle like it was money and Terrence walked back to the car in the drizzle. When he was out of sight, I set one cup next to the tombstone and kept one for myself.

“Well, Jane, I told you he was fine.” For a moment, I allowed myself to believe she’d speak back to me, or maybe her ghost would talk to me and I’d get some sort of miraculous closure and spiritual enlightenment. I didn’t know where to start so I started with an icebreaker.

“The last time I was at a graveyard…Well, you know the story.” I thought I’d hear her breathy laughter one more time but, crickets. I sat there just staring at her dirt mound and felt silly talking to myself. So, I pulled out my phone and sent a text message she would never get to read.

ME: Dear, Jane…

ME: I know you may not see things this way, but I must apologize for failing you.

ME: I replay that day in my head over and over again and I—I hate myself for not having arrived sooner. 😭

```
ME: I know that I cannot change the past
and that I cannot bring you back.

ME: But, there has never been a time
where I wish I could do just that more
than I do right now.

ME: I hope that you and Steve have found
each other up there…

ME: That is how it works, right?

ME: Or, is everything they say about our
kind true? Condemned to hell?

ME: In my blanket of darkness, you were
a source of light and for that, I am
forever in your debt.

ME: I love you and I will cherish every
memory with which you have so graciously
blessed me.
```

I took a nervous breath in and paused with uncertainty as I stood over Jane's grave, tears falling into the dirt mound and my hands unable to hold the coffee steady as I tried to take a sip. I leaned down to pour a little of hers into the ground, our last drink together and that's when I saw it. The epitaph. It threw me into a tearful rage.

Here lies Johnathan Mallard, beloved son of Edward and Tonya Mallard.

It was the single most disrespectful thing I had ever seen. Not even in death would her family respect her identity. And what was worse, was that Steve's grave was nowhere to be found. The very distance that that tortured her into her final days followed her into the afterlife! If I knew Jane at all, I knew this was not in her dying wish. Although I had no power to make a change for her, I decided to let Jane's story be a lesson to love and to fight for love because a life without love is a life lived in vain.

The violet sky lit up with sparks, so I poured Jane's coffee over her grave, grabbed my tea hurried back to the car. As soon as I shut the door, I kissed Terrence passionately on the lips.

"You wanna come over? I just restocked my candy dish and I'm about to watch Scandal. Got your favorite!" I wanted to ask him what he thought my favorite was, but I thought it would be interesting to see how much he paid attention to me. When we arrived at his apartment, the scent of fresh linen and pineapple lifted my spirits. I turned the corner to the kitchen to see a tray full of fresh pineapples cut into little squares just the way I like them, and macarons neatly placed on a plate. All I could do was smile. It was comforting to know that he knew something about me other than his way around my pants. While I snacked, he lay in bed texting on his phone.

I was damp my shoes squeaked as I walked over to grab one. "Go take a shower, you smell like grass and sweat." I didn't feel much like talking anymore, so I just shrugged and did as I was told. When I got out of the shower, I climbed into bed with him and as promised, we watched Scandal. I watched him eat Laffy Taffy after Laffy Taffy out of his candy jar from the corner of my eyes the whole time. I remember wondering how the hell he hadn't slipped into a diabetic coma, but for now, I would join him and have a few Laffy Taffy, pineapples, and macarons.

When Scandal ended, he got up to smoke a cigarette on the balcony. I joined him but smoked a blunt instead. He lit the little cancer stick as he gazed out over the parking lot and blew the smoke in my direction. I squinted my eyes and swiped it away. I hated the smell of it, but I tolerated it. "You know, my heart was heavy when I found out about your situation with Ms. Jane."

"Yeah. It's fucked up." I said. "I'm trying not to think about it anymore."

"It really hit home for me because when I was younger, I used to be a cocaine addict." I was so caught off guard, I didn't know what to say. I had assumed his problem was with alcohol. But then understood what Jarvis meant when he said that he was substituting one for the other.

"Wow. I'm sorry. Are you—"

"Don't worry. I'm clean." He was sure to warn me as he chased down 3 pills. "These are for blood pressure."

"I wasn't worried." I lied. "How long have you been clean?" He paused to put another Laffy Taffy in his mouth.

"7-years. Thanks to Jarvis" He sounded like he had a mouth full of cotton balls, but I was still fascinated with him. He was physical perfection, but a tragedy on the inside. It made him feel real and less like the fantasy I was having the privilege of acting out from time to time with him. "It was my mother's dying wish for me to get clean. When she passed, she left one of those VHS tape recordings behind for me. The attorney told me I was to watch it alone. So, I did, and she read me my rights. Cussed me and called me all kinds of names. But at the end of it, she cried and begged for me to get myself together."

"I'm sure she would be proud of you if she were here. How long have you known Jarvis?"

"8-years as of a few weeks ago." There was a part of me that felt what little issues I had going on, failed to compare to battling for sobriety. My problems just didn't seem that important anymore. I just nodded after that. I didn't want to pry, and I was beginning to feel even worse. How is it his mother was able to help him from the grave more than I was able to help Jane when she was sitting right across from me?

"You can't blame yourself, love." He said. I winced, trying to make sense of his words.

"What do you mean?"

"The look on your face and the regret in your voice. I recognize it because it's the same look my mother had every time she looked at me. I would hear her at night when I would show up at 3 and 4 in the morning, high, with no place to go."

"She turn you away?"

"Not always. She would feed me and let me sleep it off on the couch while she cried in the room next to me and prayed to God to forgive her for failing me."

"Why would she blame herself?"

"Because..." He hesitated as if you were contemplating whether or not I was ready to hear what you had to say. "Because my uncle molested me when I was 7 and again when I was 9. When I told her about it, she accused me of lying, called me a faggot, and kicked me out of the house. I was only 15." He did not hold for a response and I did not have one for him. I was overtaken by a need to hold him.

Not everything warrants a verbal response and so, I moved closer to him and he wrapped his arms around me, tight as if he were protecting me from something. He fell asleep soon after, snoring the paint off the walls. And I laid awake. This time, by choice and not because of my mysterious sadness. I admired him in his messy slumber and saw him in a different light that night. He was a survivor and I wanted to spend all my days getting to know him.

All I Want For Christmas

Some people wish for a new car, designer shoes, or a new iPhone for Christmas. Not me. I treated myself to gifts year-round, so I had no desire to ask anyone for anything. All I wanted for Christmas was to go to Atlanta. Aside from it being the season of Mariah Carey, festive lights, extravagant decorations, and vacation time, I was a little indifferent toward Christmas.

The holiday cheer seemed fake to me. Call me a Grinch, but maybe it was the forced exchanges of Merry Christmas between strangers that bothered me so much, or maybe it's the cold weather? Mid-day in May is more my speed. Or, maybe it was the fact that I hated how it brings everyone together when all I wanted was to be alone. Is it wrong to not want to be around loved ones during the holidays? Are self-care days non-existent during Christmas?

I didn't want to go to my mom's house for the holidays for a number of reasons. One of them being that I was still feeling guilty about Jane's discharge letter. Still, I felt inclined to buy my mom a gift. I was browsing the Galleria Mall for something that said I'm sorry for putting her practice and life's work at risk. No pair of Red Bottoms, not a single designer handbag, no Tiffany bracelet…nothing, could possibly make up for that. She's never been into all that stuff, no matter how much money she made. It didn't help that she's one of those people that has everything.

Something was better than nothing, so I finally settled on a new Apple Watch in rose gold to match mine. I was anxiously waiting for the sales rep to bring it out so I could run over to the Coach boutique and snag up a messenger bag. I never made it there after buying my mom's watch because Terrence called and suddenly, he was all that mattered. "Heeey." It was sultry, but with enough twang as to lightly suggest southern roots. Every time he opened his mouth to speak, it sounded genuine, whether it was or not. He made you believe it without even trying. And if you didn't believe it, you wanted to. "What's up?" I said.

"Just givin' you a buzz. How's your holiday shopping goin'?"

"Awful."

"Really? How so?" The next thing I knew, we were in a full-fledged conversation about how I was struggling to find a gift for my mom. He told me how he was out spending too much money on his kids. I used to think he was likely overcompensating for his absence as a father figure in their lives.

"Well, baby… I stopped and got you something while I was at it." I was dumbfounded and not the least bit prepared for such a random act of generosity.

"Oh really? Now I feel bad." We hadn't discussed exchanging gifts, though I had given him plenty. That would be the first time he'd ever gotten me anything.

"Well, playa, it's no big deal. You do a lot for me anyway. But, you still got time to get something if that's what you're worried about, love. I just need my car note paid and maybe one of those swivel flat screen mounts for my new TV" I laughed uncomfortably and told him to hold his breath.

"How big is the TV?"

"Uhh, 70. I think."

"Noted. I'll see what I can do."

"If you're not busy Christmas Eve, I'd like to give it to you then." He said. I had every intent on booking my flight to Atlanta that night but I didn't. My plan was to spend the days leading up to Christmas in Atlanta sleeping with other lonely gays who were estranged from their families in some sort of way. Same thing as last year. How's that for a holiday tradition? Christmas Eve with Terrence sounded like the domestic fantasy I daydreamed about.

"Um. Sure. I think I can stop by then." When he hung up the phone, I re-routed to BestBuy. I was wheeling Terrence's mount out the door when I had an unexpected run-in. When I got to my car, I was a little nervous having spotted a man struggling to get a 70-inch tv in his little red 3-Series BMW with blacked-out wheels. Had to be between an 09 to 2011 model. The E90 body style was a dead giveaway. It wasn't just any 3-series though. It had a dual exhaust and a shiny M-badge on the trunk lid. Assuming he bought it new, it had to cost him a pretty penny, which made it that much more of a shock to see him nearly scuff the seats trying to get a whole 70-inch TV in the backseat. More importantly, it was parked right next to my Benz.

I just knew if he opened the door any wider, it would have surely scratched my baby. I was cringing. Without seeing his face, I offered to help him, being sure to remote start my car, so that he knew it was my Benz he was teetering on the edge of scratching.

"Oh, Hey man. I'm sorry." He said as he tried to catch his breath. His head was buried in the backseat as he tugged the box toward him. I could have easily gone to the passenger side and given it a little push. At least that way, nobody would have to make a call to insurance and make a claim that would depreciate the value of both our cars any more than it did the moment we drove them off the lot. He peeped his head over the lip of the roof and the street lowering above us, lit up the front of his face. I was shocked to see it was Jarvis. After getting a good look at me, he raised his eyebrow and pursed his lips.

"No thanks. I think I got it." He said. His black sweater vest was disheveled and the red collared shirt he wore underneath it was lopsided.

"Clearly, you needed help." If I had known it was Jarvis before offering my help that night, I probably would have turned back around, and gone back into the mob of people in BestBuy.

"I'm good." He insisted.

"Are ya sure? I mean, how are you gonna be able to see out the back?"

"I'll figure it out. Thannnnks."

"You might just want to let the seats down and put it in the trunk." He looked around as if to scout for any other help.

"Fine." He said. I parked my cart with the mount in it and helped him maneuver the box around in the trunk. We had to let down the rear seats and slide the passenger seat up as close as we could get to the dash. It was snug, but we got it in there.

"Thank you." He said. Our eyes met under the ambient street lights. His eyes looked like chestnuts and he had dark hair that suggested he was Persian or something mixed-ish like that. Kinda cute.

"Good to see you can do something other than spread your legs for married men." He said.

"That's quite the attitude to have considering I just did you a favor."

"What you diiiiid…was create a monster. You made him relapse!"

"I can't force a drink down a grown man's throat."

"Tuh!" He paused to catch his breath. "Drink? Oh, honey…You have no idea." I wanted to tell him that I hadn't seen Terrence drink all that much in our time together for the sake of being right and proving a point, but I didn't want him to know that we were still seeing each other.

"Terrence and I are done," I said. "I haven't seen the guy or heard from him in months. No telling who he could have fucked after me." His foot tapping drew my eyes to his signature loafers. His feet looked wider in them than usual.

"Just stay away from him. He's not well."

"And that's none of my concern. Merry Christmas." I said before getting in my car and burning rubber. He didn't say it back. Probably because he knew I didn't deserve it. I didn't know what he was referring to about

Terrence not being well, but it made me question whether Terrence had been completely honest about his addiction. Was I asking the right questions?

The next day was Christmas Eve. Terrence told me to come over around 7. How was I supposed to ask him about his sobriety without it seeming like I was antagonizing him or accusing him of lying? Considering that Jarvis was my source, I thought mentioning that I ran into him would likely cause problems I was unprepared to deal with. It was my first Christmas with a man I had feelings for, and I had to go into it suspicious and worried. Go figure.

The last thing I wanted was drama. It was the precise reason I was avoiding my mom's house. Rather than dwell on it, I figured whatever was done in the dark, will eventually come to light. Besides, other than the mixed signals I was getting from him, I had no reason to suspect that he had been drinking. Instinctively, I played Mariah's "All I Want For Christmas Is You" on a loop the whole drive. It was the appropriate thing to do. I was finally starting to feel the Christmas spirit when he opened the door and I spotted his white tree with red and gold decorations shining in the far corner of the living room. He placed it in front of the window so that it could be seen from the street. The real star of the show, however, was the giant rectangular box behind the tree wrapped in red paper. The thought crossed my mind that maybe it was for me, but it was a long shot.

"Wassup, homie! Merry Christmas!" He said when I walked in the door. My first thought was to ask him when did I become a homie? We hadn't discussed labels yet, but I was sure I graduated from homie the moment he stuck his dick in me and told me he loved me.

"Merry Chris—" I was cut off by the initial shock of seeing two other bodies emerging from the bedroom. Two teenagers.

"Don't be alarmed." He hurried to say. "That's my son Brandon and my daughter Tiffany." They both smiled and waved to me from the living room. Brandon was taller than me and I had Tiffany by maybe 3-inches. It was a little embarrassing, but when you're a mere 5'7 and a half, you'll rarely be the tallest person in the room. Brandon walked over to give me one of those straight guy hugs. He shook my hand first and pulled me in. "Good to meet you, bro! He talks about you all the time!" He smelled like hot chips and his dad's cologne. Tiffany just waved and said hello. I was hoping the squint in her eyes was from the glare in her glasses.

"Oh, man! If I would have known you guys were gonna be here, I would have thought to get you a gift."

"Well, my dad remembered us this year. So, we good." Tiffany said. I didn't know how to respond to that, so I just grinned and looked at Terrence for help. I was smiling on the inside having heard that Terrence talked about me to his kids, but the warm and fuzzies were shut down quickly. I was leaning down to put his gift under the tree when he tapped me on the shoulder and told me to meet him in the bedroom. He shut the door behind me and whispered. "Tiffany doesn't know about me like that."

"What you mean?" I asked.

"She doesn't know I'm gay."

"What the hell? How?"

"When I went to prison, she stayed with her momma, been with her ever since." The click from him locking the door made me scowl inquisitively.

"Oh, I see," I said. "What about Brandon?"

"He knows. But I need you to pretend we're just friends." I wanted to ask him why, but when it came to parenting, I did not have a leg to stand on, especially being a manstress and all. Instantly, I caught this weird case of performance anxiety. I didn't know what kind of straight guy I was supposed to portray. I wasn't the most macho in the room. My 29-inch waist and fitted shirts were not the most convincing.

"That's easier said than done," I said.

"Think of it as role play." He said as he approached me slowly. My eyes were allured to his hands as he unbuckled his belt. The bulge in his briefs met my face. "Don't worry, baby. I got something to help you relax."

"We can't do this?" I said, softly pushing his hips away.

"Why the hell not?" At first, I thought he was joking but the straight face he wore quickly changed that. If he was cool with it, then why not? Right? After a silent quickie, we returned to the living room where Brandon and Tiffany were sitting by the tree organizing their gifts into separate piles. It wasn't much, about 5 gifts each. Brandon looked back and smiled at me. "I put your present over there." He said, pointing at the sofa. I looked over to see a gift box wrapped in shiny gold paper, topped with a red bow.

"Thanks, man." I looked over at the big gift still sitting behind the tree. "Should we start with the biggest one, or are we saving it for last?" Tiffany chuckled to herself.

"Nah. That's my dad's gift." I turned to face Terrence, who was in the kitchen preparing everybody's dinner plate. He was not the same man who had his dick down my throat all of 5-minutes ago as if we weren't in a 1-bedroom apartment with two teenagers he rarely spent time with sitting in the living room.

"Ayyy! That's my dad comin' through with the Jordans!" Brandon said with a proud grin on his face, holding up a red and white shoe box. Tiffany, on the other hand, ignored him and opened her first gift to reveal a pair of black Gucci slides. Her eyes lit up.

"Oh my god, Daddy! Thank youuuu!" She said, in this high-pitched slightly raspy voice. Terrence had become daddy all of a sudden. Brandon followed suit and unwrapped a brand-new iPhone. Instantly, I wondered how the hell he paid for Jordan's, Gucci slides and an iPhone, considering I had just sent him the money for his car note on Cash App for the month and the previous month. Surely the money he used for all of that could have gone towards paying his car note. "You gonna open yours?" Brandon asked, slapping me on the shoulder like we were on the basketball team together.

"Oh, right!" I said. Having been so distracted with all that had just gone down in the bedroom and the charade we had to put on, I hadn't thought to open my gift. I sat down on the sofa next to Brandon, the same one Terrence and I had messed around on many times before. Terrence laid down on the loveseat opposite me and lit a blunt. I wanted to hit it but didn't know if it would be too gay to do it in front of kids. Overthinking as usual. It was for the best anyway. Smoking would have loosened my tongue to the point of no return.

I slid off the bow and removed the top. My jaw dropped slightly. Turns out he paid more attention to me than I thought. A pair of white Beats! "I figured you'd like those for your runs at the park." He said through a small cloud of smoke. It was the first time a guy had given me anything other than a wet ass and nervous trips to the clinic. I wanted to kiss him. "Thanks, bro," I said, trying not to cringe.

"Got a frog in your throat, Khai?" Brandon said, laughing. Terrence nodded and took another puff. "Come hit this." He passed me the blunt. After taking a few puffs and letting it marinate for a few minutes, my eyes drifted back over to the sparkling tree.

"I'm ready to see what's in this big one," I said.

"Me too, bro!" Brandon erupted, egging me on. I pulled the box from behind the tree and pushed it in front of Terrence. He nodded at Brandon to do the honors. Instantly, I spotted the Samsung branding. You could see some small dents on the edges of the box where Jarvis and I had beat it up a little when we were trying to stuff it in his car.

"70-inches! Yeahhhh boy! I can't wait to play Madden on this!" Brandon shouted. Salty, I immediately pulled out my phone and shot him a text.

ME: 👀 You played me, for a TV mount, huh? Who bought the TV? 👀

TERRENCE: Nobody played you.😒 I bought that TV myself. I've been saving up.

ME: "When have you ever saved anything!"🙄

TERRENCE: I had it on layaway. Why are you trippin! 🤨

Me: …layaway? Okay.

"Wow! 70-inches! Who knew you were such a size queen?" I said, with an intentionally cocked brow. A raspy laugh got everybody's attention. We turned to see Tiffany having the time of her life.

"That's what I'mmmmm saying!" She said after catching her breath. Terrence shrugged it off and told me to be careful with disapproving eyes. I was boiling inside. "Oh! Don't forget about this one." Tiffany said, reaching for my gift. She ripped off the paper to reveal the TV mount Terrence conveniently insisted he wanted for Christmas.

I didn't know they even still did layaway. I knew right then that there was more to Jarvis than Terrence had led on. Still, I couldn't tell him I knew he was lying. Not in front of his kids. Plus, I would have had to tell him about my run-in with Jarvis and I didn't want it to seem like I was jealous of his sponsor. How desperate would that have looked? It wasn't worth the risk, or the headache. Brandon and Tiffany unwrapped the rest of their gifts and I set the table for dinner. Every now and again when I would look up from my plate, I'd get a glimpse of Terrence looking me up and down. Considering he gave Tiffany more food than me, I knew he was watching to make sure I didn't overeat.

It may seem a little controlling, but when you are on the bottom diet, intermittent fasting and portion control are your best friends. Nobody likes a messy bottom. I was hungrier than what my diet allowed, but knowing Terrence and I would soon be intimate again later that night, made it worthwhile. After dinner, Brandon left to go ice skating at the mall with his girlfriend and Tiffany decided to join them. She had a new Ralph Lauren sweater that she was itching to wear. Meanwhile, Terrence and I snuggled up in bed and looked for a movie to watch. No matter how hard I tried to avoid thinking about why the hell Terrence would lie about Jarvis buying him the TV, it burned like a cold sore until he hit me with a headliner.

"What's your favorite Christmas Movie?" He asked. I could smell the watermelon on his breath from the Jolly Rancher in the corner of his mouth. It took me a minute to answer. Nobody had thought to ask me that question before.

"The Grinch," I said. "The Jim Carey version is my favorite."

"Ha-ha! Why am I not surprised?"

"What's that supposed to mean?"

"It means, you seem like someone who would like that movie. That's all."

"You calling me a Grinch?"

"Did you put up a tree at your place?"

"No," I said, suddenly realizing that spending Christmas Eve with him was the most festive thing I'd done in a while.

"Well, my family has never been big on Christmas, or holidays in general. We sorta just go through the motions. It never feels real to me." I could have mentioned that the brewing tension between my brother and Lee made things awkward during both Sunday and holiday dinners. They never failed to get into a heated argument about my brother's slacker-jack tendencies and unwillingness to stop selling weed to my mom's patients behind her back. Last year, Lee went on a rant that made my brother flip a table and burn rubber on his way out the driveway, according to my mom. I was grateful to have been away from it all. "The Grinch embodies a harsh reality about Christmas some of us choose not to acknowledge. Everyone is so consumed with the idea that everyone should be expressing joyfulness that they forget that not everybody feels a reason to fake holiday cheer." "Working with all those depressed ass patients has gotten to you huh?"

"I was a Grinch long before I got involved with them," I said, laughing.

"Well, love. Hopefully, this year will be better. I know it's not much, but it's a start for us." Considering our arrangement, it was more than I could have asked for. It was the closest to an actual relationship I had ever been in. He pulled me in and I laid on his chest, trying to fight the waterworks that normally blinded me when the Grinch finally grew a heart. The sound of his heart beating and the vibrations from his chest as he told me he loved me, silenced the angry thoughts in my head. The Grinch was in his sleigh full of stolen gifts careening down the mountain towards Whoville when Terrence and I started making love.

When I rolled over, all sweaty and basking in the glow of an orgasm, I was finally feeling the Christmas spirit. That was until I got a text from my mom.

I had to go home before Brandon and Tiffany got back from their outing. Terrence swore it would have looked suspicious to Tiffany if I was still there when they got back. I wasn't too upset about it until the next day. I woke up on Christmas morning alone in my condo. There was no Christmas tree, no decorative lights, and no sign of Christmas. Cade was scratching my pajama pants, begging to go outside. "Merry Christmas, buddy. I guess you'll have to see Atlanta next year." He looked at me like I was crazy and ran to the door. As Cade did his business, I stood swaying back and forth in the grass, contemplating how I could get out of going to my mom's house. It was as impossible as trying to catch a last-minute flight to Atlanta on Christmas Day.

TERRENCE: Merry Christmas, love. I love you. 😘

ME: Merry Christmas, baby. I love you too.

TERRENCE: WYD?

ME: Getting dressed. Gotta go to my mom's house today. Wanted to see you later…if possible.

TERRENCE: Nah, love. His family is here.
It would look weird if I just left.

ME: Oh, I'm sorry. Some other time.

TERRENCE: 🩶🩶

MOMMY DEAREST: Khai, I'm sure you're planning to be out of town this year, but I need you to be here.

ME: Why? Besides, I've already booked my ticket.

MOMMY DEAREST: I need your support getting dad on board to allow your brother to come back to the practice.

ME: IDK. It hardly seems like the time. I'm not trying to be in the middle of all that…

MOMMY DEAREST: It's not optional.You can't spend your life avoiding confrontation. This was a courtesy. Be there, or I'm docking your pay.

ME: Yes, ma'am.

I clipped Cade's new Louis Vuitton collar on his neck and took him outside. Afterward, I lit a blunt and reheated some of the leftovers Terrence cooked, spiked my eggnog with rum, and downed a shot before getting dressed to go to my parent's house. I thought about how It would have been nice to spend Christmas Day with Terrence, but with our arrangement, that was a luxury I couldn't buy.

My parent's house is located in one of those neighborhoods on the outskirts of Houston where all the homes sit on at least 3 acres of land.

Aside from the impending blow-up between Lee and my brother, there was also the Jane issue I was avoiding. I worried about whether or not she would bring it up and what that conversation might look like.

Would I have the balls to fess up? Probably not… maybe some other time when I was ready. I hoped.

Parked outside their driveway, I looked up beyond the acres of pine trees, tractors, and ranch-style mansions and up to the skies. Thoughts of cutting my losses feel easier. The repercussions of disobeying my mom, be damned. The idea was fowl. I know, but that was the default response I had to battle with every day. Running away came so naturally to me. It's what I was always good at. Hell, I have the medals to prove it. I couldn't make a decision fast enough. The grinding and squeaking from the garage opening was a sign that it was too late. The door was halfway up and I could see Lee's long black fingers fiddling with the buttons on the wall. Every 3 out of 5 trips to the garage he managed to press the wrong button. He blamed it on age. I didn't disagree.

"Bring yo ass in here boy and get off that damn phone!" He waved from inside the garage with a small barbecue rib in his hand. Poor rib never had a chance. The camouflage long-sleeve he was wearing rode up his stomach high enough that I got a glimpse of his underbelly. I waved back from my car before getting out to come inside. The smell of my mom's peach cobbler lured me to the kitchen where I found her wafting away the steam with an oven mitt.

The safe beige walls paired with warm brown crown molding welcomed a stolen moment where my mom looked at peace. It brought a smile to my face. "Smells so good!" I said as I leaned over her shoulder to get a sniff. I tried to kiss her on the cheek, but she wasn't having it.

"Go sitcho ass down, Khai. You ain't even wash your hands yet. All in here breathing on the food and shit. Go sit down somewhere and don't let me catch you in my bathroom stealing my Bath and Body Works!"

"Breathe, mom, before you pop a blood vessel."

"Anyways. Have you heard from your brother? He's supposed to be on his way." She rolled her eyes and shook her head. "I'm not worried about it. If he shows up, he shows up. If he don't he don't."

"He'll be here," I said. "You know he's got to get those two boys up and going. They are a handful."

"Stop making excuses for him like you always do. He should've been up and moving earlier. Hell, I'm surprised you even made it here on time given the way you've been moping around here lately."

"I have not been moping!"

"You need to quit that, Khai!"

"Quit what?"

"Trying to deal with everything on your own? It's not healthy. Have you been to see Dr. LeRoy?"

"Merry Christmas, mom," I said, handing her a little white gift bag with the Apple Logo on it. She sighed and put her hands on her hips. "Merry Christmas." She said. "Put it under the tree. We'll do the gift exchange after we eat."

"No Christmas music?" I asked.

"You can play something if you want."

"I seized the opportunity to play Mariah's Christmas album. It certainly put me in better spirits to hear her voice than the sound of my mom scolding me. The door slammed and peppy footsteps grew louder and louder. I turned around to find my brother and Lee walking in with my two nephews behind him, dashing toward the Christmas tree in the living room.

"Woah! Nana! It's huge!" One of them said. The tree was flooded with gift bags going in all directions. As my parents got older, they grew less patient with gift wrapping, so they just stuffed everybody's presents in gift bags and stapled them so that we couldn't see what was inside, and put them under the tree. I was scanning the area for a place to put my mom's watch when Jordan interrupted me. "What's gotten into you, Mr. Grinch? Since when did you become Mr. Christmas? Shouldn't you be in Atlanta?" Little did he know, I was just trying to change the subject because the conversation with my mom was headed down the wrong road.

"Just wanted to do something different this year. Where's Erica? " I asked. "With her mom. She's been in the hospital for a week now."

"Oh, wow! Is she okay?" He was about to respond until Lee walked in and plopped down next to me on the sofa. My first instinct was to make up an excuse to get up and move, but I figured it would look a little shady, so I sat there silent and eyeballing my brother, who turned his attention to his phone. My two nephews sat on the floor by the tree and talked about what they thought was in each bag. They were both going on and on about how much they wanted a new Playstation. The last one they had lost a battle with orange juice, to make a long story short.

"What's up with ya Lil bit?"

"Chillin."

"You not going to Atlanta this year?"

"No, sir. Something came up."

"Well, that's a shock. You how antisocial you are unless you're all in Atlanta chasing behind some ass." Rather than take the bait, I just nodded. My mom announced that it was time to eat, so we made our way to the kitchen. We stood in a circle around the center island and held hands. She said a brief grace and we all went to piling food on our plates.

When everyone was seated and had a good minute to swallow their first few bites, my mom decided to break the silence, and all hell broke loose. "So, while everyone's hereee..." Everyone turned to face her. She removed her glasses and cleared her throat. "Effective January 1st, Jordan will officially be the supervisor in the Billing office." Lee choked on his Mountain Dew. "Bullshit!" He said as he was coughing into a napkin to clear his throat. "Say's who!" My mom looked at me for backup.

"Khai and I talked about it already. "Considering how much money we've been making, we'd feel a lot safer with a family member overseeing the finances of the clinic. Right, Khai?" I nodded. Lee shook his head.

"Hell to the no! Am I the only one who remembers how he was selling weed to patients! Talk about a fucking liability!" To his credit, what my brother did, wasn't the most ethical by the books, but many of the patients had seen a decrease in anxiety and depression, so my mom was able to overlook it in some cases.

"That was three years ago, dad. Let it go." My brother said back in defense. "I've apologized too many times for it already."

"That's your problem. You just, sooooorry." The two locked eyes and my brother put down his phone. I looked across the table and watched as my mom sat at the head of the table eyeing Lee down like she wanted to say something, but was refraining. I could see the tension in her jaw. It was festering inside her like a rat in a burning box.

Lee turned his attention to me. "Khai, did you let your mother talk you into this bullshit?" How I managed to be caught in the middle of an executive decision, I don't know. My job was to see patients and report to her. Period. If my mom wished it, it was my command. After all, it was her executive decisions that had made us rich over the years. Why question her now? Everyone had turned to look at me for a response. Was my opinion the deciding one?

"Can this wait until after we open gifts?" I asked. I released my grip on my fork and pushed my plate away. "Stop avoiding the issue, Khai. It's a yes or no question." I looked back at her and conceded. "No. She did not force me to agree with her. Jordan is much better at math than I am. Plus, trying to see patients, and manage the company finances would be too much for me to handle right now." Never mind the fact that I was still trying to process how my dad hated me being gay so much that he killed himself. Or, at least that's the way I interpreted it. Lee stood up from the table and delivered an ultimatum.

"If you bring Jordan back into the clinic, I QUIT." It sounded more like a promise. My mom remained seated at the end of the table.

"Lee, he's family! And I built this practice for my family! Yes, he made a mistake, but he's still my son and I'd rather have him in there than some bitch I can't trust!"

The bitch she was referring to was Linda, a Cuban Medical Assistant we hired to supervise the Billing office. Linda was a hard worker and loyal to the company, considering she had been the only employee outside the family to last more than 2-years working there. The problem was that she was way too friendly with Lee. My mom just plain didn't like her. She was convinced Linda wanted him, but she just couldn't prove it.

"Do what you want, Dr. Evans. That's what you always do."

"Lee!"

"You right. It's your fuckin' practice!" He yelled, just before storming off and slamming the front door. My ears perked when I heard the rumble of a diesel engine pulling further and further away. Then, it was quiet and everyone was looking around.

"So, are we still opening gifts?" I said, trying to break the awkward silence. My mom got up to go to her room and slammed the door behind her. My brother and I exchanged glances. "I guess Christmas is canceled," I said.

"I'm not worried about it. He's just an asshole. He'll be back."

"What makes you so sure."

"I'm not."

"Daddy? Can we go home?" My nephew said. He was bent over behind the tree collecting gifts. "We finna go right now." He said. Moments later they were headed out the front door with all their gifts and I was sitting there alone. When I went to check on my mom, she called me on my phone and told me to just go.

"We'll talk about this later."

"Now, who's avoiding the issue?"

"It's not the time, Khai. Please." I slumped down on the couch and tried to sleep. My imagination kept telling me Lee was going to come back and kill us all. I never believed he was all the way there since retiring from the military.

It was after midnight when my mom decided to come out of her room. "You still here?"

"Yup. I got you something." I pointed at the little white bag with the Apple logo on it.

"If I open it, will you promise me, you'll go home and stop worrying about me?"

"No promises."

"Fine." She said as she snatched the bag from underneath the tree. With the shiny band in one hand, she wiped her eyes with the other and sniffed. "It's beautiful. Thank you."

"I know I can't buy more time with you or buy back time lost, but I want you to know I love you more than anything in this world and I will spend the rest of my life..."

"I love you too, Khai. You and your brother are all I have and I will never abandon my boys, no matter what a man has to say." She embraced me with a hug and I squeezed as if she were trying to run away. The tears in her eyes were all the response I needed. In the midst of dysfunction and chaos, I was able to take in a stolen moment and see her smile. Genuinely. And that's all I wanted for Christmas.

The Ultimatum

Terrence flaked on me on New Year's. He said he had a family emergency. Never mind the fact that he wouldn't bother to call or text me throughout the whole holiday. Not even a cheesy text that said, *Happy New Year, baby*. Silence. Maybe I was asking too much, being a manstress and all, but I still couldn't help feeling left out. That's one of the hardest things about "dating" someone who has already started a family without you. There are times you will be reminded that you're an outsider. How was I supposed to get to know him this way? How was I supposed to make him mine?

My intuition kept warning me not to chase this man but my mind was made up, and I was going to see this chase to the end. He called me three days later and acted like nothing happened. I was fed up. It was over and he was week-old leftovers as far as I was concerned. Then, he hit me with a headliner:

"Hey, baby. You coming over later?" I was triggered.

"Yeah. What time?"

After fucking around that night, Terrence lay in bed on his back and lit a cigarette. The sheets were still sweaty and the steam from his touch still hovered over my skin. His face was blank, and uninterested, and I was still craving more. The feeling didn't seem mutual. Normally after sex, he would kiss me on the forehead repeatedly, tell me he loves me, and ask me to rub his back. As I admired him, he barely found time in between smoking and scrolling on his phone, to look at me. I loved rubbing my hands across all his prison tattoos and listening to him talk about all the houses he saw on Zillow that he didn't have the credit or financial means to afford.

When I asked why he was so quiet, he said, "Warren is sick."

"With what? A cold or something?"

"No, he has a heart condition that has been getting progressively worse." When he put it like that I felt like I was sinking into quicksand. It's terrible, but my first thought was about what would it mean for us.

"Is he in the hospital?"

"No, but they put him on meds."

"How are you feeling?"

"I don't know. Warren saved me from a lifestyle that was destroying me. I will forever be in debt to him for that. If I can do something that makes him feel good from time to time, I have to try."

I didn't want to pry any more than I already did, and decided to change the subject after that. I didn't want to upset him. There was always this nagging fear that he would find someone else more suited for him. I didn't want to make it easy for him. I couldn't tell him that I understood where he was coming from. I couldn't possibly understand his struggle, having grown up sheltered my whole life.

"I respect that," I said.

"It's all good now. I'm just worried about how I'm going to pay my car insurance and pay for Tiffany to get her hair done and pay for Warren's medications." I guess the subject change was my cue not to ask any more questions. He gave me enough to shut me up, but stopped before it got too deep. I've seen it before when I first started seeing Jane because she would come in and express how much she wanted to be in a better place, but would always shy away from the uncomfortable memories in detail, especially when I tried to get her to talk about her transition. Every time I tried to revisit those memories with her, she'd tell me it wasn't relevant. With Terrence however, it was not an option. The more time we spent together the more he talked about money.

In the few months that we dated, I had spent over $5,000 on buying Terrence shoes, clothes, groceries, weed, household cleaning supplies, and paying the occasional utility bill here and there. Things I thought his husband was doing based on what he told me about their "marriage" agreement. His bills were supposed to be paid. He should have been able to pay for Warren to get his medication at the very least. It didn't add up, but what did add up, was the cost of "dating" him. He was kept. Nothing explained why so many of his bills were past due. In the meantime, I was feeling insecure about our relationship, since Terrence got so much attention online, and had a dying husband at home. I wanted a label.

It's no secret that I love a good label. Christian Louboutin, Yves Saint Laurent, Dior, Chanel…You name it, I had it. Unlike most people, I appreciated labels both in my closet and in relationships. With a label, you always know exactly where you stand. Top, bottom, verse, fuck buddy, friends with benefits... Boyfriend. Labels made sense of the world for me, but when it came to men, figuring out which one was the right fit was a bit more challenging than just strutting down the halls of the Galleria Mall and snagging all the extra small and slim-fit Ralph Lauren cardigans I could get my hands on. Of all the labels, I could have worn, I wanted the one I couldn't have...Boyfriend.

So, I found a new hobby—posting racy couple photos of us on Instagram. Terrence didn't seem to mind me claiming him, he wanted people to know I was taken, but not him. The attention was fascinating. I definitely understood the appeal and why Terrence was so into it. More importantly, I felt like I had him all to myself.

One week, Terrence kept making excuses for me not to come over. He kept saying he was too tired from work, or that his husband was coming over to visit. Sometimes, when he was gone home to Warren for the weekend, he'd have me go to his apartment and clean up. Without fail, I found a different condom wrapper in the trash when I'd go over there. The sad part is that it didn't seem like he even tried to hide it. It got to the point where I would hide the lube in specific areas in the room before I left his place and looked to see if it had been moved when I came back. I've put it in the window seal, in the sock drawer, under the kitchen sink, you name it. When I came back, it would be on his nightstand next to his red candy dish.

When I would ask him about it, he would swear up and down that he wasn't fucking anybody else. Over time, I graduated to eyeballing how much lube was in the bottle after we had sex to make sure he wasn't using it when I wasn't around. He failed that test almost every time, and would cover it up by saying, he used it for himself and Warren, or that he used it to masturbate. My favorite was the infamous, "I don't have time for other dudes, baby." Lies, lies, lies, and more lies! Somebody had his attention. I was sure of it. Either he had a condom fetish or, I had stupid written all over my fucking forehead. Still, I took off my clothes, laid on my back, and let him hunch me to completion. Afterward, he told me he loved me. All was right with the world again.

One day after work, I hurried to Kroger to get a few things Terrence told me he needed to cook dinner. If the man couldn't do anything else, he could certainly cook. My stove was more for decoration, so I was glad to have a man who liked to use his. I walked in wearing a smile and carrying a hand full of groceries. After I sat the bags on the counter, he kissed me on the forehead and hugged me. That's when I noticed he didn't have Anita Baker's love ballads playing in the background and there was no laundry sitting out for me to do.

"Everything alright?" I asked.

"Yeah, why?"

"I dunno. Looks like you cleaned up."

"Yeah. A little."

"And the money?" I asked, pointing at the stack of cash sitting on the table. He was looking down at me and smiling. When he paused as if he were reconsidering what he was about to say next, I knew something was up. I tried to ignore it. I had learned to know when he was lying. You see, Terrence never told the whole truth. What makes his lies special, was that 50% of what he said was true. It was like how he told me he was married to a woman and that she just supported him financially when in reality, he was married to a man. I was too afraid to hear the truth aloud more times than not. It was like I wanted him to lie to me to spare my feelings or something.

"Jarvis gave that to me. Not that it is any of your concern." My thumb twitched slightly the more I thought about who could have been in there.

"So, wassup? You don't have on Anita, so you must have something on your mind." He sighed and looked at me sharply.

"Look, Khai. Whether you like it or not, things are about to change. I'm going back home to Warren. He says he needs me to be there right now."

"So what, we can't see each other anymore?"

"No. It just means we can't see each other as often."

"How is that fair? I guess I'm just one of those things you play with when it's convenient for you, huh."

"Let me ask you something, playa." He looked like he was 3-seconds away from a nasty eye roll. "Are you gonna pay my bills?"

"Last I checked, I was."

"Boy! You ain't paid my child support, or paid on my student loans! I got kids, fucked up credit, and a felony!"

"Yeah, but I helped you pay your rent, car note, insurance, funded some of your shopping sprees… Oh, and don't forget you have cable and internet because of me!" I couldn't believe it. I was leveraging money as a means for him to stay with me. My mind told me I was scum. My heart told me it was the least I could do. His wide eyes and busy hands were reaching for a cigarette.

"I thought you didn't need him?" He hesitated and put the cigarette in the corner of his lips.

"I have three kids. Do you know how much a divorce would cost me?" He wasn't exactly dad of the year, I'm no parent, and I had no intention of being one.

How could I possibly understand what it was like to be in his position?

"You can stay here tonight, or as long as you want. But I'm going home."

"Looks like you're going out with all that jewelry and cologne you got on. It's the middle of the night. Seriously?"

"Warren and I are going to the movies with the kids as a family."

"I thought Warren was sick?"

"He has a bad heart. He's not crippled."

"So, what now? I just sit around waiting for you to have time for me?"

"You're welcome to come here anytime. You have a key." He didn't even stick around to have dinner or to get in one last quickie. A kiss on the forehead, then he walked passed me like I was trash on the ground. The door slammed and I lost it. I couldn't believe it! We had no idea when we would see each other again and all he had for me was a fucking forehead kiss? Really!

I stood on the other side of the door, hoping he would come back. Hoping it was all a joke…He never did. That's when I got disappointed in myself all over again. How did I allow myself to fall for a married man, who essentially had no means of supporting himself? The disappointment lingered until it became an obsession. I was pacing back and forth around the house, re-running it all in my head. The Hoe-Tale, to The Agreement, to the night at the Marriott. I remember the orgasms and peaceful nights. It was as if they had all suddenly been taken away from me. Something had to be done. Then I remembered I had his location, and that's when I got the grand idea to follow his ass to his house. The GPS led me to an elaborate Spanish-colonial-style home in what one could call your average upper-middle-class suburban neighborhood.

There it was. Terrence's other home. It was only a 10-minute drive from the apartment. It had these dramatic arched floor-to-ceiling windows in the front that caught my eye as they reflected a smudgy red image. Terrence's Impala was parked on the corner. Meanwhile, a red 3-series BMW and a Black Tahoe bogarted the driveway. With my car parked across the street, I watched lights go on and off in different rooms, and tried to make sense of the shadows running about in the house. The constable patrolling the neighborhood was a sign that I was doing the most.

But all I could think about was the frustration of being told I couldn't have him. It made me ignore all the signs. It was now or nothing. I sent him a text.

ME: I'm outside.

TERRENCE: Bullshit. Don't
play like that!

ME: WHAT IS JARVIS DOING HERE!

TERRENCE: Have you lost your damn
mind! I'm coming outside. Don't fuckin' move!

That shook things up pretty quickly. Within 5-minutes he had made an excuse to leave and met me outside. A crack of lightning formed an electric zip-line in the sky. He charged up to my window and started pounding.

"Unlock the goddamn door, boy!" Honestly, I was too chicken-shit to do anything. He looked like he was ready to whoop my ass. It was understandable, considering my little intrusion. I waited for him to stop beating my window before I rolled it down. "I'm not going to hurt you. Just let me in, please!" I realized he wouldn't want to go back to prison, so I unlocked the door and he hopped into the passenger side.

"Go!" He demanded.

"Where?"

"Anywhere! Just get the fuck away from my home! What the hell was you thinkin, boy? Are you crazy!" Carefully, I drove the car to the next street over and cut off the lights. It occurred to me at that moment that I hadn't thought this whole thing through. What could I have possibly accomplished going there? It was too late. The damage was done and I had to defend my actions.

"When were you going to tell me Jarvis is your husband!"

"What are you talking about, boy?"

"I saw him walking in the house. I'm not an idiot!"

"You shouldn't have come here. And if I was a different man, I would have choked the shit out of you."

"If you knew you were never going to leave Jarvis, why would you entertain me at all? Why would you lie to me about who your husband was?" The blank look in his eyes, I'll never forget. I wanted answers. I wanted him to make me feel better. Tell me none of it was as it seemed. I needed the comfort of his smoke and mirrors. He looked through me like I was begging him for a dollar at a stoplight in the middle of Downtown. I was a bum on the street. Then, in true Terrence fashion, he hit me with a headliner:

"I tell everybody that, playa." Something about it I wasn't comprehending. My wishful thinking tendencies made me want to believe he was being sarcastic.

"So, you just go around telling everybody you love them? Is that some kind of twisted fetish?"

"You need to calm down! I do love you." I stopped to feel the words as soon as they kissed my ears. It was exactly what I needed to hear.

"Then, why all this? Why can't I have you!"

"You're too young to understand, Khai. I really hoped you would."

"Fuck that! I need to know, now! Am I wasting my time, or what?"

"I don't have time for this right now! Jarvis is looking for me. We'll talk later. I promise." He was looking frantically out the corner of his eye. The porch light came on and he started reaching for the door handle.

"I need to know! I love you, Terrence. I dunno what else to say."

"I love you too. But that ain't enough." I searched his eyes for sincerity, but his emotionless expression did not match the words that left his lips. I knew better than to believe he loved me, but I needed him to mean it, so I conceded. His phone rang in his back pocket, causing him to jump and spring open the door.

A lashing rain attacked the leather on the door panel as he got out of the car. I spotted Jarvis standing in the doorway scanning the area for Terrence. I reached for him in a panic. He paused to eye me down. It was my turn to give the ultimatum.

"If I leave, I'm not coming back."

"It's all or nothing huh? You making threats now?" I nodded. He didn't even look back at me as he ran to Jarvis. For the life of me, I couldn't comprehend why that had failed. So much for asserting my self-respect, and proclaiming my love. Raw and uninhibited by ego. My ultimatums sounded more like a threat. Terrence took it as a challenge and decided to prove me wrong, to show me that I was not as important to him as I desperately wanted to believe I was, and that he had no problem moving on. The slip of his hand leaving mine crushed my spirit.

I wouldn't stand for it. The storm trapped me in my car. No way I could leave. As I sat behind the wheel, waiting for the rain to stop, I grew angrier. Forced to watch from the outside as Terrence retreated to his family life. It wasn't fair. Not in my mind. Something had to be done.

Don't Forget About Us

Almost anything has the potential to be addicting. That's what they told me in school. All addictions can be traced back to one basic human desire…We all just want to feel good. Maybe Jhene Aiko was on to something when she said, *most of us are hurting*. I don't know if I'm ignorant on the matter, but some people just seem a lot happier than others. Or, maybe some of us find comfort in pretending the pain is not there?

One thing's for sure, when I find something that makes me feel good, I tend to do whatever I can to prolong the rush of energy and the temporary relief from the sadness that hangs. over me. Terrence was my addiction. Some say love is the greatest addiction of all. The euphoria it induces is comparable to any Sativa you can scoop up from your local weed man. I believed this wholeheartedly until I met Terrence.

We had something, and it felt very much like love when we were getting along. In Terrence's absence, I considered the possibility that maybe love and lust are twins. Lust is every bit as charming, sexy, euphoric, and desirable as love. The difference is, lust is a little more aggressive. I like to think of her as Buttercup from the Power-Puff Girls. She's got spice. She's hotheaded, passionate, and has a hard time with the word no. That said, I guess my middle name must be Buttercup…

I had just finished with my last patient for the day and was sitting at my desk charting when the office phone rang with a call from a paralegal requesting Jane's medical records. I still needed to buy myself some time, so I told him we never received the request and that he would need to resend it, along with paying the medical records processing fee my mom charged. He put me on hold to verify with his boss if it was okay to pay for the records with the company card, so I sat on my phone scrolling through Terrence's Instagram messages. Stalking his social media accounts became part of my daily routine, and you know what they say about what happens when you go looking for something. He had been with at least 11-people that I could track from reading the messages between him and guys he met on Instagram and Tumblr within the first week of us splitting!

"Hello, Mr. Allen? Are you still there? I'm ready to pay." I tuned the man completely out. When did Terrence find all this extra time to fuck? He was supposed to be tending to his sick husband. That's what I was stuck on. It didn't add up and it haunted me.

Whether having the passwords to all his accounts was a blessing or fuel to feed my unhealthy obsession, I still don't know. All the evidence screamed he didn't give a damn about me. It was all documented on Tumblr and every-damn-thing else. It was like reading a travel log of hookups. I could have looked past these little indiscretions, but there was one fucking constant. A bug on the windshield. Someone else had filled in for my position as the favorite, and it wasn't his husband. This one he liked screw a lot more than the others. Ivan…

"Hello? Mr. Allen? Can you hear me?"

Ivan was the same gym rat from Atlanta that Terrence lied about not flirting with on Snapchat on Halloween. He's the same one Terrence swore had recently recovered from temporary paralysis or some shit. It baffled me how he had the balls to show me who he was about to cheat on me with months ago and made me look crazy when I showed signs of being jealous. I didn't know what to think. All I could see was red in front of me.

"Mr. Allen, can you hear me?"

"Yes. I'm sorry. You were cutting out." I tuned back in to process his payment. As soon as the phone clicked, I was back scrolling. The more I read Ivan's messages to Terrence, the angrier I got. I shut down my work computer and hurried home before my mom could even get the chance to say goodbye and touch base with me about a few patients who weren't doing well.

I thought if I went to bed early then the sadness would pass faster. I thought I could forget about him. It failed. For several nights, I'd find myself tossing in turning, trying to shake the thoughts of them being together from my head. After a month, he and Ivan had been together just about every day from what I could follow in the messages between them on Instagram.

> TERRENCE: Hey, love. How was your day?"
>
> Ivan: It was stressful, baby. Had a hard day of physical therapy. 😩
>
> TERRENCE: Well, when you get home, I'll run your back. Then i'ma put this dick in you.🍆
>
> Ivan: Haha! Ur so sweet, babe.🍑
>
> TERRENCE: See you soon. 😈

As the messages came in, they drove me to drink. My blood steamed like an iron over polyester over how much they were liking all of each other's pictures, commenting on each other's stories, and all kinda bullshit. The flirting and nudes they swapped back and forth on Instagram sickened me. He was saying things that he used to say to me. I was starting to think it was all a scam and that Ivan was an opportunist who used his recovery story as a means to get attention from men.

Not that Terrence's attention was hard to get. Almost any good-looking man with a nice ass and body caught his eye. It was just hard to keep it, and that was abundantly clear with all of the people he led on just to screw and move on to the next that were still sending him messages asking why he hasn't returned their calls or texts. Ivan, however, had done the impossible. Piqued and kept his interest. He dropped me like a bad habit and it was as if our time together was a hazy insignificant memory of the past.

It was Thursday night and I was feeling nostalgic about our old regularly scheduled hookups. The loneliness and jealousy made me desperate for his attention. So, I did the most desperate thing anybody could do. I downed a couple more bottles of wine, smoked some weed, and sent him a drunken text hoping he would throw me a lifeline.

ME: I miss youuuuuuu…💔

TERRENCE: I miss you too, love.

ME: Can I call you? 🥺

TERRENCE: Come over later.
I'll be at the apartment.😈

His response caught me off guard. I wasn't expecting him to reply considering he hadn't reached out to me in a month. Still, I hoped that he would miss me as much as I missed him. A welcomed breeze blew over my shoulders as I leaned over my balcony and downed the last swig of Stella Rosa left in my glass. After cleaning myself up, I was on his doorstep an hour later. He looked me up and down as he stood in the doorway with black sweats and a white wife-beater. What was his angle? I didn't bother to consider because all I could do was admire him from head to toe, and wait for his signal.

I missed his gaze. It was magic, the way it seemed to cast a spell and seduce me into believing everything he said. So when he told me he missed me, I believed him. For a moment, all the questions I had and all the unfinished business which led to our time apart, no longer mattered. He just made me stupid! I didn't want to bring up the fact that I was in love with him and the idea of sharing him just didn't fit into the picture anymore. The last thing I wanted to do was ruin the mood. Or worse, provoke him to the point he asked me to leave. Never mind the matter of his marriage still being intact. Never mind all the guys that have been in and out of his bedroom in my absence. Here and now was all that mattered.

He invited me in to sit on the sofa. His tone was calm but not all that welcoming. I looked around the room for signs of other men. I hadn't learned my lesson about looking for things because I spotted an open bottle of lube sitting on the floor next to the couch. Still, I thought there was a chance he planned on using it for us, so I didn't ask any questions.

Not that I needed to see the lube or any of the messages I read on his Instagram and Tumblr accounts to know that someone else had been in the house. There was something in the air that felt different. Maybe it was because the trash was overflowing in the kitchen, and the dishes were piled in the sink. Or maybe, it was because the coffee table was filthy. The glass was smudgy and it had white residue splattered around the corners. There were two shot glasses and an empty bottle of Jack Daniels knocked over on top of each other.

"Damn. You just let the place go, huh?"

"I told you I missed you baby."

"Yeah, right. You're so full of it."

"I'm fa real, boy. You ain't been giving my booty away to nobody have you." He sounded a little tipsy.

"No. I don't have the time." His eyes were red and he was sniffling.

"No, go on and tell me you missed me. I know you did. You ain't gotta lie about it." He sniffed so hard, I thought his nose was about to bleed.

"I missed you too..." Are you okay? Do you need a tissue?"

"My bad. It's too cold in here. It messes with my sinuses." He walked over to the thermostat and turned it off. "So, talk to me." He said as he dimmed the lights. I didn't know what to say and I didn't know what to make of the warm light that suddenly relaxed me.

"I'm sorry…" I said. "It wasn't fair of me to ask you to choose between the two of us."

"I love you, baby. But I will never leave Jarvis for you or anybody." I didn't understand how he had gone from coming home to an empty house and Jarvis asking him for a divorce, to—*I will never leave Jarvis*. When he sat down next to me, I lost my nerve and couldn't restrain myself from looking into his eyes. He wrapped his arms around me, and I got a whiff of his Versace. It made me want to sit closer. A lot closer. His aroma was exciting. My body couldn't help but lust. The delicate kiss he placed on my forehead as he wielded his arms to lure me into the comfort of his chest, made me believe the words I was yearning to hear when he said them.

When he said he loved me, I believed him… I struggled to wrap my head around the fact that a month had come and gone since I felt the warmth of his embrace. Instead of moving on in his absence, I found myself growing fonder. The days spent doing his laundry, washing his dishes, cleaning ink stains out of his carpet, rubbing his back after work, getting him off before he called to tell his husband goodnight, and funding his shopping habit just to see him smile, started to feel nostalgic. Yeah, I was bitter that he had moved on so easily, but I still had plenty of love to give.

The sound of his heart beating and the vibrations from his chest as he told me he loved me, silenced the angry thoughts in my head. Without warning, he grabbed my hand and slid them down his pants. I had a hand full of balls and a man to please. He carried me to the bedroom and climbed my back. Everything was going fine until his dick softened like a soggy breadstick from Olive Garden.

"Is everything alright?" I asked, face down on the pillow and ass pointed towards his lips. It took him a moment to respond.

"Just tired. Probably just need to watch some porn." Since when did he need to watch porn to stay up?

"Do what you gotta do."

"Cool. I gotchu, love." He pulled a bag out of his drawer and emptied 3 pills into his hands. After downing them with two shots of Jack, he pulled out his iPad and opened Pornhub. Eventually, he rose to the occasion after scrolling through a few flicks and would pump me like a blow-up doll. Not once did he look at me. The squeaking from the mattress sounded more like a ticking clock and I was dreading every second of it. It made me feel like shit. Insecure and worthless.

Later that night, he got a call that made him jump out of bed and go outside. Initially, I figured it was Jarvis so I didn't think much of it. Then it started to marinate. Even when I still thought Jarvis and Warren were two different people, he usually didn't mind talking to Jarvis in front of me as long as I was sure not to make any noise. About 5-minutes later, I decided to peek outside to see if he was still on the phone because I couldn't hear him talking. When I stepped out onto the balcony, that's when I noticed he was in the storage closet. He was speaking so low, I couldn't make out what he was saying. When my eavesdropping failed I decided to knock on the door.

I didn't give him a chance to open it. It was swinging open with fury the moment I got a firm grip on it. He turned to face me in shock. The phone was still glued to his ear and without a word, I just glared at him. He quickly hung up and stepped to me like he was ready to fight.

"Why the hell are you spying on me!"

"Why the hell are you in the closet on the fuckin' phone!"

"I was cold."

"Bullshit! Why not come inside!"

"Uh… I was talking to Jarvis."

"Bullshit! You've talked to Jarvis in front of me plenty of times. Cut the crap! Who the hell was you talking to!" I asked a question I already knew the answer to, but a small part of me remained stupidly in love and optimistic that he wouldn't say his name.

"You need to leave!" He ordered. "I ain't got time for this. I got work tomorrow."

"I'm not going any damn where until you tell me who the hell you was talking to on the phone! Got you hiding in the closet and shit! Mothafucka! Do I look dumb!"

"You need to calm the hell down Lil boy. You in business you don't belong in."

"You are my business!"

"No, I'm my husband's business. The sooner you learn that. The better off we'll be. I was talking to Jarvis. And that's that. I don't wanna hear no more about it! Give me my key and go home!"

"No! Please!" I begged.

He dared me with his raised eyebrows and tightened jaw. "If you don't give me my damn key, I promise I will change the locks and you will never see me again!" Desperate. I pulled it out of my Coach bag and handed it over. After snatching it from me he said, "I'll call you in the morning." I knew he didn't mean it. I didn't want to leave because I knew I would not be asked back, but what choice did I have? I couldn't stay where I wasn't wanted.

I was halfway home when I decided to check Terrence's inbox. He had a fresh set of messages from Ivan.

IVAN: What happened? 😨

TERRENCE: He started trippin. He
Is gone now. So you can come on.

IVAN: Cool. Y'all broke it off?

TERRENCE: Yeah. I told him I ❤️
you. It didn't go well.

IVAN: Aww! I love you too!!😍

TERRENCE: I got you a gift.

IVAN: What is it?

TERRENCE: 🔑

IVAN: OMG! I'm on my way!

TERRENCE: 😈 🍆 🍑 💊

There they were. Those three devastating little words packed more punch than Louisiana hot sauce on crawfish étouffée. His words hit me like a hurricane. How could he say that? How the fuck had Ivan managed to steal his heart! Was that even makeup sex we just had all of an hour ago? Was it a pity fuck? And this fucker was getting a fucking key? My fucking key! Are you kidding me! I wouldn't stand for it.

The roar from my revving engine told me to get a grip on my emotions, but the tears slowly blurring my vision, told me to turn around and get answers. I was pushing 90 trying to get back to Terrence before Ivan could get there and claim his key. All I could see was red down the highway until blue lights started flashing behind me. Suddenly, reality set in. The danger. The consequences of recklessness. All of the reason and good sense in the world came flooding in too little too late.

I was shaking when I pulled over to wait for the State Trooper to get out of the car. I didn't have time for it. Finally, after about 3-minutes, a tall slender figure leaned his head toward the window. The way I fumbled around with the window switch before finally letting it down, you would have thought I had just pulled off the lot with fresh paper tags and had no idea what any of the buttons did.

"Sir, Do you have any idea how fast you were going?"

"Uh–I…" I paused to think. I hated that question. It always rattled me. I've always thought that it was some sort of weird American custom to lie about it. My anxiety just ran with it the whole time he was eyeing me and pointing a flashlight in my eyes. Two different nervous voices argued back and forth in my head about what my next move should be.

If I lie, he's going to know I'm lying because that's what everybody does right? So why lie? Why not! Because, that would be an admission to guilt, and who is dumb enough to do that? Right? No! Lie! No, Don't! You're going to jail Khai!

All these questions and social theories bounced around in my head like a 6-year-old with untreated ADHD. Not to mention the blowout I was having with Terrence and the whole Ivan situation. I could feel my heart slamming against my chest.

"Sir, I'm gonna ask you one more time." My eyes drifted to the small band-aid on his chin that looked like it had come from a shaving accident. I was fixated on it until it seemed like it was warping. A crisp click from his flashlight startled me enough to force a response.

"Yes, sir," I finally said. "I had some bad Panda Express and I'm honestly about to shit on myself!" I pointed to the empty takeout bag in the passenger seat that had speckles of soy sauce splattered in random spots inside of it. "License and registration, please." He ordered. I handed it to him through the window, but my hands couldn't seem to maintain a steady grip, and everything fell on top of his black leather boots. "I'm so sorry, officer. Sometimes, I just get so anxious, I can barely hold anything." I admitted. It was the partial truth because it definitely wasn't my case of fake runs that had me wired like that. After bending down to pick everything up, he studied me for a bit.

"Are you alright?" He asked. "You seem rattled." Maybe the red in my eyes was not only visible to me. Did he see it? The bitterness and devastation fueling the fire behind them?

"No sir. I just don't know how much longer I can hold it. Not to be dramatic or anything."

"Was it the one on FM 2920?"

"Yes, sir."

"Oh, myyyyyy man! I'm sorry bout that! Been there. Done that and ain't goin' back!" He was laughing when he said it. "I tell ya what, let me see what I can do for ya." He tipped his hat and chuckled a little bit more to himself. Without another word, he walked back to his car, spoke on his walkie for a bit, then came back and issued me a warning.

I still wasn't sure he believed me. The paranoia in me told me that the cop would follow me to see if I had the flying shits, so I took the nearest exit although I was still about 5-miles from where I needed to be. I had to commit to the lie for my peace of mind, so I wasted 10-minutes in a nasty Texaco stall.

I finally arrived at the gate to Terrence's complex and couldn't get in because the gate was closed. I needed him to buzz me in, so I had to sit and wait for somebody to come in or go out. The fact that it took another 5-minutes for someone to come through the gate irked the shit out of me. I had no control over my hands banging repeatedly on the steering wheel as I fought unwanted thoughts of the three fucking words he had the audacity to say to someone else just moments after uttering the same bullshit to me and sending me on my merry fucking way!

Did he mean them when he said it to me? It sure didn't feel like it. When he said it to Ivan, it carried more weight, considering that's who he was spending all his time with. The thoughts tortured me and I floored it the moment an old white Chrysler Sebring was buzzed in. With my fist pounding on his door desperately, I begged him to open it. Knees to the ground and head tucked in disgrace, I burst into tears on the other side of the door as he said to Ivan, "Ignore him. He'll go away."

"You need to go talk to him." I heard Ivan say back. His voice was softer than I imagined for the gym rat he was. I couldn't believe that he was in there acting like he was some sort of voice of reason. There I was, looking immature and desperate, hoping that if only he saw this as a grand gesture of my love, he would reconsider. Maybe he would take me back and tell me he loved me and mean it in the way that I needed him to. There I was again with my wishful thinking. I sat outside his door for over 30-minutes as people passed through the hallway looking at me crazy. He finally decided to call me.

"Go downstairs. I'll meet you down there." He said. I submitted and within minutes, he had me cornered against a brick pillar. For a moment, I was unsure if he was going to bash my head in or kiss me. The brick beat up the skin just above my elbows, leaving behind a few shallow scratches. His chest sat high up and in my face. The heat radiating from the groove in his neck made my heart race.

"Are you alright? Because you trippin. Have you been sleeping?" What was that supposed to mean? Hell no I was not alright!

"I'm fine! Just go. I shouldn't be here!" I said. He grabbed both my hands, pinned them to my thighs, and looked me up and down. I returned the favor by glaring right back at him.

"I don't understand! What does he have that I don't?" He ignored me and looked the other way. "You need to go home before you do something you're gonna regret." He was so nonchalant with it, I wanted to slap him.

"Fuck you! And him! If you think I won't tell Jarvis about this, you got another thing coming!" The way he was looking through me told me I had nothing to lose. The ash from his cigarette fell and crumbled on my sneakers and in between the laces.

"Look here, ya Lil mothafucka! I will kill you and your family! You might be crazy, but I wasn't in prison for petty theft. I will hurt you!" He shook me repeatedly, daring me to try him. "That's your problem! You don't know how to stay in your place. Go home, now! Or, you can forget about us!" How was I supposed to know my place when he blurred the lines? He had me believing that his marriage was over and that there was a possibility of us being together when the dust settled from the ruins of divorce.

I couldn't bring myself to ask him why he would lead me on. But the fact that there was another man upstairs that had managed to get Terrence to love him in the way that I so desperately desired, fueled a fire within me known as envy. I wanted both of them to hurt as badly as I was in that moment.

I shouted in his face. "And you're a piece of shit father, lying to Instagram for likes and comments! I hope you snort that Xanax all the way to the fucking grave!" He took a step back and shoved me against the wall.

"Annd! You'd still want me." He was right. But did that mean nothing to him? He grabbed my hands and pinned them above my head. "Go home! I'll call you in the morning." He tossed me to the grass and pointed behind me to the parking lot. "Go!"

The blank expression on his face pierced my heart. He was cold. I didn't recognize him that way. After regaining my balance, I looked up to see Ivan peeping over the balcony with two shot glasses in his hands and a joint tucked in the corner of his lips. He had front-row seats to witness his win. I wanted to take my bat and beat the smirk off his face. It wouldn't solve anything, but the idea was satisfying.

I accepted my rejection and retreated to my car just in time to beat the storm. The rain stomped on my moonroof, awakening the storm cloud that resided in the corner of my mind as the rage of a bull took the driver's seat. Every man lies. And I cannot sit here and pretend that I am somehow special to have fallen victim to pain caused by a man and his lies. It also doesn't mean I'm not allowed to be pissed off about it. Now, when I think of addiction, it hits a little harder.

Addiction is… not being able to sleep in my bed at night because he hasn't called to say goodnight. Addiction is the chill creeping up your back in the lonely hours because he isn't there to hold you. Addiction is when you cannot focus or start your day until he's told you good morning. Addiction is when you know he's lying but you don't mind it because his lies coddle you. He knows just what to say. It is every bit of knowing the truth and avoiding life decisions that do not fit within the hopeful but misguided fairytale ending you have imagined.

Addiction is the stomach cringing and irritability you get when your gut is screaming out to you that he's in bed with someone else. Addiction is when you still yearn to be with him. Addiction is when you're feeling like Whitney Houston because you're saving all your love–ooh! You're saving all your love for him! You find yourself asking the same questions even though you know the painful answers. You ask only to see if he will lie. Of course, he lies. You find a way to cope. Suppression works the best. It makes you numb. He still cheats, but you don't mind it. You tell yourself he loves you and maybe he'll change, though none of his actions reflect it. No! God no! You can't let him go. Not yet. It's not over yet!

Addiction is when you give more than you can stand to see walk away. You find your aching heart singing, baby dontchu, dontchu forget about us! It's bruised egos, hurt feelings, and everything else in between. Addiction is when toxicity starts to feel normal.

West Dallas Street

Valentine's Day. It was the first time since Rick that I cared about a man enough to want to celebrate it. The only problem was, the man I wanted to be my Valentine had moved on to someone new. I was back to getting only 2 to 3-hours of sleep again. Groggy, and emotional from looking at all the happy couples on Instagram, I reached out to Terrence. I hoped that maybe Valentine's day would open the door for reconciliation.

ME: Happy Valentine's Day! WYD? 💗 💗 💗 Can I call you?

TERRENCE: I'll call you later. I'm at the movies.

ME: With who?

TERRENCE: My sister.

Terrence told me he'd be spending Valentine's Day at the movies with his sister who had been diagnosed with

Cancer. I knew he was lying because the guy he was cheating with had just posted on his Instagram story that he was going to see the same damn movie. Hidden Figures. Plus, Terrence had already seen that movie a month ago with his son. I couldn't very well tell him that because I'd have to explain how I knew what I knew, and that would require me to tell him I had been reading every message he got on social media for the past few months.

It was a cold February night and Terrence had left me completely untouched, unwanted, and unloved on the day of the year when you're supposed to celebrate love. My bed was cold without him and his bed was not an option. I couldn't sleep through the night without waking up screaming. I had to leave. Find warmth somewhere else. A 30-minute cruise down the highway, living on adrenaline, bitterness, and several Mariah Carey heartbreak songs later, I got a group of messages on Jackd. Again... So, I found a date on Jackd. It was a quick fix. At least that way it would be harder to think about it. My first date that night was an epic fail. I drove 35-minutes south of Downtown to meet this guy who tried to use what was left in the corners of a struggling tube of Vaseline for lube.

I was so turned off by the smell of feet and pickles in his place, I didn't bother to offer to use the lube in my bag instead. I told him that I left the dog out and didn't want him to piss and shit in the house. When I left, I ended up getting a message from another guy named Grant that I was also talking to on Jackd. He wasn't replying fast enough earlier otherwise, he would have been my first stop.

From our messages and photos exchanged on Jackd, I knew he lived in a much nicer part of town, was better looking, and had a porn-star dick. We broke a rule by exchanging numbers. The app kept crashing and we were both chasing a fix. I'm sure I can speak for both of us when I say, we didn't have the patience for that. Grant stayed in a luxury hi-rise in Midtown off West Dallas Street. I knew the street well because it wasn't far from Buffalo Bayou Park and the Dunlavy. I passed it up all the time on my way to the park. I had to drive 10-stories up a parking garage and waited for 5-minutes for him to buzz me in the building. I had to take the elevator down to the 3rd floor after that.

ME: At the door.

GRANT: It's open.

I hesitated for several minutes before knocking. I was unsure if I wanted this. What I wanted, I couldn't have. At least not in the way that I needed to have him. And so, when I walked in, I found Grant laying on a massive fluffy gray sectional stroking and smoking. His brown skin was a welcomed change in pace from the yellow bone I had been riding all this time. My eyes couldn't help but drift up his legs and straight into his crotch. I couldn't believe how big it was. He motioned with his head for me to come join him. When I was within reach, he grabbed me and pulled me on top of him.

In a low but stern voice, he said, "Take that shit off." He gripped my ass and pulled me in close for a kiss. I had become desensitized to breaking rules at this point. Or, maybe I missed the memo on kissing being part of hookup culture. His grip was firm and more aggressive like he had something to prove and he was lean like he ran track in his day. Just my type.

Once he stripped me naked, I let him manhandle me all over his couch. Everything was hot until I looked at the clock and realized it was 3:00 a.m. and he was still stroking me. Every time he'd get close to cumming, he'd pull out and hold it.

"It's getting late, man," I said.

"Nah, boi. You don't have to go. You can spend the night." He said. He kissed me some more and laid down beside me. The vigorous pounding in my chest told me I'd better slow down or I'd be coming out on a stretcher. Still, I didn't listen.

He was laying on my back, pinning my hands to the bed when he licked behind my ears and said, "Man, that shit was feeling so good, I didn't want to cum." I don't know why that made me smile, but it did.

"Can you cum?" I asked. We were both sweating and trying to catch our breath, so I figured he'd tap out.

"Hell yeah, boi." He rolled me over on my side, hiked my left leg up, and slid inside me. His assertion was so attractive it had me wanting to do whatever he said. He moaned and groaned for an hour before finally finishing and collapsing on my back as if he'd just run a marathon. I wasn't able to finish, but I enjoyed having him hold me all night, at least until the sun came up…

TERRENCE: I KNOW U SEE ME CALLIN!!!🤬🤬

TERRENCE: If I don't hear from u tonight,
LOSE MY FUCKIN NUMBER!

TERRENCE: I won't call again!
You can forget about us 👋

The regret flooded in without warning and my heart sank through the pillow top and deep into the springs of Grant's mattress. What I thought would ease my pain and jealousy, had only made things worse. I was about to lose him. For real this time and I wasn't sure that's what I wanted. Sometimes, I wish I had met Grant under better circumstances. He was a successful business analyst, younger than Terrence, better in bed, and most importantly, single. But in the heart of all the chaos, I was in no place to jump into a new relationship. But knowing that did not keep me from trying.

I had already begun romanticizing the idea of me replacing Terrence with Grant. The possibility of seeing Terrence jealous for once made me want something more with Grant than just sex. It wasn't right, but I figured I'd keep coming around to see where things went. Grant became a rebound and a damn good one. I did not drive down West Dallas Street with the purest intentions. I came to him, broken. Grant offered me a distraction and like a fish to worm on a hook, I took the bait. I convinced myself that maybe if I saw more of Grant I would forget about Terrence.

Grant and I had started hanging out a few times a week. Turns out he worked at AIG Financial, he was a Rice University Alumni, he was the kind of guy with a résumé that would bring a tear to my mom's eyes. He also confirmed that he ran track in his day. We had that in common. One Saturday afternoon, I was getting ready for my evening jog. The blossoming springtime air had me feeling a little better. I hadn't been on a run since the breakup with Terrence, so I was looking forward to getting back to some sort of normalcy.

I was busy loading my car with my duffle bag when Terrence called. I ignored him because Grant was calling on the other line and I wanted to believe that I was capable of moving on. Grant was educated but he still had that southern edge to him. He called me "shawty," and I liked that. "Wassup, shawty? Whatcha doin'"

"Not much. Just about to head out for a run."

"Oh, word? You want a partner? You know I can keep up." It turned me on to know that he could, but when he asked if he could join, I was a little hesitant because I normally prefer my jogs to be a solitary act. It gives me time to clear my head and discover a better space mentally. It was almost like a high and I didn't want to ruin that. Then he hit me with a headliner.

"If you serious about us getting to know each other, it would help to include me in things that you enjoy, shawty." I suddenly felt inclined to agree, so I came up with a compromise. To ensure I had a little alone time with myself, I told Grant I would be there around 6:30 when I'd be there at 5. When I pulled up to my usual spot, I was dumbfounded to find Terrence there waiting. He was sitting in the grass just off to the side of the paved trail with his shirt off and grinning at me. I turned my lip up at the small group of people surrounding him wanting to take photos. There were two women, one wearing a pink hoodie and another wearing a blue one, and a tall man who was wearing nothing but blue compression shorts. His ass was huge and his arms looked like they could bench-press a horse. All of them were going on and on about how they followed his Instagram and love his photos.

It was annoying to have to stand there and observe how desperately hungry in the pants for him they were. When he spotted me walking in the opposite direction, he said to his groupies, "I've gotta go." After hugging the guy with the muscle booty, he hustled up to greet me.

"Sup, boo?"

"I guess I'm boo now? Where's Ivan"

"Now why you gotta go bringing up old shit." There must have been something on my face because his groupies shot me a nasty side-eye. I was rolling my eyes and decided to hug him, hoping it would piss them off. The wind blew and I got a whiff of his cologne. Instantly, I was thrown back into the memories of rolling around in his sheets. His hair was uncut and he looked tired with all the bags under his eyes. He smelled like sex and heartbreak at the same time. He placed his big hands on my petite shoulders and with a firm grip, he shook me playfully and said he was ready.

"Boy, go on somewhere with all of that. We are in the middle of a public park. And, I'm not even supposed to be talking to you right now. I have a date."

"A date?"

"Yeah. A date." He looked out the corner of his eye and bit his lip. I tried to look away, but he stepped up to me and slid one of his hands up my bright yellow shorts, squeezed my cheeks and kissed me on my neck. "You sure about that?"

"Absolutely." I was aroused but gently shoved him away and started jogging down the trail. Terrence stayed behind to tend to his groupies and I called Grant to have him meet me a mile in the opposite direction. When he arrived, I couldn't help but smile. He had on shorts similar to mine but they were black and he wore white compression shorts underneath. "Glad you changed your mind, shawty."

"Me too."

"You look good." He licked his lips and I tried to shy away from the compliment by offering to help him stretch. After I helped him warm-up, we took off jogging together. For the first half mile, he kept up, occasionally falling a few paces behind me. I would slow down so I could hear him go on and on about how he used to run track when he was in high school and college. Although talking and running was not my idea of a smart workout, I was intrigued. It was the first thing I noticed we had in common.

"What events did you run?"

"All the sprints." He said, trying to catch his breath.

"Well, it wasn't anything over the quarter-mile that's for sure," I said as I laughed a little under my breath.

"Uh-What makes you say that?"

"Because it looks like you're struggling to keep up and we haven't even hit the mile marker yet."

"Ha-ha! Fuck you. I knew you was a hater when I met you."

"You call it being a hater. I call it, the truth." We both laughed and he shoved me towards the bushes playfully. The sun was out, but thunder roared and it was quickly followed by another Houston unexpected rain shower. My first instinct was to head back to the car, but Grant seized the opportunity to have a little fun. He grabbed me by the waist and pulled me into his chest, which was soaked in sweat and rainwater. My left cheek was pressed up against his nipple and I could smell the manly sweat radiating off his skin.

"Where you goin', shawty." He said. I said nothing for a while and avoided staring into his tender brown eyes. The next thing I knew, I found myself looking down at the ground as my feet went up and wrapped themselves around his waist as he carried me into the bushes. One lingering roar of thunder, rhythmic rain patter, and the moist sound of a tongue circling the tips of my nipples were all it took for him to seduce me. Afterward, we went back to his place, showered, and hopped in bed.

I lay there staring at the ceiling, bearing the stench of promiscuity. The fan spun round and round and I struggled to believe I was there again. In this empty space. This stranger wasn't what my heart desired. I didn't want him or the one to follow. Although a suitable and more qualified candidate, the timing was not right. Sure, his bed was warm. But, did not engulf me in goosebumps in the way that Terrence's did. I missed the way he used to wrap his arms around me, kiss my neck tenderly, and uttered those three addictive words:

I. Love. You.

His voice, so effortlessly sensual, it aroused me deep within the depths of my spirit even when he was miles away. It was a psychedelic high I long for, day in and day out. From one stranger's bed to the next, I found myself trying to replicate that warmth. Trying to mend the shattered glass, that remained of my heart. A fool's pursuit. I would say that I wish I could let him go, but that would be a lie. Replace him. Or, so I thought. More fish in the sea. Or, so I thought. It was dark and lonely in my mind more than ever since Terrence took his affection away. I needed a cold shower. The warmth in Grant's bed grew sticky, stuffy and outright unbearable, reminiscent of a Houston summer.

It was baffling, almost laughable, that no matter how many warm beds I found to lay my head at night, no bed brought me the warmth I felt when Terrence's chest was pressed amongst my back while he snored in my ear and kept me warm all night. I gazed out the window and spotted the street sign. West Dallas Street. It was not my home and not where my heart ached to be.

Broken

Have you ever choked on a fishbone? I have, but not in the way that you might be thinking. Let me explain...You see, growing up I always believed my parents to have had the perfect marriage. Lee was happy as long as my mom was happy. At least, that's the way it seemed. I'll never forget the day my mom cried in front of me.

We were in the middle of our busy afternoon clinic. At least 10 patients were waiting out in the lobby. The phones were ringing off the hooks, and I was busy charting on a grieving father whose son shot himself 6-months ago while they were sitting in the car together. I remember thinking how hopeless that situation sounded. How is one supposed to heal from that? How was I going to help him? I was scratching my head and clicking my pin like I had turrets so, I decided to take a break and headed to the break room to pop my lunch in the microwave. My mom grilled salmon, mashed potatoes and asparagus for me and brought it to the office. As I was chewing a piece of my mother's perfectly seasoned fish, I heard Lee shouting and cursing at someone in the hall.

"Fuck you! Shut the fuck up talking to me!" A door slammed and a dinging bell sounded from the lobby door. I thought maybe he was on the phone because he was good at going off on telemarketers in the office like they had called him out his name or something. I peeped out the hall to see the whole clinic stop for a very, very brief moment of awkward silence. If you blinked or scratched your nose, you would have missed it. Everyone returned to their regularly scheduled programming and I returned to my desk. 5-minutes later, my mom walked in and told me to meet her in her office. I walked down the hall a few paces behind her, passing by one of the nurses and the patient she was ushering into her office to triage.

I tried to pretend their stares weren't there. After closing the door behind me, she told me to sit down on the couch in front of her desk. She watched me as my back sank into the purple pillows. That's when I saw it...The look in her eyes told me she was hurting. The slight wiggling in her pupils and hard swallow told me she was fighting tears. "Khai, I don't know what else to do! I don't know what's wrong with him. Why is he so angry? I–" Her voice was horse and faded.

"What are you talking about?"

"He's mean, Khai. Just mean." She shook her head no as if she was telling herself not to cry. "He calls me stupid, tells me I don't know what I'm doing, and that this whole clinic will fall apart without him. You don't know how many times I get up in the middle of the night to cry in the bathroom. He's just angry. Explosive. Nothing I do makes him happy!" I wanted to vomit.

"Mom, has he hit you!"

"No!" She said quickly. "But his words hit just as hard as any slap to the face." With my arms wrapped around her, I uttered a thousand tearful apologies and squeezed her like I would never see her again. "I'm doing everything I can to make him happy! He's just miserable and I don't know why. I'm seeing a lot of patients, finding new ways to bring in money to the clinic, hired two therapists, and a Nurse Practitioner, running labs... Every damn thing! Khai, we're making more money than we've ever made! I cook, I clean, put up with his negative ass attitude...I just can't do this anymore. He always has something to say. He makes me feel like I'm nobody!"

Being in my own world, when my mom needed my help and support, made me feel like shit. I could never escape the prison inside my head when it counts. "Oh my god! Mom! Was that you he was screaming at!" She just looked at me and nodded. How could he have humiliated her like that in front of an entire staff?

"I told him your brother would be coming in 3-times a week and that on those days it is best he stays out of the office. He just lost it after that. Khai, I was trying to compromise and keep the peace. I don't know what else to do!" She was devastated. I could hear it in her voice. Where was I when my mom needed me? I felt like scum. Then she hit me with a headliner:

"I feel like I might need to see somebody. I...I... Khai, I'm..."

"Mom, please!" I didn't know if I was ready to hear what came next. "I'm broken..." she said, completely ignoring my plea to avoid hearing yet another hard truth. I didn't recognize her with the hopelessness and devastation in her eyes.

"I cry almost every day on my way to the office in the morning. Do you know I have to sit out in the parking lot 10-minutes before clinic to get myself together so I can be there for my patients? Khai..." She paused and clenched her teeth. "I do this for a living. I recognize the symptoms!" Her head fell into my chest and she wept like she had been holding back 47-years of tears.

A sudden constriction gripped the inside of my vocal cords. The pain was so sharp I thought I had choked on a fishbone. The sight of my mother's tears evoked an instinct I didn't know I had. It fucked me up. Tears poured from my eyes without warning. Her pain was my pain. Feeling helpless, I just squeezed her harder. How does a child comfort his mother? How do I save her? Save her from herself and the man who claimed to love her... How could I not see my mother was broken? I was not equipped with the tools to save myself, let alone my mother.

Guilt overran me because of that. For the woman that has given me everything, the very least I could do in return was ease her mind... Ease her heart. But I couldn't. Through her sobbing, she uttered, "Sometimes, when he's out fishing or out hunting I wish he'd fall out of a tree and break his neck or, drown." Finally, I grew angry enough to respond.

"Mom, you know what you have to do. You can go see somebody all you want. Take all the medication in the world... But If you don't make the necessary changes to your environment you will continue to exacerbate the problem. You can't—" She interrupted me... "I know. I know." She said. "Just promise me you won't say anything, Khai. You know how you can get."

"I promise, mom." I wasn't sure I could keep that promise. I wanted him dead. He had one job. Make my mother happy and he wasn't even doing that. What good was he? What respect should I have for him? It took me years to let that man into my heart after my dad's death. I thought he made my mom happy, so I tolerated him and eventually grew to like him. He taught me to fish, how to change the oil in my first car and how to change a flat. Hell, I learned everything from landscaping down to laying bricks thanks to him. Skills I would make sure I never had to use, but I had them nonetheless.

After wiping her tears and assuring me she would be okay, she sent me back to my office so that she could prepare to see her next patient. I was sitting at my desk, with my arms folded and a stubborn wrinkle on my forehead when she sent me a text.

MOMMY DEAREST: Hey, I forgot to ask about Jane's case. Did you get everything sent over to the Attorney General's office? They still threatening to report me to the Board.

ME: I'm sending everything now.

MOMMY DEAREST: Thank you. One less thing to worry about.

ME: I love you, eternally.

MOMMY DEAREST: I love you too.

I had done no such thing. But after Lee's blow up and my mom's unexpected and heart-breaking confession, I knew I had to do something fast. That's when I decided to finish writing Jane's Discharge Letter and upload it to her file. I had to back-date it so that it would reflect that the letter was sent prior to Jane committing suicide.

11/27/2016

Dear Ms. Jane Mallard,

This letter is to inform you that I will no longer be your mental health provider effective immediately due to the reasons listed below.

- Failure to adhere to the recommended treatment plan.
- Failure to maintain a consistent follow-up regimen
- Failure to comply with office policies and procedures regarding attendance and medication management.

Should an emergency arrive within in the next 30-days, I will a be available during regular business hours. In addition to providing you with 90-days worth of medications, I have provided a list of referrals that accept you insurance and are accepting new patients. This should give you enough time to find a new provider.

I will be more than happy to provider your new provider with a copy of your medical records. I f you have any questions, please feel free to contact the office using the contact information provided below.

Sincerely,

Dr. Valair Allen, MD

Tel. 832-555-5555

Fax. 877-400-713

Referrals

- Holistic Care Group: 1994 Stonehollow Lane, Suite A-500 Kingwood TX 77339
- West Houston Outpatient Psychiatry: 1283 West Gray Street Houston, TX 77074
- Woodland Grove Mental Health: 1835 Rayford PL, Conroe, TX 77380

To seal the deal, I attached a copy to the personal letter Jane wrote to me before she died to prove that she had knowledge of her discharge. It wasn't that hard to prove, considering Jane was never consistent with her appointments to begin with and my mom had the progress notes to show for it. It was desperate, morally corrupt and all those things, but all I could think about was how my mom carried the family on her back for years. The least I could do was attempt to carry some of that load for her and not add to her stress.

The fact that Jane's family had the nerve to try and profit from her death when they refused to accept her for who she was and couldn't give her the burial she deserved didn't sit right with me either. After work, I was feeling resentful towards the world. I decided to reach out to Terrence. I remembered how he was there for me when I had to say my final goodbye to Jane. I hoped that maybe he'd have the time to coddle me with his lies, even if it was only for one last time.

Break ur Heart Right Back

One last time. That's what I was telling myself I needed to get Terrence completely out of my system. Grant would serve as his replacement and all would be good. So when Terrence called and told me he missed me. I thought I had the upper hand. Keyword. Thought…

It was a Friday evening. I was supposed to be meeting Grant at the park for a run after rush hour. "Wassup, shawty? How's your day going?" Grant said through the phone. I got up from my desk to close my door.

"Meh. It's alright. I've got some progress notes to get done, so my mom can review them.

"Oh, word? Do your thing, shawty. I have a surprise for you later, so hit me up when you done."

"Wow! Really? What kind of surprise?"

"The kind that you have to see in person, so call me later, boo." His confidence was enticing. He and Terrence had that in common. The problem was, we had been seeing each other for a couple of months and I still knew very little about him outside his profession and how to make him cum. It was hard to take him seriously.

"Hah-ha! Okay. Well, let me call you later then. We can figure something out."

I figured something out. We were laying in bed smoking a blunt and talking about LA, and how much he wanted to move there. "If I could find a job out there, shawty, I'd pack my shit and yo fine ass and just go." For a minute, I allowed myself to imagine us in a nice hi-rise condo in West Hollywood. It was a pleasant thought. Then, I imagined the same scenario with Terrence, and it brought a smile to my eyes. There I was fantasizing again. That's what got me in trouble the first time.

His room had a beautiful pink glow thanks to the LED strips he mounted on the walls. I knew something was up when he got all sentimental and rubbed my eyebrow with his thumb and looked into my eyes like he actually cared about me. He placed a gentle kiss on my lips, then leaned over the side of the bed and pulled an envelope out of his nightstand.

"So about that surprise." He said, with a grin. I loved how full his beard and goatee formed that perfect square around his mouth and accented his jawline. His brown skin looked sensual under the pink lights. He lifted the envelope in the air and dangled it over my head.

"What about it?" I said, reaching for it, only for him to pull it away. Kiss me and It's all yours. I rolled my eyes and kissed him. My breath was taken when I opened the envelope to see a plane ticket. I looked up to see him on one knee, wearing nothing but a smile and a hard dick. "Meet me in LA" he's said." He made it jump at me. "Are you bribing me with dick?" I said, laughing. It was far bigger and fuller than Terrence's. That's what made the decision so hard. "It's whatever you want it to be as long as you say yes." I was lost for words. No man had ever thought to take me on a romantic getaway. That's the kind of romance I believed only existed in movies. Surely he didn't expect me to be so hesitant, but as far as I knew, Grant had no reason to suspect I was seeing someone else. We never talked about labels anyway. He didn't know that this was the exact kind of gesture of affection I wanted from Terrence. Why was I still holding on to the possibility that things would eventually work out for us?

I nodded and smiled. "Somehow, I thought you'd be more, I dunno…excited?" Truth is, I was elated on the inside, but I was also disheartened that Terrence never thought to do something like that for us. It was bittersweet. I wasn't ready to return from my Terrence trip yet. He was my drug and Grant was merely a supplement. That wasn't fair to Grant, which was why I had such a hard time accepting the tickets. "Sorry, I'm just in shock," I said. "So, are you up for round two or not?" He paused to process. "Hell, yeah. I gotchu, shawty."

We were deep into kissing and nipple play when I got a call from Terrence. For the first time since we initially met, I ignored him and didn't fear the consequences. This time, I wanted him to miss me like I missed him. I wanted him to long for me in the way that I longed for him. It was his turn to be the one up all night worried about who I was fucking. I wanted him to know that I was capable of moving on too. What I wanted more than anything was for him to love me in the way that I loved him. That was something he was incapable of doing, and so I settled for a little payback.

After I let Grant score round two, I called Terrence back. "Sorry, was taking a nap. What's up?" Taking a page out of Terrence's playbook, I was trying to be all nonchalant "You wanna come over? We should talk." I couldn't say yes fast enough in my mind. The new and improved me would make him grovel a little bit more, make him prove that he meant it. New and improved… Yeah, right.

"When?" I asked. "Are you sure it's okay?"

"Yeah…Why wouldn't it be?" Was he serious? Was I supposed to ignore the fact that he was still married and had three disgruntled lovers? "Let me rephrase. Should I be making an appointment before or after Ivan's?"

"I'm sorry." He said through the phone. Even though it sounded like he was smiling when he said it, I held on to those words like a white girl walking through the mall with a Prada bag. He told me how shit hit the fan with Ivan because he found out that Ivan was seeing some guy in Dallas the whole time they were "together." Karma. She doesn't always work fast, but she's always on time. It was everything that I had hoped would happen. In the midst of all the cheating, lying and deception, he would realize that I was the one. That's how I imagined it. That was the fantasy. I showered and kissed Grant goodbye and told him I'd call him to let him know I made it home safely despite his pleading for me to stay.

I was in front of Terrence's door an hour later. As soon as I was inside and the door was closed, he hugged me and kissed me on the lips. “I missed you, love.” He softened his voice. “You know I luuuve you. Always have. Things just got so…complicated.”

“I hear you.” All the things that had gone wrong were replaying in the back of my mind and that’s exactly where I decided to keep them.

“Hold on. I gotta take this” Grant was calling and I didn’t want to miss it. I decided to pull one of Terrence’s moves and went outside to talk to Grant.

“Hello?”

“Wassup, shawty? Did you make it home safely?”

“Yep. I’m just a little tired. I’ve got a lot of work to get done.” It wasn’t a complete lie. I did have to do that, but just not in that moment. “Cool. Just wanted to say good night.”

“Good night,” I said. He moaned playfully. “That’s what you had me sounding like earlier!” He said, giggling. “See you in LA, shawty!” I hung up the phone, suddenly relieved that I managed to buy myself some time to finish with Terrence. The door wasn’t halfway closed behind me when Terrence decided to confront me. He was in his boxers and his print was showing. It was hard not to stare.

“Who the hell was that?” He asked.

“My mom. She had some questions about a patient I’m seeing.”

“Oh. Okay. How are things with you two? Did you figure out that Jane situation?” I couldn’t tell him how I back-dated my incomplete letter and uploaded it to her medical records to make it look like she had been sent out a formal discharge letter and also had the audacity to upload her the letter she wrote to me as proof that she knew about the discharge. My ethics were questionable at best, but I did what I had to do to protect my mom’s practice.

Channeling my inner Olivia Pope, "It's handled, I said.

"Good. Now, get naked and come handle this." He grabbed his junk and raised one eyebrow. I did as he said and got in the bed on all fours and played with myself how he liked it. Two fingers at a time while he watched porn on his phone and looked at my ass in his face. It was so impersonal. He was struggling to get it up though. It couldn't quite stand at attention.

"Who have you been fuckin?" I hoped he would notice the difference, but I wasn't sure if he would.

"What are you talking about?" I said, trying to play innocent.

"Somebody been fuckin you. I can tell, mothafucka! Annnd, they dick bigger than mine!" Out of nowhere, he grabbed the back of my neck and pinned my head to the bed.

"Who the hell have you been fuckin!" His grip was tightening and I couldn't speak with my face smushed into the blankets and pillows.

"It's none of your concern," I said.

I turned to see his reaction. His face was flushed and the veins in his neck were protruding. The disappointment in his eyes made me reconsider. It was too little too late. The damage was done, meaning my booty was loose thanks to Grant's anaconda.

"Why should it matter! You fucked around on me plenty of times! Don't be a fuckin' hypocrite!" I stood up and looked up to his eyes.

"You can get yo shit and go, playa." He said it so calmly that it startled me.

"Excuse me?" I was butt naked and looking around for my underwear.

"I'm not playin' with you, boy!" He gathered my clothes and threw them over the balcony outside, and pushed me out the door. Reverse effect. It all happened so fast, it made me light-headed and dizzy.

"Get out!" He barked. I was unable to catch my breath momentarily, and unable to form a coherent thought. It was over. Just like that! How was it so easy for him? It was the ultimatum all over again. With nothing but my hand to cover my crotch, I prayed the sprinklers wouldn't hit me with an unexpected shower while I desperately picked up my clothes off the grass. I looked up to see Terrence watching and making a phone call. He didn't say anything, just watched like I was some stranger in the street. The first thing I grabbed was my underwear. I rushed to put them on and balled up my shirt, pants, and what was left of my dignity, and ran to the car.

I was sitting at my desk, mind racing. I was playing the revenge game, but the gamble wasn't worth it. I realized that I still wanted to be with him. The more it marinated the angrier I grew. Humiliated and rejected. Is this what he wanted? The petty inside me refused to let it go. I had to do something. Anything to return the favor and break his heart. That's when I started going through my phone with the intent to erase all our photos and homemade sex tapes together. It was time to move on. I wasn't ready of course, but I just couldn't stomach to see his face. It made me burn inside with envy that was dangerous for me. I didn't know what evil I was capable of until that night.

Maybe I listened to Mariah Carey too much, but I truly believed that if it was meant to be, then he would return to me. The problem, however, was that my mind didn't like the idea of waiting. I had done too much waiting for him to be all mine. The universe needed a little nudge in the right direction. Terrence didn't love me how I wished, so I couldn't hurt him by sleeping around. That proved to fail. Then, I thought that maybe

I could hurt him by taking away the thing he loved most. His "sponsor…"

Taking away the sugar baby lifestyle that he had become accustomed to, was the only way I could think of to truly hurt him. Then it hit me. Why not send all our photos and sex tapes to his husband?

When Love Calls

Summer of 2017. The city was on high alert when the announcement about Hurricane Harvey hit the airwaves. Predictions were all over the news. It was around noon and I was hiding out in my condo in The Woodlands. My car was a safe 4-stories high in the parking garage, and I was chilling out on my balcony smoking a blunt, munching on pineapples and cackling at cade while he shamelessly begged me for something to eat. The air was still and a friendly mist wet the tips of leaves and dampened the grass.

I hoped that in the event of a natural disaster that Terrence would at least call to check up on me. But I guess after taking that blow to his ego, it was foolish to think that he would care. Wishful thinking again.

It was a quarter till three and not even a text. Grant called, however, and told me to come over before things got bad. Harvey was predicted to touchdown later that evening. The fantasy of being trapped in the house with Terrence to weather the storm was romantic. It was a special kind of humiliation that hit my fragile ego when the truth dawned on me that he didn't want the same thing. Where was he? What was he doing? Who was he doing it with? He was on fucking Instagram posting videos of him lounging around in a towel and talking about how he was not going into work. After seeing that, I decided to take Grant up on his offer.

He left the door unlocked for me, so I walked right in. I smelled something burning. "I know you are not tryna cook!" I said, laughing. Grant peeped his head out the entryway to the kitchen.

"Heyyy, shawty. Glad to see you." I kissed him on the lips once, but he pulled me back in for three more. "You ready to ride out this storm with me?" For a hurricane to be coming, he sure was chummy.

"I dunno. Midtown is not the best place to be during floods." I said, suddenly realizing I was much safer on my side of town, where it typically doesn't flood. The things I do for love…I removed my cardigan and sat on the sofa. Grant already had Real Housewives playing for me.

"Grape juice?" He asked, handing me a glass full.

"Absolutely. It's my favorite!"

"Mine too. You got good taste I see." He said, flexing his pecs at me.

"Maybe a little."

"Did you call into the office today?"

"No. My mom closed the clinic until the storm is over. It all worked out." Grant took a sip from my glass and swallowed. Then I got a text from Terrence. I didn't bother to look at it.

Later that evening, after a quick round in the shower with Grant, the sky turned purple and the city was eerie. Thunder slapped and I suddenly felt an unwelcome chill creep over my shoulder until Grant walked up behind me and kissed me on the neck. His smile was big and bright as if he were laughing all the time.

"You aiight, shawty? You look nervous."

"I am. We are in a flood zone." I said as I was peeping out the window.

"Aye, If we gotta swim outta here, ima carry you on my back and we gone dip."

"Ha-ha! You laughing. But we might have to do just that."

"I'm down. As long as you're with me."

That's all it took. I was sitting on the couch when an agitating sense of urgency overtook me. The faux tiger skin rug warming my toes started to feel like it was burning. When Grant went to put his arm around me and flip the channel all in one motion, I ducked.

"Grant, I have to go. Something's come up." I jumped up, grabbed my clothes and rushed toward the door. Grant jumped up from the couch and got in front of me. He stood in front of the door wearing nothing but a bath towel and some Nike slides, his brown skin looked tempting. "Where are you going? It's not safe out there, shawty." My phone was ringing with a call from Terrence. I tried to ignore it, but I couldn't help but look down and glance at the screen.

TERRENCE: I know we not on speaking terms, but I need u.

The photo I took of him in the shower filled my screen and all I could do was look down.

TERRENCE: After this, I promise I'll leave u alone.
TERRENCE: NVM. Don't come. Please don't come!

Grant sighed and kissed me on the forehead, I knew then, that I couldn't avoid the truth. Whether my desire was pointless or not, Grant didn't deserve this. I turned to him and looked him in the eyes.

"I'm sorry, I began, "Sometimes when I'm with you, I want to be with him. I know it makes no sense, but he's everywhere in my mind and my heart." There was a moment of silence, as I searched his eyes for signs of forgiveness.

"When you find the answers you're looking for, let me know, shawty."

"I'm sorry for wasting your time. Really. I thought I could move on."

"Nah. You ain't waste my time. It's too soon, shawty. Understand, our day will come." He kissed me on the forehead and hugged me. My face was pressed against his bare chest just how I liked it. He wasn't backing down. An alpha. I liked it. I could feel his heart beating a part of me wanted nothing more than to say fuck it all and stay right there in his arms and out of the storm. A new life in a new city with a new man sounded like the treatment I would have ordered for myself. Running away without having seen things through with Terrence would have bothered me to no end and I hated it. Terrence baited his hook and I foolishly snagged it.

Grant shook his head and stepped to the side and sped-walked to my car. I couldn't believe I was about risk being in a hurricane to get to Terrence. The roads were barren and a steady mist stuck to my windshield. I was deep breathing, but the moment I glanced over the hood and saw the water on the road, it immediately looked like ice and it took my breath away. My mind had tricked my brain into believing my car was skating on thin ice and it was only a matter of time before I crashed and burned.

The only thing keeping me pushing was the idea of getting stuck on the highway when the rain finally came. 40-minutes later I arrived. I had to sit in my car for a minute to get my nerves together. My heart rate was up and my head was hurting. I called Terrence and he didn't answer.

There I was again, standing outside my man's door. Uninvited and unannounced. I guess I didn't learn my lesson the first two times. I knocked and no one answered. Instead, I got a call from Brandon.

"Khai, you gotta do something! My dad doesn't look good!"

"Brandon! Open the door!" I yelled.

"Promise you won't do nothing crazy."

"Boy? What! Open the damn door!"

"He's in here with Ivan." He said in a panic.

The next thing I knew, I was running out to my car. I returned outside his door with my cold steel bat in hand, driven by pain and what I perceived to be a betrayal. There was no time for hesitation. Do you remember that old pinball game that used to be on all the old Windows computers? Space Cadet 3D? Yeah… That's what was going on in my head. All the different ways in which Terrence was screwing Ivan, pinged, pinged, pinged around in my head. Brandon opened the door and pleaded with me to calm down.

"Khai you gotta help!" I didn't hear him. Like an angry bull, all I saw was red and I charged in. The humidity in the room stuck to my skin as I swung my bat at anything bold enough to be in my way. The two marble statues I bought for him and put in the entryway met the meat of my bat and shattered to pieces. All the photos on the walls that I took of him, and some of the ones his other play toys snapped, were reduced to bits of wood, glass, and laminated paper. I smashed big gashes into the center of the TV screen that Jarvis bought him for Christmas. I put holes in just about every wall that crossed my path. No words. Just rage.

I turned the corner to the living room and what I found was not at all what I was expecting.

Terrence was laid out with Ivan on the same white leather couch Terrence and I once had angry make-up sex on. Terrence looked barely conscious, his nose was bleeding, and he was wearing nothing but briefs and white tube socks. Ivan was completely naked with his face buried down in the cushions. His arms looked purple and his body was still.

Like a cherry to an ice-cream sundae, a small rectangular razor blade decorated the mound that looked like coke sitting on the smudgy glass dinner table. When I saw my old prescription for Xanax on the table, I was stunned. I didn't even know you could snort Xanax! All my anger retreated to the front door. My hands lost their grip on the bat and I ran to him. I placed my head on his chest, his faint heartbeat was faint. I shook him and shook him but couldn't get anything more than a weary grunt.

My mind kept repeating nine, one, one…nine, one, one! But my fingers couldn't dial fast enough. It threw me into a panic and I couldn't keep my hands steady until a jarring shake on my shoulder snatched me out of my pitfall. "Khai, please! I think he's dying!"

It was Ivan. His eyes were red and snot was dripping from his nose. It was the Hoe-tale all over again. "Breathe, Khai! You gotta breathe! Help my dad! My dad! Please! Y'all gotta help my dad!" Brandon was hysterical on the phone. He was lost for words. His voice cracked repeatedly and with every crack, it broke my heart. And suddenly, a sense of urgency surged from the pit of my stomach and bench-pressed the weight off my chest. I snatched my phone back from Brandon.

"911, what's your emergency?" I stumbled over almost every word, but when she asked me if there were any other people there in need of medical attention, my head drifted over to his new manstress lying on the couch. His lips were blue and his mouth was open. Her voice was calm yet I was still shaking with anger. I stuck my foot out and kicked the naked bastard. He didn't move. I wanted to take the blade on the table and slit his fucking throat. If I could have gotten away with it, I would have. No hesitation. I wanted him gone. Period.

Why was it so hard? Why was choosing the moral high ground so hard! Evil, revenge, and petty, came easier, like second nature. Who was this monster I had become? Bitter and scorned over a man who was never mine to begin with? I didn't recognize this evil. I looked at Terence in my arms and up at Brandon who was begging me with his eyes to do the right thing and not leave Ivan's dead body for them to find when they got here. I wanted him to suffer a miserable death. A lonely death. I wanted his body to wither away in a ditch where nobody would ever find him.

"Sir! Sir! Are you still there?" The breath I had been holding in to keep from bursting into hysterics broke the silence and what I can only describe as divine intervention, spoke into the phone told them about Ivan. Ambulances and guys in navy scrubs were outside making a scene in the parking lot and rushing into a place that I wanted so badly to believe was our home. As the coroner and his crew zipped Ivan up in a black bag and carried his body out on a stretcher, I resented all the deceit, hookups, affairs, scandals, drugs, and betrayal that consumed us all only to end in death.

Looking In

Oh…This is what heartbreak feels like. It was an epiphany and devastating in the way every tragic romance and every sad love song ever written described. I could hear the raindrops pounding the pavement and the thunder roaring outside the hospital walls. I sat with my back pressed up against a white pillar just outside a room on the 5th floor, room 512 to be specific, contemplating how I ended up looking from the outside in. Ignored and unnoticed as if the affair had never existed.

I was in a fog. Everything around me seemed to slow down. I could hear every rapid beat of my heart and every unsteady breath. The squeaking of the nurses' clogs treading back and forth as they came in and out of various patients' rooms, the shuffling of papers, the whispers of a couple standing just outside the room of a loved one who was most likely not doing too well. I knew this because both sides of the woman's flushed cheeks became swathed in her greasy reddish-brown hair as she drew her hands to her face and unleashed a silent cry so violent, that it looked as though she was coughing.

The wind and rain clashing together sounded like cars passing freely on the highway if you listened closely enough. I winced at the moist sound of lips kissing a forehead gently. The painful sight of two thumbs curling over each other as Jarvis and Terrence held hands, hurt my soul. I plugged my fingers in my ears in an attempt to drown out the squeaky footsteps squashing up and down the hall, gusting their rough wind and rubbery scent under my nose.

I was envious. Terrence lied in the hospital bed, his eyes barely open and gripping his husband's hand as if afraid to let go but also at peace with him around. There were IV's in his arm and bandages on his forehead and the bridge of his nose. In my lover's hour of need, I was forced to watch from behind a cracked white metal door a few feet away—not too close that I would have been spotted inappropriately staring, and not too far to not have been a witness. I was forced to watch from a stiff chair with no arms and a back of which offered no support as Terrence took his final gaze into Jarvis's eyes and Jarvis into his. I saw history, a connection, and a love with which I could not compete. I found myself wishing I could swap places with Jarvis. How evil that thought was. Jarvis had done nothing to harm me or anything to my knowledge that would justify such a punishment. And here I was, wishing heartbreak and suffocating loneliness upon a grieving spouse. Though I could not understand how they could go on as if the home-wrecker that destroyed their marriage was not lurking just outside the door, it wasn't my place as a mistress, no, Manstress, to do so.

It was then I realized my true place in Terrence's heart: Hovering—No, orbiting, around its sultry gravitational pull but never once being able to break through its atmospheric layers and land on its surface. That space was already full, and I had to make a decision I wasn't prepared to make. I accepted my defeat and prepared to make my exit.

I was standing up from the hurtful ass chair when my phone slipped out of my CoCo-Buttered fingers and smacked facedown on the floor. The shaking made it impossible to maintain a grip. Just my fucking luck. As I was leaning down to pick it up, Jarvis spotted me. I called myself trying to flee. Where was the nearest exit? The fastest exit? I couldn't bear to wait for the elevator, so I took the stairs. I couldn't find them fast enough. I flung the metal door to the stairwell open and when I turned around, everything seemed to happen in slow motion as Jarvis charged at me like a lion after a gazelle.

He got all in my face and eyed me down. "Why are you here!" It was a hard whisper from the meatiest part of his throat, but it was stern. I wanted to tell him had it not been for me, he wouldn't have made it to the hospital, but I choked up. What was I doing there? I didn't belong. I had done my due diligence by making sure Terrence at least got help.

"I—I..." Cat had my tongue. He was breathing heavily and his eyes were blood-shot red from all the crying. He was taller than me but just as slim. Terrence had a type.

"If he dies, I blame you for this!"

"How can you blame me? I wasn't the one in the house with him when he was snorting that shit! If anyone is to blame, it's you! You allowed him to have affairs that did nothing but enable him to feed his addiction. For a sponsor, that's pretty lousy!"

"I am also his husband! Which means I love him! When you love someone, you accept them as they are. Don't waste your time trying to change them. We found what worked for us, and that's not your place to judge." I wanted to say I loved him too but that hardly seemed appropriate, but I didn't have to. "Let me tell you something about MY husband." He paused and looked me up and down. His eyes were stretched out and his bottom jaw was clenched. "He will suck the life out of you. Break you down. Make you feel like nothing. And then turn around and make you feel like you're high on LSD. I've been putting up with his shit for 8-years. You've been putting up with it for 5-minutes, and you THINK you have some right to grieve? To stand on the other side of his deathbed?" He paused again, wiped his forehead, and took a deep breath. At first, I thought it was for dramatic effect, but the way he grabbed his chest made it seem like it was tasking for him to do. When he caught his breath, he let me have it.

"It was your little stunt that caused this whole fiasco, honey. I got the photos and videos you called yourself sending to me. I finally cut his ass off and now he's in the hospital doped up on Xanax. I don't think he has anything further to say to you." His words spat me in the face. For once, I felt worthless and it was not because of Terrence. I couldn't breathe. My neck stiffened and the tears blurred my vision. A storm was brewing. It was the same storm that swung a bat through every flat screen in his apartment and flattened his tires! I wanted to headbutt him into a coma. I wanted him dead! My shame and fear of what my retaliation might look like pulled my head down as if to tell me to reconsider. The light shined just right on Jarvis's finger and instantly, I was triggered.

The sight of the shiny silver ring on his finger and my naked one brought me to sudden tears and I had to turn away to avoid the embarrassment. I was retreating to the exit, but Jarvis followed me down the hall to the stairwell. I took off running down the stairs and he chased after me. His red soles rapidly slapped the steps behind me and echoed in the hallow stairwell. I could hear his keys jingling wildly in his pocket as he trailed me like prey in an African jungle. My tears blinded my eyes as I desperately ran down 5-flights of stairs. The thunder outside rattled me. I was outnumbered. I turned to see how close he was gaining on me, and that's when I noticed the jingling stopped. There was a hard staccato grunt as he grabbed his chest. He was struggling to find his balance and stumbled back against the rails. And then, he tumbled down the steps.

It threw me into a panic. Faster! I cried in my mind. Run! Through the swinging glass doors and into a vast parking lot. I got soaked running to my car with no umbrella. I had forgotten the danger I was in but was quickly reminded by a jarring flash flood alert from my phone. My stalled breathing and the wailing sirens from an incoming ambulance caused my head to throb. My trembling hands had me fumbling with my keys. I was unable to form an angry thought, unable to cry—unable to scream. I just stared blankly down the empty road. Water was slowly rising as the ditches became flooded and the violent wind trashed the roads with snapped tree branches, twigs, and what have you.

Meanwhile, I stood motionless, drenched in the rain, and for once wishing some asshole in a Ford F150 would speed over a puddle and splash me in the face. At least that way I would feel something rather than this overwhelming numbness and crippling fixation on the painful image of what lay beyond that damn cracked door! I had to get home. Risking my life driving in the storm was worth escaping the hospital. I cranked my car and pulled out of the parking lot, fighting every urge not to look back. No more than 5-minutes up the road from the hospital, my shaking became uncontrollable. It was too late. I could no longer grip the steering wheel. My vision blurred again, and all I could feel was the car sliding.

Bitter

I woke up a few days later in the emergency room with a massive headache and some minor scratches on my face and elbows. My mom was sitting in the corner pecking away at the keyboard on her MacBook and holding her cell phone to her ear with her shoulder. She had to have come straight from the office because she was wearing her usual power pantsuit and telling someone to reschedule her afternoon patients.

Before she met my gaze, I tried to quickly shut my eyes, hoping she would think I was still out cold. "This is what happens when you internalize everything, Khai! Why didn't you talk to me or somebody?" Her seemingly insensitive directness, made me want to droop my ears, tuck my tail under my ass and scurry underneath the bed. "Look at me when I'm talking to you, son." I hated it when she said that. She said it through her teeth, so I knew I'd better turn or she would give me something to be unconscious about.

"Aren't you always the one talking about closure?"

"If it lands you in the emergency room, threatens your livelihood, and has a grieving family wanting to press charges, ya' neeeed to leave well enough alone."

"I was handling it! The car just spun out of control. It had nothing to do with my emotional state!"

"What were you doing leaving the hospital?" I finally broke down and told her about Terrence and all that had led to this bleak moment in my life. She didn't respond with the sympathy I had hoped for. Instead, she let me have it. "That's your fuckin' problem, Khai. You're impulsive. When the slightest thing doesn't go your way, you get completely irrational and start acting out. It's time to grow up." My head hung low and all I could do was shake my head. She released her grip and turned in the other direction to look out the window as if she couldn't stand to look at me anymore.

I made the smallest attempt to meet her gaze but it was futile. Just like that, she was cold…Disappointed. I felt so helpless. There was nothing I could say to make her feel like she hadn't failed me as a mother, and nothing to convince her that I didn't need mommy to come to my rescue every time I got myself into trouble. There was nothing left to say so one loooong minute of awkward silence lingered. And then, the Channel 5 news hit us with a headliner:

"Breaking News! Man found dead in a stairwell at Methodist Hospital, hours before Hurricane Harvey touches down in the Houston area has been identified as Jarvis Warren, Computer Engineer and a regular volunteer at the Woodland Springs Substance Abuse Treatment Center! Security footage shows him running down the stairs before taking what would be

a fatal tumble down 3-flights of stairs! Though many speculated murder, HPD officials have ruled this a tragic accident."

Murder! My breaths became shorter, more rapid, and increasingly more of a struggle. My fingers grew weak. Dizziness blinded me. And the tears, tears, tears… They wouldn't stop. As the darkness crept behind my eyes almost to the point of no return. All I could hear was machinery beeping and my mom screaming for the nurse. Imagine enduring the torture of unrequited love. Imagine seeing the person you love, look into the eyes of someone else, with all the love of which they deprive you. Imagine clinging on to the hope that maybe one day, he will see you, only to have him look through you.

And then, Murder! Jarvis was dead because of me, dead because I couldn't stay away from his husband. The realization knocked the wind out of me. The hospital air was suffocating and my gown stuck to my back. "Khai! Baby, you have to breathe!" She cried. It only made me panic more. I thought I was dying.

After I was discharged, my mom drove me home. I was a little drowsy from the meds so I was drifting in and out of sleep as we cruised down the highway. My mom broke the silence as usual. "I scheduled an appointment with Dr. LeRoy for you. Be there, or don't even think about coming back to my office. You'll have to finish your remaining hours somewhere else. I'm not putting up with it from you. I expect this kind of rebellion from your older brother, but not you."

Rebellion? Is that what she was calling it? She turned to face me in the passenger seat and gripped my left hand. I remember her smelling like Elizabeth Taylor's White Diamonds, as she leaned over the center dash with piano black trim to grab my other hand. The rain tap-danced on the windshield and the wind howled. My hands were shaking a little. I could feel my dark cloud creep over my shoulders. It made the fine hairs on my neck stand up and my hands tremble. Her motherly touch was warm and calmed me like it used to when I was a kid. She made sure to meet my eyes even though she knew the eye contact made me uncomfortable. I could see the worry in them just before she kissed the scar on my chin.

"Don't forget these." She handed me a bottle of pills. "This is what happens when you're off your meds, Khai" I took them from her and put them in my bag. She unlocked the doors and we said our goodbyes.

"I'm serious about Dr. LeRoy. You need to talk to somebody and stop being so hardheaded." Rather than protest, I said, "yes ma'am," and went inside the house, where Cade was waiting for me at the door. He swiftly crawled from underneath the bed and darted towards me, shaking his long black and white hair in the process. I motioned my hand over his head, and with his big deer-in-the-headlights eyes, he hopped on his hind legs and used his paws to play patty cake on my legs. I fell into the safety of my nightly routine. Showered, fed Cade, and drank a bottle of Stella Rosa as I watched reruns of Housewives until I got bored.

I didn't leave the house to do anything for a week. Uber eats was my best friend. When I finally got off my ass and went in to see Dr. LeRoy, I wasn't in the best mindset. I was buzzed on wine, and high on Sativa as I sat across from him with my arms folded and my legs crossed. It baffled me that he would agree to see me after the history we had created together. Professional lines had been crossed and I had no regrets.

"How ya been, Khai? It's good to see you."

"I'm alright. I guess." I said. "I'm sure my mom has given you the specifics." He nodded, and without further delay, "So, let's talk about Terrence. Who is he to you?"

"An ex."

"Is that all? Can you think of anything else?"

"An ex," I said again. This time, sharply. He twisted his full lips to the side and nodded.

"Mmm. What about, lover?"

"That's who he was to me. Now, he's an ex," I said.

"And, how would you define a lover?" He leaned back into his chair, crossed his legs, and put his fingers together in a way that formed a triangle.

"Someone who is my partner, my protector, my source of intimacy. Most importantly, he's the keeper of my heart." I had to stop for a moment because the feelings were all coming back so fluidly, it scared me. Dr. LeRoy nodded to encourage me.

"He was, Prince Charming. My happily ever after." I said, feeling a little embarrassed having heard my thoughts out loud.

"If he was all of those energies for you, then why lash out the way that you did? Why so much anger?"

"It's irrelevant."

"Stop trying to avoid dealing with the issue, Khai. That's the kind of behavior that is responsible for your episodes." He was blunt.

"Episodes?"

"What do you call them."

"I don't call them anything." I was sitting there with my lips twisted.

"I used to believe that life's struggles helped make us stronger, but now I'm starting to feel like they ruin you without any greater purpose. The by-product of it all being…mental illness."

"Well, Khai you gotta try something. Right? Or, do you want to feel this way all the time?"

I wasn't feeling the least bit optimistic about being on LeRoy's couch. Somewhere in the world is someone's mother, father, daughter, or son, overdosing on the very drugs prescribed to them, or hanging themselves. Disease of the mind does not just fade away like a shallow flesh wound. It's high maintenance and never quite heals. A few painkillers and band-aids are not enough.

"This is a waste of time," I said, as I started gathering my things. "I know how this goes and I'm not interested in mind games and hippie bullshit. So, you enjoy the rest of your day, Doc." I'd just finished playing the love game, the ultimate mind game, and I lost. The thought of giving Terrence any more of my time and energy frustrated me. Why does everything have to be about him? I didn't want to relive the anger, the suppressed devastation, and the pitiful yearning to hear his voice one more time, even if it was to tell me another lie.

"You love him. Do you not?"

"Loved. As in past tense." I said. LeRoy shook his head.

"Love is stubborn. It doesn't just go away because your heart is broken at this moment. The fact that you feel something, shows that there is love because if not, you'd be indifferent. Love lingers like a shadow, and sticks with you no matter how much you think you have moved on."

"I'm pretty sure. The love is gone. It was one-sided anyways. What's there to linger?" After 3-minutes of silence, he handed me a teal journal. It was about the size of your average book. "What's this for?" I asked.

There was a slight grin on his smooth caramel face as if he knew something I didn't.

"I have homework for you. Well, think of it as a long-term project. Have you done something similar with your patients?"

"Rarely," I said. "Nobody likes homework."

"Well, brotha, I am going to challenge you to tell your story. Have a conversation with yourself." I held the leather bound-book of blank pages in one hand, unsure how to feel. "These pages are to be inked with the unfiltered truth. Take any thoughts, emotions, memories, and stories that emerge from the corners of your mind that in some way speak to you about not just Terrence, but your relationships with other people in your life."

"So, you're giving me a diary?"

"Don't act so surprised. I'm sure in at least one of your classes in the past, you discussed the importance of journaling." Part of me considered how it would be easier to write rather than speak it aloud. I looked at him and laughed because I immediately thought about the movie, "White Chicks."

"Okay, so I'm gonna write a letter?"

"I'm serious." He said. "Denial. Anger. Depression. Acceptance. Grief's lessons hit hard. Relationships have a life cycle, whether it be one for the long term or a quick fuck in a bathroom stall. When those relationships have run their course, we must still grieve them like any death."

"Nah. I'm good. I have no desire to give Terrence and his bullshit anymore of my time."

"Stop being stubborn and try it. You need to mourn the loss of this relationship before you can move on." I wondered if he practiced what he preached because I had several ideas about what unhappiness led to me being bent over his desk and him stuffing me like a Thanksgiving turkey the last time we were in the same room together.

"Are you still married, Doc?"

"Separated." I toyed with the idea of sliding my head in between his lap to avoid the conversation, but I refrained.

"Yeah, that's what Terrence said too."

"For your first entry, I want you to write a letter to someone."

"To who? What would it say?"

"That's for you to decide. Spend some time alone. Say something you wish you never got the chance or had the guts to say to their face."

Later that night, I lounged around on the balcony, a glass of Stella Rosa in hand, and admired the clouds and planes flying above me. My eyes met the blank page finally and after much deliberation, I finally found the strength to say goodbye. I took Dr. LeRoy's advice and modernized it. Instead, I wrote a text message that Terrence would never read. It was my very own Aaliyah-style "4 Page Letter" moment.

ME: Dear, Terrence
Much like Direct Energy who warned you to either pay your remaining balance or live in the darkness, I gave you an ultimatum. One, I deeply regret. Either me or nothing at all.

ME: I am aware that I hold no such power to exile you or anyone to a life without love, but choosing to withhold the love of

which you so desperately needed and I so desperately wanted to give, is a crime worth the torment I am receiving as a result.

ME: The ghost of guilt continues to haunt me, as I cannot help but feel somewhat responsible for Jarvis's death. I hope that someday you can forgive me. Beyond your status, beyond the trauma of a young boy molested, turned ex-conn, turned escort turned addict, turned father and unfaithful lover, I see you.

ME: I see you beyond your mistakes.
I love the scars on your back and how they are shaped like spider webs that you covered up with angel wings. I love the muscles you built in prison, and I love the redness on your nose from years of abuse.

ME: Where you see shame, is where I see a beautiful man that once lay next to me while he sweated out the withdrawals. Where most saw a lack of self-control, I see a man who had to fight the monster that is addiction and through that struggle, discovered what true pain and suffering means.

ME: Though our age separated us by 20-years, you sought a chance to connect us through sharing your experiences with me in hopes that I would not make the same mistakes.

ME: I saw you as my happy ending. Yet, you saw yourself as a lesson from which I would learn hard truths. I'll miss our Friday nights and the shrimp étouffée.I must apologize for allowing my imagination ran wild with the idea that I could change you.

ME: Briefly, you arose from the flaming pit of addiction like a phoenix from ashes, with more love to give than any mere simple man or woman could ever be ready to receive.

ME: The thoughts of you with other lovers ached, but I celebrated every incremental moment of growth between us. To be an object of your desire felt like an honor.

ME: Part of those feelings may owe its respects to my crippling insecurities and shallow physical attraction towards you.

ME: Still, when most would shut themselves out, you opened yourself up to the possibility of love beyond the physical and emotional limits bound to you for a man of your pain. I once admired your struggle and daydreamed about your potential.

ME: Such an intense desire to have you in that way made me selfish and bitter. I wanted you all to myself, though you were not ready. I blamed you for the pain of which I am the sole cause.

Me: Love riddled with ultimatums and defined by labels is conditional at best, and though I never stopped loving you, the unconditional love I once professed was overshadowed by selfishness and impatience.

ME: And so, in your sudden death, I bid you this past due letter in hopes that you will hear my past due apology and plea for your forgiveness.

I sent those texts thinking Terrence was dead after his overdose and wouldn't answer. So, when I got a message back I damn near had a heart attack.

```
TERRENCE: I am heading to rehab
in Chicago. Don't contact me
again.
```

As badly as I wanted to take the time to process the fact that he was still alive, I didn't. He wasn't wasting any time thinking about me. It was time to let him go.

Thank u, Next

I've always liked stories. I see stories in everything. They are how I make sense of the world and its people. You see, I blamed Terrence for all the bitterness that provoked me to expose our affair to his husband and for a while, I felt vindicated. But, sometimes the problem with stories is, perspective. It's easy to observe other people's actions and find faults and mistakes, but it's not always easy to reflect on your own situation with the same critical eye and accept the role you played in your destruction.

My mom and I were having Sunday brunch at this Tex-Mex place called Cyclone Anaya. We were sipping mimosas. Her smile was bright and I was glad to see it again. The waitress came by and I was ready to ask for the tab when my mom told her to bring out two more mimosas and she hit me with a headliner.

"Hey, I just want to say I'm proud of you for pulling it together and getting Jane's case dropped. I got the letter in the mail yesterday. It's good to see you had your priorities in the right place for once."

"I love you, mom. And I appreciate the empire you have built for this family. I would do anything to protect it, and you." For the first time, I had no problem expressing my love to my mother. Whether she knew the shady things I did to get the case dropped, I don't know. What we had was that moment and I didn't want to spoil it with details. The job was done Lee was out of the picture for the time being, and we were well on our way to repairing our relationship. She kissed me on the forehead and proposed one more toast. At the clink of our glasses, Grant called.

"Wassup, shawty? How ya been." His upbeat spirit made me smile. His frequency hit a little differently than Terrence's. It wasn't heavy. It was light and refreshing. "I'm alright. Just thinking."

"Oh, yeah? What about?"

"Everything."

"Hope that includes me, shawty."

"What do you mean?"

"The offer still stands. I'm headed to LA tonight. I sent you your ticket on the app so take your time."

"Okay. I'll call you either way." I hung up the phone and looked up to see my mom shaking her head. "You running away again, huh?"

"No. I wouldn't be running. I'd be taking a vacation."

"Running from one man to the next will not help you work through your shit any faster."

"He's a nice guy, mom. We're just going as friends. Besides, it will be nice to get away and come back with a refreshed mind." I wanted to do what LeRoy suggested and take some time to be alone and let my heart speak through the pages of my diary. But for the first time since hearing about Jarvis's death, the last thing I wanted, was to be alone. I kissed my mom goodbye and promised to be home soon.

Later that evening I had just finished stuffing all my luggage in the trunk of my rental car and was pulling out of the driveway when I saw Terrence's red Impala pulling up behind me. I did not know what to say. I took one look at him and suddenly I had an appetite to make bad decisions. He was a little banged up and looked like he hadn't slept easy in a while, but I was elated that he was still alive. How was it possible that he still had that effect on me? He got out of the car, scratching his head and wearing a white button-up shirt that was wrinkled and unbuttoned completely. I followed the snake tattooed on his side as it slithered all the way down his gold belt buckle.

"Where you going?" He asked.

"Shouldn't you be on your way to Chicago?" I guess I shouldn't have been surprised if it turned out to be a lie.

"Don't worry about that. What matters is that I'm here. Where are you going?"

"On a trip," I said from inside my rental car with the window cracked. "Where!" He shouted. I debated telling him the truth, that I was going to LA, with the guy whose dick is bigger than his.

"It's none of your concern," I said, avoiding looking into those green eyes. Then, he hit me with a headliner.

"Baby, I read your messages."

"A little late for that. Dontcha think?"

"Look." He said, as he approached my window and leaned in to trap me in them. "I think we should talk. If we don't work this out now, I will not be here when you get back." I looked at the clock it was 5 and my flight left at 6:30. There was no time. I couldn't avoid him or making my decision any longer. Why did he still make me nervous? My jittery hands vibrated the steering wheel, which had me wanting one of those pills. I wanted him to reach through the window, grab me by the back of my neck and make me kiss him. I couldn't be around him. Not anymore.

"Please just, move!" I begged. "I hate you!" He gripped my hands and I thought he was going to do it. Kiss me. He looked into my eyes and asked, "Are you sure?" My fingers traveled over the window switch and I pressed it down. The wining sound it made, drowned out the wailing of my heart crying out for him, begging me not to go.

"You'll regret this, Khai. I promise you'll never see me again!" He said. I tried not to look at him in my review mirror. Shake it off. Shake it off, I kept telling myself. All I heard was his tires burning rubber and then he was gone. I sulked in the car for a few minutes before I finally found my nerve again.

A cold sweat overran my neck and armpits as I stood at the check-in gate, scanning through swarms of rolling luggage, unfamiliar faces, countless security guards, and ticket machines, hoping he wouldn't stand me up. Lord knows I deserved it. There was no sign of Grant, so I sent him a text.

ME: Hey, where are you?
ME: If you're not coming, please just let me know…

No reply for over 20-minutes. Would he abandon me the way I did when I ran to Terrence's overdose distress call? As I boarded the plane, still no sign of Grant, I thought about Terrence, my dads, Jarvis, LeRoy, and all the hookups I could remember. I daydreamed about the reality of all my past mistakes and imagined them differently, but better.

But, I soon realized that all the imagination in the world cannot erase the mistakes of my past. I wanted to blame Terrence for the scars I will forever have to live with, but I can't. What I can do, is accept my faults, forgive myself, forgive him, get my ass on a plane, and leave it all behind.

I was waiting at the terminal when I heard the last call for everybody to board the plane. I looked around one last time. Nothing. I boarded the plane and started feeling sorry for myself. Just when I was ready to accept that I would be going to LA alone, I looked up to see Grant smiling at me in the aisle as he stuffed his orange carry-on in the cabin above me. "Did I scare you, shawty?" He said, smiling.

"A little." He leaned down and kissed me on the forehead. "Running late, but I'm ready. Are you?" Truth is, I was unsure, but I was ready to find out. Grant on my side and Terrence behind me. We took off into the sky, and I gazed out the small round window at the sea of clouds as the plane glided above them, and looked forward to sunny days on Venice Beach and nights out in West Hollywood. Whether it was with Grant or someone else, was to be determined.

As we cruised god knows how high in the air, I recalled the scandal, the sleepless nights, blatant infidelity, suicide, dangerous lies, broken windshields, blackmail, and death. I remembered when my heart broke. I remembered when I lost my mind and found myself grateful for the struggle. I reveled in the fact that

I had a new story to begin, and so for my memories with Terrence and the shit we put each other through…

Thank you, next…

I had a new story to begin, and so for my memories with Terrence and the shit we put each other through…

Thank you, next…

www.ingramcontent.com/pod-product-compliance
Lightning Source LLC
Chambersburg PA
CBHW020941310726
48980CB00001B/3